TOUGH BREAK

THE SHAKEDOWN SERIES

ELIZABETH SAFLEUR

Elizabeth SaFleur LLC
PO Box 6395
Charlottesville, VA 22906
Elizabeth@ElizabethSaFleur.com
www.ElizabethSaFleur.com

Edited by Trenda Lundin
Cover design by LJ Designs

ISBN: 978-1-949076-24-0

1

Six Years Ago

Tonight would not be Declan's proudest moment. He knew it three steps into Maxim's. What did it matter? Three days out of Eastern Men's Correctional Facility and he had nothing better to do. Besides, he hadn't been in the presence of, let alone touched by a woman for two years. Pure hell for a man like him.

He had one last desire before he'd go down to the waterfront to see if he really had the guts to walk into the river. He wasn't disappearing into the murky Patapsco River without one last physical contact with a woman. A strip club seemed as good an answer as any to fulfill that wish.

He threw a $50 bill into the jar at the front desk for the main doorman and handed over another to the slight young brunette behind the register for the entry fee.

Her deadpan expression morphed into a bright smile. "You look like a man who deserves the private tent."

Sure, he did. A few days' stubble on his face in a plain white shirt and blue workman's pants—the dead opposite of how he entered prison—wasn't private tent material, but nothing mattered to anyone here except money. "No, sweetheart. Tip rail's fine." He leaned against his cane. His leg throbbed, and he needed to sit his ass down for a bit.

His cellmate couldn't stop waxing on about how, once free, he'd be going to Maxim's. *Got the most gorgeous dolls there. Make you feel real good,"* Mick had said with that faraway look that could get you killed in prison, leaving yourself open for being jumped.

"You sure? I can get you someone special just for you." The main doorman, a stocky fellow with jet black hair and a nose that appeared broken a few too many times, quirked his lips at him. "Perhaps two?"

"All good here." He didn't need a private VIP area for a bit of attention. The girls here may be instructed to never object to what the client desired—so long as it wasn't recorded or traceable—but his goals were modest. The lack of their true consent for that last part roiled his gut, but here he was, buying into a system where a man could buy a bit of imaginary love. A few touches, a few smiles, that's all he required.

The doorman eyed him. "You a cop?"

"Not even close."

The man circled his shoulder, glanced around and then dropped his voice low. "You need somethin' special, give me, Trace, a shout. I'll hook you up with some pussy." The guy's gaze dropped to Declan's cane. He'd gotten used to that look —pure pity for the crippled half-man. No matter. He could take down a man twice his size if needed, another skill learned over the last two years out of necessity.

The guy scratched his chin. "We've got quite a few women who'd love to spend some time with you."

More like his money. "No, thanks." With a quick head

shake, he freed himself from the unwanted offer. He seated himself on a cracked black vinyl stool at the tip rail.

Prostitutes weren't his style, but he'd accept a dancer's feigned interest. They likely needed his money more than he did. In fact, he may never need money again.

A thin blond woman swayed her hips against a pole and eyed him. Of course, she sized him up. Was he a Kmart shopper who'd spend very little or a holy roller?

"Best vodka you have. Straight up," he said to a cocktail waitress who'd sidled up to him.

Declan laid a stack of $20 bills, all creased down the middle, on the lip of the stage. That was all it took for his status to be established.

The dancer slunk to her knees and crawled toward him, a smile plastered across her face. "Hi, handsome. I'm Heaven." He held out a $20 to her, which she took with her teeth. She rose to her knees and gyrated her crotch in front of him while another dancer on the floor drew closer to him. She walked by him twice, eyeballing his cane but not stopping.

Heaven dropped to all fours and slithered closer. The scent of freshly baked cookies rolled over him. Had women always smelled this good? Her cheek, as soft as a baby's butt, brushed his as she whispered a thank you. Her hand slid down his forearm to his hand, which she grasped and raised to the silky skin on her neck.

Up close, she resembled a little girl, all pink, pouty lips and round face. Was she even of legal age? After two years of never touching another soul, the feel of her matched her name. Her gesture was such a small thing for such a big impact, but there it was—powerful beyond measure.

He memorized the flush across her smooth chest, the warmth of her skin in case he got to carry it with him to wherever souls like him went in the hereafter.

As soon as his drink arrived, he withdrew his hand. He

threw back the vodka and pointed to the stack of bills. "They're all yours." She blinked as if she hadn't heard him right.

The doorman appeared. With one meaty hand on the rail and the other on the back of his chair, he leaned down to him. "You look like a man seeking something special. Blonds not your type?" His gaze shot to the stage and back to him. "Or did she—"

"Heaven was perfect." Declan rose and pressed both palms into the end of his cane. He wouldn't be responsible for any black mark on her reputation here—and this guy seemed like someone who'd take any chance to lower these girls' status by any imagined infraction.

The guy's fake smile was back. "I got something for you." He raised his hand and snapped his fingers at a redhead across the floor. "Hey, Red!"

The woman straightened from her lean over a table of women—an unusual sight in a strip club. The doorman jerked his head in a "get over here" gesture.

With a roll of her eyes, she moved toward them.

"We're breaking her in." He cocked his head toward Declan. "For a little extra, I'll make sure she does you extra. You got the cash, you got access to whatever you want."

The woman's saunter held a grace he hadn't seen in a while—like she'd been on a runway once or a performance stage. As she grew closer, her blue eyes sparkled like the waters off a Caribbean island.

"Hi, I'm Phoenix Rising." Her gaze dropped to his cane quickly and then back to his face. Not an ounce of pity showed in her face, a gift she probably had no clue she'd given him.

"She'll get a rise out of you, for sure," the doorman chuckled. "You know what they say about redheads, right? Firebrands... the lot of them. She gets too hot, you've got that cane." He lifted his chin. The man was giving him permission to hit one of his dancers? He'd seen enough, gotten enough. A few inhales of feminine perfume, a bit of skin-on-skin contact was all he could hope for.

"Heading out."

The doorman gripped her arm. "She'll do whatever you want. Won't you, Red?"

She tried to yank her arm free. The guy held it so tightly her lower arm grew paler from restricted blood.

"Let her go."

The guy dropped his hand and huffed. "Like I said—"

"Lap dance." The words tumbled out of his mouth. "That's all I want." He pulled out a hundred from inside his jacket—one of three he'd put there with thoughts of slipping them under St. Mary's of the 2nd street Episcopal church door before ending things. His one last gift to the God that had abandoned him long ago to put *Him* in Declan's debt for fucking once.

The doorman snatched it, and the woman glared at him. "You came in after eight. You know what that means."

Mick had told Declan what that meant. The time of day the girls arrived equaled the percentage they got to keep. The later they arrived, the less their percentages no matter what they did when they were there. Phoenix wasn't seeing any of that hundred.

"Phoenix." Declan dipped his chin. "Do me the honors." He held out his elbow, his other hand gripping his cane. He could at least get her away from the fucking doorman.

"Of course." She took his arm and papered on a smile. With one last glare at the doorman, she led him to a set of curtains.

The private rooms in back were small, a six-foot-by-six-foot space with a double-wide chair illuminated in dark red and purple light. Piped-in music floated down from the ceiling. After making a point to leave his cane out of his own reach, he lowered himself to the double-sided vinyl chair.

"What's your name, gentleman?" She ran a hand up and down the arm the doorman had gripped, angry red finger-print marks blooming.

"Declan."

"Well, Declan. I'm so happy you came tonight."

Sure, she was. "Sorry he grabbed you like that. I'll make sure you're paid."

Her lips twisted in amusement. "Is this your first time to a strip club, Declan?" She softened her voice as if willing up some innocence and took two steps forward.

"No, but you—"

"Don't. Worry." She placed a finger on his lips and strad-dled him, her thighs barely touching his. "I'll report him to the stripper's union." One side of her lips inched up and her hips rolled over his legs in sensual undulations.

His single backpack left back at that motel with all his possessions weighed more than she did. She was like a rare, tropical bird—flaming red hair over skin as white as milk. He'd give anything to have bare legs, to feel the skin of her thighs on his. He hardened instantly.

Her full breasts brushed softly across his face, and her scent—cinnamon cookies—rose up a warm ache in his heart. Bruises marring her delicate neck caught his attention.

He touched her skin there, and she flinched. Their eyes locked.

"He give those to you?"

She didn't answer. "Where are you from?" Her eyes cleared as if she'd mentally shaken something from her mind.

"Here. But I've been away."

She put a little space between their chests but kept her hips rocking. "Vacation?" Her eyes lit up, an obvious act. She was more intelligent than she played. All that blue flickered with attention and thoughts.

"Prison."

She eased off him. She wouldn't want to touch him after learning that. Instead, she lifted her hair and let it cascade over her shoulders as she swayed. "You just got out? Congratulations." She undulated and flitted thin fingers over her hips. Had he ever seen anyone so pale? She glanced down at his hard-on attempting to punch through his pants.

"Sorry." Hiding his reaction to her, however, was near impossible.

She laughed. "That's the point." Her knee slipped between his.

The urge to run his hands over her shoulders, her arms, down to her tiny waist obliterated his thinking.

Red hair covered his face as she placed both hands on the back of the chair and leaned toward him. "Besides, if you didn't walk out of here with a huge hard-on, it means I've failed."

"I don't think you could ever fail."

She pulled back a little so he could peer directly into her eyes. His heart wrenched at the sadness he found there.

How did she end up here? How did he? Why did he believe going to a strip club, a pathetic attempt to get a little humanity before ending things, was a good idea at all? How had anything happened the way it did?

Before prison, he'd lived a good life—at least, until the MacKenna family got him in their sights. Now, he was a former antiques dealer who'd gone to prison under a set-up because he wouldn't play nice with that mob family—a group he didn't even realize he'd been related to most of his life.

As soon as they'd learned of his existence, a long-lost cousin and nephew to the family's patriarch, his life had shrunk like a corpse in the desert heat. First, they'd tried to lure him into the family business. When he'd balked, the threats came. Then, when their strong-arm tactics didn't work, they'd set him up for vehicular manslaughter, thanks to some tampered with brakes. Antiques dealer to prison in less than one afternoon—what a bad made-for-TV movie.

"I went to prison for an accident." He needed to explain. He didn't want her scared of him.

"I'm sure it was."

"It was."

"I believe you." Her pink tongue darted out to lick her top lip.

"Good."

She let out a soft half-laugh. "Why do you care if I believe you?" She spun and presented her backside—perfect, tight, alabaster white. She rocked her hips over his erection.

"Don't want you to think I'm a criminal who's violent. Like your doorman."

She turned to face him. "Don't do anything." She backed away. The music had died. "I hope you enjoyed your dance." That fake smile was back. "Come on, I'll escort you out."

"You deserve better." Why was he talking to her like this? Maybe because she didn't belong here. He didn't either, but then he didn't belong anywhere. But this woman? Her skin, like cream, didn't belong against the glaring colored lights, cracked black vinyl chairs, and stained red carpets. Her eyes —God, those blue eyes that held so many secrets, full of intelligence but also anguish and pain—didn't match the smile she'd forced on her face.

"How are you here?" His mouth couldn't stop questioning this inexplicable dichotomy.

She held out her hand. "Oh, didn't I tell you? I have a master's in Shakespeare studies. I'm just having fun here." She winked and helped him stand, which was humiliating as fuck.

"'All the world's a stage and all the men and women merely players?'"

"'They have their exits and their entrances; And one man in his time plays many parts,'" she completed and handed him his cane. "I always did like a man with a cane. It's elegant and…" She stopped short and a peach flush bloomed across her cheeks.

Jesus, she was beautiful.

He handed her his last two $100 bills, all the money he had in the world. "Thank you. And keep at least one of these bills for yourself."

"Hey." She stopped him from stepping through the curtain. "How about a second dance? On the house as a congratulations for getting out. I can tell you're one of the good ones."

The good ones? Hardly. "You'll get in trouble."

"I'm always in trouble." She winked. "Firebrand and all."

She led him to the couch and straddled him anew. "It must have been hard on the inside." She then placed her small hands alongside his neck and it felt so fucking, insanely good because she'd dropped the stripper act for a minute.

He shrugged. "Life is funny that way." He swallowed down the emotion that threatened to rise. "How'd you end up here? You don't seem like you belong at a strip club."

She stopped moving, stared into his eyes. "Neither do you."

The curtain swiped back, and the doorman barreled inside. "You only paid for one dance."

Phoenix jumped off him and stood with her back flattened against the wall. She held up a hundred. "Oh, he did."

The guy reached over and yanked the second hundred from her bra. "And this? You skimming now?"

"No, she's not." Declan set his cane out in front to block the guy.

"Yeah, yeah. Take it outside." He inclined his head. "This ain't your problem anymore."

"Listen—"

"Get out," the man said to Declan.

No, he wouldn't. He stayed between the ass and Phoenix, but two more bodyguards showed up and had no trouble yanking him out. Just as he was through the curtains, the sickening thud of a man's fist against flesh filled the air.

Declan wrenched around, slipping from one of the guys' grasp. Phoenix was crouched to the floor, hands against her cheek. All her red hair waterfalled over her perfect shoulders, hiding her eyes. Trace curled his hands into her hair and yanked her up. Declan had never wanted to pummel a man so badly.

One of the goons who gripped his arm growled, "Leave it. She's used to it."

"I'll be back," Declan said right into her gaze.

The doorman took Phoenix by the arm, yanked her past him and toward another set of curtains.

"Don't bother. We got better girls." The bodyguard jerked him in the opposite direction.

No, they didn't—and he would be back.

Fate, kismet, whatever anyone wanted to call his visit, Declan wouldn't leave her here.

He wasn't walking into that river.

2

———————

Present Day

I quit.

The ink feathered and the cocktail napkin ripped at Phoenix's hurried writing, but the words were visible, which was all that mattered. No one was judging her penmanship, and no one could blame her for quitting Shakedown—immediately. Not even her sisters, who she'd convince to go with her, would argue. Any place was better than a burlesque club owned by someone with ties to a local crime family.

She glanced around Declan's office until her eyes landed on the perfect spot to place her resignation letter. She propped the wilting napkin against a picture of the three of them—herself and her sisters, Starr and Luna.

She tromped to the door just as Declan opened it.

A mask of pure boredom dropped onto his face. "Have a seat."

"I'm leaving." She stepped back to let him in—and her out.

He entered but stopped in front of her and blocked her way. "Not going to let me explain?"

"There's nothing to explain." She crossed her arms. "You are a member of the MacKenna mob family—the family that almost killed my sister..." Jesus. Her voice had cracked. She pried her gaze from Declan's perfect silver-gray eyes framed by his perfect eyelashes—eyelashes that should never be gifted to a man.

Declan's cane thumped once on the ground as if making a point. "I'd have killed them all before I let that happen. Take a seat and let me explain." He moved closer to his desk, stared at her note.

He lifted the napkin toward her. "Take. A. Seat. Phoenix." His voice was pure iron, which was rich, given what she'd just learned about the man.

After the year they'd had? Learning he was related to a mob family? Even she hadn't thought things could grow worse after one of the MacKennas almost killed Starr.

Her sister had to fall in love with Nathan, an ex-con that started this complete mess. The MacKenna mob family wanted him dead. Starr got in their crosshairs and... *stop, just stop.* She rubbed her forehead as if that would erase the image of her sister curled up in a hospital bed that arose every time she even thought the name MacKenna. Her stomach roiled a little from the remembered antiseptic smell, a scent she'd grown familiar with at too young an age thanks to their deadbeat, alcoholic father who'd nearly killed *her*. Too many men throwing their weight around, using them as punching bags...

"Six years, Declan. I've danced for you for six years." She held up her fingers. "And you didn't think to tell us yourself that you... you..." Jesus, she might stop breathing. Her chest was going to explode. Her hand moved to over her heart. It ached, an honest-to-God pang even though she knew where heartache lived. Only the romantics believed pain lived in that blood-pumping organ. Anguish took up residence in your bones.

He sighed and dropped to his chair that gave off a loud complaint. "It's not what it seems." He rested his cane against the edge of the desk.

"Oh, really? Did I not hear Nathan say the words on your loading dock *'your MacKenna relatives'*?" She and Starr had been rooting around the back looking for costumes and came upon Nathan and Declan chatting under the dock door. Nathan uttered those words and Declan did not deny them.

"Well?" she gritted out.

He studied her. "Are you going to wear a hole in my Oriental carpet next?"

She halted in her tracks, placed both hands on his desk, and leaned forward. "You know why I can't stay. You know my past. I could dance here because it was safe. But now? You're related to the family that almost took my sister away from me." She couldn't talk anymore. Her throat squeezed shut, maybe forever. Now if she could only keep the torrent of rage at bay.

How could he have been someone she didn't really know? All this time? For so many years, she'd wondered what it'd be like to be with a man like Declan, someone who appeared perfect. She should have known better. Perfect lied.

She stared at the little flowers and swirls woven into the carpet under her feet. Finally, more air entered her chest now that Declan's face wasn't in her sights.

What would it take for she and her sisters to live a life that didn't involve being worried about anyone getting cut, punched, kidnapped, threatened, blackmailed, and any other crap that had gone on in their lives?

It would take going far, far away.

"Phoenix, please, look at me."

Her lids lifted, lured by the gentleness in his voice. He had that uncanny ability to do that—hook her by kindness and bring her back to him again and again. But it was time for them to break the pattern.

Declan's eyes softened. "I'm related to them. I'm not like them, you of all people know that."

He spoke the truth. He wasn't like them—at all. "But they are dangerous." Her words were barely a whisper.

"They are."

"So, you'll have nothing to do with them?"

His silence answered. He couldn't *not* deal with them—not when they were coming at this club and the people inside it with both barrels raised.

Still, she had to hear the words straight from him. "So, they could be around…"

"I'm working on making sure they're not."

"But they still want something from you. So, you're wondering why I'm leaving? I won't let them traumatize my sister anymore. I'm going to protect her from that."

"Like you always do." His soft smile loaded with so much kindness her heart nearly cracked in two. She had to toughen up, curl that hard shell around her.

She wheeled away from him once more, unable to look into his eyes anymore.

A long sigh emitted behind her. "Do your sisters know you are quitting? Leaving them to hold the bag on the show tonight?"

Her sisters shouldn't pay for his fuck-up, but she had to hold her ground. "I'll dance tonight, but then…" Her throat closed anew at the thought of really leaving.

Shakedown had been her world, a safe place for her and her sisters to dance, the only thing they knew how to do. Declan had shown them a different kind of life than the one they'd been thrust into far too young—stripping and demeaning themselves to have something to eat. Now? This place was as dangerous as Maxim's, only instead of fists, she'd have to stand in front of bullets to keep Starr and Luna protected.

Declan cleared his throat. "And then what? Where will you go?"

She swallowed. That was the problem—she didn't have anywhere to go other than Shakedown.

"Phoenix."

She couldn't face him or she'd lose control. His gentle ways would ensnare her, take over.

She strode to the door. His hand fell to her arm, and she jerked herself against the door. God, he'd moved quickly. He'd been out from behind his desk, across the floor, and to the door in seconds, his cane barely making a sound across the thick Oriental carpet.

She'd reacted as she always did and how she always would when it came to being touched by surprise. She'd flinched. She'd always cringe, even from a man like Declan, because that's what survivors did when they'd had so many men abuse them. They stopped drinking from the well that poisoned them.

He held up his hands in surrender. "I didn't mean to take you by surprise, but please, tell me you're going to be okay."

"I'm going to be okay." Her words were truth because, honestly, what was okay, anyway?

"Tell me you won't go back." He wisely let his words die off. They both knew where "back" was—Maxim's strip club.

"I'll never go back to anything like that again." Thanks to him, she wouldn't. She'd also wise up.

Perhaps now her illusions about their boss, the too-good-to-be-true gentleman, could finally take a rest. Declan Phillips was her constant the last six years—her perfect, out of reach fantasy she kept at bay. Declan wanted her in all the ways a man wants a woman, but such a relationship was impossible for her.

Perhaps this recent development was God's way of calling the last shot. Because God knew Declan wouldn't have liked what he found once he'd wormed himself inside her.

She yanked open his office door and jogged to the dressing room before that lump lodged in her throat broke loose.

For now, she had her next move to play. Starr and Luna had to go with her so she had to find the right words to convince them of leaving. She'd wait until the show was over tonight. They'd fight it, but no way was she leaving without them and losing the only people who truly understood her. Declan would be fine without them, but Phoenix wouldn't be without her sisters. They were all she had, and if Starr and Luna wouldn't protect themselves, she would do it. She'd lay down her life for them. In fact, she already had more than once.

3

Declan's gaze softened as he tuned into the saxophone's wail. He couldn't get a lock on the music tonight—the melody, the harmony, or the beat.

He should go. He should be back at his own club, Shakedown, and not hanging out at Henry's Jazz Café on a Saturday evening, of all things. His mood—and utter disinterest in hanging around his own place—was all that woman's fault. He'd needed time to think without seeing all her red-gold hair and wide blue eyes aiming utter disgust at him over what she'd learned about him.

"Look what the fat cat dragged in." Henry dropped into the chair next to him. "Shouldn't you be at your own place?"

"Yes." He jerked his chin toward the stage. "See you got someone new in." The saxophonist was new and was taking improvisation turns every chance he got. To many people, jazz music sounded like a hot mess. While most people wanted the structure and pleasant progressions of pop or classical music, he rather enjoyed the unpredictability of jazz. It kept him alert.

The man grinned. "Yeah, the kid's good. Can't seem to drag him off the stage."

Declan motioned to the waitress he'd take another cognac.

For long minutes neither man said anything, just enjoyed the notes dancing in the surrounding air. The silence between them didn't last long because Henry couldn't ever leave well enough alone.

Henry sucked in some air. "Okay, what'd she do?"

"Who?"

"Whenever you show up, I know your brain is full of The Sunset."

The problem was worse than that. His brain was *always* full of Phoenix Rising, the woman who once saved his life and didn't even know it. She danced for him, ignored him, and repeated the pattern five nights a week—well, until tonight, when she, his lead dancer and general pain-in-his-ass, quit. On a fucking napkin.

Shit. Phoenix had been warming up to him when his past had to come rearing its ugly head. Finding out you were related —estranged as he was—to one Irish wannabe mob family like the MacKennas would turn any woman off to you forever.

A fresh glass of cognac appeared in front of him. "What else can I get you, Declan?"

The pretty, single, and available waitress, who also was Henry's niece, smiled down at him. He only knew her statuses because she repeatedly announced them. Her eyes trailed down his chest and back up to his face. *This* was a woman he should be involved with—not some overly dramatic hot-head like Phoenix.

"We're good, Lady." Henry gave her a wink.

After she scooted away, the man resumed his study of Declan.

"Go on. Say what you're dying to say." Henry would eventually come out with unwanted advice, so he might as well get it over with.

"When you gonna get off the duff and make it happen?"

"Nothing to make happen."

The man chuckled. "Employee manual doesn't allow you dating her or something?"

He should have never confided his obsession with Phoenix to his friend—a late-night boo-hoo-fest after a particularly lonely evening. He'd gone on about her and how she'd turned him down for the hundredth time. Dinner, coffee, a drink at Shakedown's bar—she wouldn't accept a single offer.

Declan huffed and took a sip of cognac. "Came here to get away from my troubles. Not air them."

"Shit, man. Women are trouble whether you're with them or not."

Truth in spades. Managing a club of twelve regular dancers—most of them women, including three sisters who were identical triplets—meant he regularly found himself immersed in female energy that could swallow a man. Dealing in antiques a decade-and-a-half ago was much easier. Furniture and paintings didn't rebuff you.

He'd tried everything he could think of with Phoenix. Avoiding her. Staying close to her. Giving her space. Slotting her in the employee box in his mind. Putting her out of his mind—fat lot that attempt did. He'd run out of boxes to shove her in. Any sane man would have shaken their obsession with someone like her by now.

His hand found its way to his hair as if he could tug out memories of the last twenty-four hours so they no longer mattered.

Henry scratched the divot above his top lip. "Hey, I'm still glad you stopped in. Got word on the street some guy is buying up clubs up and down the East Coast."

He swung his gaze to the man over the abrupt change in topic. "You get approached?"

"Some guy named MacKenna. Made a very generous offer. Too generous, if you know what I mean."

Jesus. "Don't trust them. I don't."

"You, too, huh?"

"Repeatedly."

Henry slanted his eyes. "How dangerous are we talkin'?"

"Defcon one." That family had a way of destroying everyone around them but walking away unscathed.

Declan placed his elbows on the table, lowered his voice. "This is what I can tell you. They're buying up music halls, clubs, warehouses, anything they can get their hands on, all waterfront. For what purpose?" He shrugged an answer to his own question. "They specialize in import-export if you get my meaning."

Figuring out MacKenna's next move should be his focus, not how to make sure a certain woman worked for him so she could continue to torment him with her snubs.

Henry stood, turned his chair, and straddled it. He dropped his voice to a whisper. "How much you muscling up over there?"

"All of it." Declan's attention split for a second to the man's nephew who guarded the door, a large black man who'd stretched the limits of his camo t-shirt, and then swung to several other men assessing the leftover crowd. He was glad his friend had bodyguard coverage, but it wouldn't be enough to go against a family who'd seen the Godfather movies too many times and took out their frustrations on people you cared about.

His friend continued to assess him. "So, you know these guys."

"The MacKenna family and I don't get along... long story." No need to share the familial bond. He himself didn't want to know those facts and blabbing about it would only raise hopes he could sway that bloodthirsty family. He couldn't. Instead, he had to hold his own ground and make sure Henry did the same.

"Muscle up hard, Henry." Declan reached for his cane and pushed to standing. He drew out his billfold.

"On the house." Henry rose.

Declan threw down two fifty-dollar bills. "Give it to your niece, then." All of Henry's employees were family in some shape or another. It'd be a shame for him to lose his music hall but more so if he lost people he loved. Perhaps finding himself at Henry's Café tonight was a gift—one where he could alert his friend about MacKenna's plans.

Henry held out his hand. "Thanks for the warning."

"Don't tell them we're friends." He returned his friend's handshake. "I won't be back anytime soon now that you've been approached. For your safety."

"That bad, huh?"

"Watch your back, Henry." He broke the man's grip and made his way to the exit, not knowing when he'd return. No way would he jeopardize his friend's club because of his fucked-up situation. If the MacKennas knew of his connections, they'd use them to put on more pressure.

All his theories as to why the MacKenna family needed Henry's or Shakedown so badly proved worthy of the movies but not reality.

Shakedown, like Henry's, was on the waterfront, so they wanted to pick up running drugs using the Patapsco river as their highway.

Shakedown was profitable—very—so why not want it?

Shakedown employed people with records so they'd be

easily manipulated (they thought) and could be easily used in crime situations.

None of it made sense, though, because his club was only successful for one reason—the entertainment was unparalleled on the East Coast. And just like that, Phoenix Rising's face—fuck, every detail about her, from her delicate feet to that red hair streaked with sunlight—breached his mind. If she quit, her sisters weren't far behind. Too bad moving locations wouldn't take them off the MacKenna's radar screen.

As soon as he got to the parking lot, he eased himself into the '57 Chevy Bel Air and goosed it with some gas. While he waited for the engine to settle, he ran his hands over the steering wheel. They didn't make cars like this anymore. It'd been a little self-indulgent—and risky—taking her out tonight given the November weather was unpredictable as hell these days, but he'd needed something to remind himself of less-complicated times.

Just as he was about to lurch his car into drive, his gaze fell on a black limousine idling near the parking lot exit. Not a usual sight in this part of town. Hell, not a usual sight in Baltimore at all.

The window was down. Carragh MacKenna was easy to spot sitting in the back. His ice-blue eyes shone through the dark. Declan had been followed, or perhaps the man was back for a second offer to Henry. Neither possibility was good.

Turns out he was wrong on both accounts because when he strode over to confront the man, Carragh cracked open his door and gestured for him to join him. "You got a second, Declan? Get in."

4

When dancing, there was sometimes a moment when the music took over Phoenix's body. Some nights it took a while to get blessedly lost in the movement and music. Sometimes it didn't happen at all, and she would have to tap into every ounce of her dance experience to give off that effortless air. On rare evenings, total immersion happened as soon as she stepped through the heavy velvet curtain onto the stage and the spotlight warmed her skin.

Tonight was not that night—and not because it was her last hurrah at Shakedown. A gun—not allowed in the burlesque club—peeked out of a man's suit jacket as he splayed himself out in a chair close to the stage.

At seeing her step on stage, the man cocked his head toward the guy sitting next to him. Their shoulders and arms nearly burst the seams of their suit coats. Their size was menacing enough, but their dark and assessing eyes turned her blood to ice.

Please, not tonight. It was a futile prayer.

The two men's gazes trailed her body as if they were picking which part they'd try to own first. A familiar sneer across their face was next, its message clear. *Don't disappoint me.*

Adrenaline pumped through her body hard, too hard to be useful. Instead, a familiar nausea crept up her throat. An even more familiar urge to run, throw off her heels and make a break for it, threatened on the edge of her consciousness. God, it angered her to the core that the man, the scum, could have any effect on her.

He took a lazy sip of his drink, eyes trained on her over the rim of the glass. When he pulled the glass away from his lips, the scuzzball licked the edge. Itchy heat prickled her skin as an instinctual alarm hummed in the background of her mind. His hand reached down under the table, and his body shifted a little in his chair as if the guy was rearranging his balls. Then the hound winked at her.

Her insides clamped shut.

She loved that something as simple as a leg kick or smile would light up the audience. Sometimes they crossed a line, however, where their need for fantasy morphed into their need for her submission—like those two guys' attitudes.

Only her years of dancing experience kept her legs from marching her off the stage. She was a professional and wouldn't run. Instead, she gazed into the darkness that shrouded the audience.

Body shapes moved and flashes of diamond bracelets broke through the dark. A slight pang hit her chest at the thought of leaving Shakedown, even if it was the right thing to do. Declan's club wasn't a cheap night out, and for that, she was ever-thankful. No sweaty palms filled with dollar bills approached the stage. Here, patrons laid down platinum American Express cards to pay for bottles of Macallan and rare wines Declan found.

Where the hell was he, anyway? Was he not here? He'd never let armed reprobates waltz in and take the best seat in the house. How did they get past security with guns? Her eyes, the traitors that they were, lifted and searched for Declan at his usual place—leaning casually against the end of the polished wood bar, the brass rail gleaming under pendulum lights. Not seeing him, her nerves threatened to break through what little courage she had to keep dancing.

She pranced across the thirty-foot stage and tried to forget all about men with guns and mob relations and what happened to Starr mere months ago.

She spun in a series of three-point turns, the beaded fringe banging against her thighs. The crowd cheered, and an intense, intoxicating power filled all her limbs at the sound. The feeling soon vanished as she was back at stage right in front of those two barbarians again.

The last horn notes of the song crashed over her and she caught the end of the boa in a final rainbow toss over her head. For a brief second, the ensuing applause cooled her unwelcomed fear.

The guy's hand still curled around his tumbler, his gaze still running up and down her body. Her own gaze seemed to have a mind of its own, like telling yourself not to look at a car accident you passed but being unable to divert your eyes. The guy lifted his tumbler to his mouth and licked the edge once more, slowly and deliberately.

A memory surfaced. She'd seen those two men before— outside the hospital where they took Starr after Ruark MacKenna attempted to kill her. The men were with Tomas MacKenna, the head of the MacKenna clan.

Their presence only meant one thing. Declan was in serious trouble, which meant she and her sisters were, too. In fact, what was she doing still standing in front of him like a deer caught in headlights?

Maybe it was because she knew she was soon leaving, or maybe her taking a stand with Declan emboldened her, but a flicker of some inner mettle sparked. Letting men get away with this kind of shit only meant they'd do it again to someone else.

Cherry stepped from behind the curtain and hooked her arm into Phee's. She urged the crowd to clap louder, harder for Phee's routine. Such a good emcee—and blind as hell since she must not have seen that guy's gesture. Cherry didn't take kindly to gross behavior either. Neither of the men clapped but rather toyed with their empty glasses. Phee got off the stage as quickly as she could.

As fast as her heels could take her, she got to the main floor. She hunted down Max, who was standing in the back on the handicapped ramp. Her message was simple. "Two guys, front row, guns. What the fuck?" She hated herself for that last question, but the man was usually more vigilant than this. He tossed people out left and right if given the chance.

Max nodded once and darted to the floor in a flash. One quick glance up by the stage and she saw both men had vanished. Maybe them being here was a blessing in disguise. They solidified her decision to leave Shakedown.

"Oh, man, you're great," a male voice boomed behind her.

She recoiled and the black curtain separating the main floor from the hallway leading to the back rooms caught on part of her costume. She froze as the man exhaled liquor breath over her face. She fumbled but managed to split the curtain and get on the other side of it. She slapped her hand over her chest as she wobbled a little on her heels down the hall. Adrenaline thrummed through her body.

It was one thing to dance on stage, an invisible wall between her and the audience. It was something entirely different to be within a foot of someone, liquored up and eyeing her like she was a doll that could be played with. It made her understand why pregnant women got so miffed when people reached out to pat their round bellies as if their body was somehow now part of the public domain.

The dressing room door was wide open and laughter from her two sisters spilled into the hallway. She dashed for it then gently closed the door behind her and leaned against it. One long second passed as she caught her breath.

"What?" Luna stood. "What happened out there?" Of course, she read Phee's face. The three of them had been inside each other's heads since birth.

She pushed off the door. "I quit Shakedown tonight."

Starr slowly swiveled her head and put down her lipstick on her makeup stand. "You did what?"

"You heard me." She unclipped the metal hooks of her corset—maybe for the last time—and sucked in another long breath. "It's not safe here. Not even a bit."

She raised her hand before Starr could voice the objections that shone across her face. She needed a second to re-center and then she'd convince them. She had to.

And, if she wasn't here, Declan could find someone who didn't flinch every time he got near. He was a good man who deserved a good woman.

5

———

Declan was a fool to slip into the back of Carragh's limo at midnight, but the second someone showed fear, the MacKennas pounced.

A blond woman with a dress hiked up to her crotch had one leg draped over Carragh. Her thick, fake eyelashes dipped down as she ran her gaze over Declan.

The man drew her face to him and brushed hair off her cheek. "Sweetheart, give us a minute."

She looked aghast. "You want me to get out?"

"Go sit with Sean."

When she didn't move, his eyes narrowed. She slipped off him, cracked open the door, and got into the passenger seat up front. The privacy screen raised immediately.

"You're going to pay for that move later." Declan adjusted his overcoat.

"She doesn't care enough." Carragh lifted a vodka bottle his way in offering, which Declan shrugged off.

"Having women trouble?"

"Once a woman is trouble, she's no longer my concern."

What a prick. The limo lurched, and they were off to God

knew where. He kept one eye out the window to keep his bearings. "Want to tell me where we're going?" Declan wasn't here to discuss women.

Carragh poured himself a healthy portion of the Grey Goose. "Around the block. We need to talk and this might be the most privacy we'll ever get." He set the bottle back in its holder.

"Then out with it."

"I appreciate a man who cuts to the chase." He adjusted his suit coat and took a sip of his drink. "Regarding our potential business dealings..."

Declan raised his hand. "Let me stop you there. There is no 'our.'"

"That's because you believe we are proposing an older business model."

"Is that what we're calling dealing drugs now? An older business model?"

He had the gall to smirk. "My father has new interests. Nothing illegal—"

"Bullshit." The limo turned right, he noted.

"Stand down, Declan, and listen." The man sighed. "He's out of the drug game. Now, he wants to be more into legitimate businesses. At my urging, I'll add."

"You done quoting *The Godfather* to me? Because I have a few things to say. One, my club isn't for sale. Two, I know what legitimate is, and your father isn't it. I know that, and my mother knew that. The man doesn't deserve to be near any woman ever, and certainly not my dancers."

"You think we'd hurt our assets?"

Such a MacKenna saying. "And therein lies the heart of it. You consider my employees 'assets.'"

"Most businesses do." Carragh took a sip of his drink, the ice clinking against the glass.

"They're people. With real lives."

"Who will continue to have real lives. With more protection—"

"From what? You?"

Carragh took in another long lungful of air and blew it out, which was patronizing as shit as if he steeled himself to explain something to a toddler.

"Trying your patience, am I?" Declan asked. Another right-hand turn. Perhaps they *were* going around the block.

"Protection from the vagaries of the entertainment world. Times are changing." Carragh swirled the liquid in his glass. "One recession, one shift in the market demand, and your little Phoenix there—oh, yes, I know all about your obsession with her—is back stripping at Maxim's."

Hearing Carragh say her name lit up his spine. And how the hell did he know about Maxim's, anyway? He wouldn't give the man any satisfaction at seeing his words had an effect, however. "My dancers can get gigs anywhere—far from you. And nothing is recession-proof. Not even the mob."

The man raised his eyebrows. "And therein lies *your* problem, Declan. You don't see us as we are. We're a family that owns many businesses—a family business—with the management acumen to weather any storm. And believe me, things are going to be run differently from now on."

"Tomas finally giving up his crown?"

"Let's just say I know how to make him come around."

"I seriously doubt that, and I have no interest in being folded into the family."

Carragh ran his finger over his top lip. "I'm very sorry to hear of your mother's passing. I regret we never met."

"She didn't."

He chuffed a little. "No, I suppose not, given she disappeared for, what, forty-some years?"

It would have been longer if it weren't for an overzealous

obituary writer in Kansas City. Some kid trying to make a name for himself connected the dots that Declan's mother, Kate Louise MacKenna Phillips, was related to a family that had recently gone through an expensive and fruitless money laundering case that captured headlines. The most innocuous detail—a traffic violation—uncovered her given name. It didn't take long for the MacKennas to find Declan, the long-lost nephew of Tomas MacKenna, who had some pathological need to know where every ounce of his DNA had settled.

"It was damned impressive, though, that she stayed hidden with a son for so long." The ice in his glass clinked too loudly. "Damned impressive, indeed."

"Jealous?"

A sliver of something flashed across his eyes. Maybe Carragh was jealous. Being born into the MacKenna family couldn't be fabulous. They had mapped his future out for him since birth. They'd done the same for Declan's mother, which she vehemently rebelled against. Getting cancer and dying at age 62 was the icing on the shit cake of her life. She may be dead and buried, but she'd saved Declan from the family, getting him away before he was even born. He wouldn't let her sacrifice go to waste.

Carragh examined the contents of his glass. "Consider having a discussion—with me. That's all I'm asking."

"I already have."

He raised his gaze to Declan. "No, you balked the second any idea was brought up. I realize my brother, Ruark, was a bit heavy-handed in delivering the original offer but—"

"Heavy-handed? Is that what we're calling kidnapping and assault now?"

"The incident with Mr. Baldwin and Miss O'Malley was unfortunate. It won't happen again. Ruark is doing time, for God's sake."

"As he should. But you're right. It won't happen again."

He'd take a bullet before he'd let any one of them near the O'Malley sisters—or any of his Shakedown family.

"Time, Declan. Just asking for time."

Something wasn't right here, but he'd be damned if he spent another nanosecond ferreting out what Carragh was up to. None of it would be good, anyway. "Let me out," he called. The limo had made another right-hand turn. So, Carragh at least told the truth about going around the block. It was likely the only truth Declan had heard since seating himself in the pretentious vehicle.

The limo lurched to a stop. "I don't need time, Carragh. I need you to forget you know me."

Carragh shook his head. "You can't deny your own blood. The more you keep denying it, the more this family is going to want to grow close."

"Is that a threat?"

"Consider it a heads-up. That's one area where I agree with my father. Family is important."

Declan cracked open the door. They were done here. He slammed the door shut before the man could say another word.

He wasn't kidding. He owed his mother to fulfill her last dying wish—to remain independent of her family. He strode up the street swinging his cane, just one block from where they'd started. He didn't give a single backward glance at the limo.

Perhaps the walk would give him time to figure out how to keep Phoenix close to him because one, he was in love with the she-devil, and two, it was the only way to keep her safe, even if she believed the opposite. He was burning that napkin.

6

———

Luna's eyes widened like twin moons. "You can't quit. You have the matador act to do in fifteen minutes."

"No one cares." She waved her hand and leaned down to pick up a dress that lay in a puddle at her feet. It was probably Starr's. She was such a slob.

"Everyone cares." Luna crossed her arms. "What happened out there tonight? Something most definitely did."

She lowered her voice so only her sisters could hear. No reason to scare Aspen, who sat ten feet away at her makeup table. "Two guys. Guns. Front row. It's only the beginning." She hung the dress on the garment rack.

"Did you tell Max because he'd—"

"They're already gone. Now we need to be. Don't worry, I will figure something out for all three of us."

Starr's eyes darted to Aspen, who pressed her finger against her false eyelash and blinked at herself in the mirror. "Hey, Aspen, you able to fill in for Phee in fifteen?"

The girl shrugged. "Sure." She rose. "Not getting in between you three. I'll be in the kitchen."

"Thanks." Phee nodded at her. Their fellow dancer understood something important was going down.

After Aspen had closed the door behind her, Starr's telltale left eyebrow rose as it always did when she wasn't buying whatever was being sold. "And where, pray tell, are you expecting us to go? Burlesque clubs aren't exactly de rigueur on the entertainment scene anymore."

"Does it matter?"

Luna's hand landed on her forearm. "This is about Declan, isn't it? And what you heard? I, for one, am not surprised about it."

"Why aren't you?" She shrugged off her sister's touch. They'd reported what they'd learned about Declan to Luna. Her response? A shrug.

"It might make things easier."

"Easier? You're kidding, right?"

Luna cocked her head in disapproval. "Phee, like I said this afternoon, Declan can't help it if Tomas MacKenna wants to buy him out. But Declan would never let anything happen to us. He's proven that."

"Like he'd never let anything happen to Starr?" That blind trust led to her being kidnapped a few short months ago. Sure, Nathan, her fiancé, was probably more to blame for that one given he was the one in the MacKennas' sights, but still…

"That wasn't his fault." Starr tapped her blusher against the countertop, spraying the top with tiny flecks of red. "Remember, Declan struck a deal with the MacKennas, too."

"Which I don't trust. It's probably time anyway, right? I mean…" Phee pointed to the bouquet on Starr's nightstand. Nathan had sent flowers complete with teddy bear and a balloon that read, "Just because I love you." Her sister would soon be married and move out—something Phoenix should have been prepared for long ago. But how could she have understood the depth of that cavern forming behind her ribs? Not living with her two sisters? An odd twist formed in her belly.

"Is that what this is about?" Starr rose from her stool. "Nathan and I haven't decided what we're going to do. It's not like we're moving overseas or something. We'll still be here in Baltimore."

"And I'm here." Luna's taffeta bustle rustled as she drew closer. "And whatever happened to talking things out with us? Our pact?"

Phee raised her eyebrows at her sister, who rolled her eyes in return. Luna got her message. *Are you kidding me* wasn't even close to how Phee felt about Luna's moves this past year.

Even though the three sisters forged an agreement years ago after they'd been separated across foster homes to always keep each other in the loop on all things that impacted all three of them, Luna had broken it spectacularly five months ago. She'd taken it upon herself behind Phee and Starr's backs to not only find their deadbeat father but to attempt a reconciliation. Fuck that. The hole in Phee's chest deepened another inch.

The man was in some halfway house for alcoholics, the address she'd never learned because no way was she visiting a man who landed her in a hospital at eleven years old.

If she thought about it—really thought about it—she could raise up one molecule of understanding around Luna's motivations. Her sister wanted to give Phee an opportunity to confront him. Phee wanted more than that. She wanted him obliterated from her memories, her life, her body. She rubbed that place on her forearm, felt the little ridge in the bone there where the baseball bat had landed.

Phee turned away from her sister and pulled out her matador costume. Someone—someone likely named Starr

—had moved it to the yellow section of the garment rack. Phee thrust it back into its rightful place so it aligned with the other red dresses. She plunked her butt down and eased her stocking off. "Whatever happened to our dedication to safety? First, you find the deadbeat, then Declan turns out to be a MacKenna, and now you want to hang out here?"

"Phee," Starr's soft voice interjected. "I'm fine. We're going to be fine. Remember, Declan—"

"God," Her breath puffed out in a long moan. "Declan can't do anything!" The MacKennas may have called a tentative truce where Nathan was concerned, but that didn't stop the fact their boss was one of them. He also was a single man, not an army—not to mention a pure gentleman with manners and impeccable taste, neither of which would help in this situation.

Jesus. Her eyes filled. She couldn't afford to fall apart now. "Frankly, you two are being far too cavalier about this whole affair."

Starr suddenly clutched her belly. "Ooof."

Phee swung her gaze to her. "What's wrong?"

"Not feeling that great today, that's all." Starr rolled her shoulders and groaned a little again.

"Where is Declan, anyway?" Luna started toward the door. "He can sort this out."

"I don't need more talking. I need out."

Luna turned and glanced at Starr. They quieted. So, the sudden silent technique? They thought she'd rant and get it out of her system? They were sorely mistaken. On this topic, she was unmovable.

"Declan's not here, L." Starr kept her eyes trained on Phee. "So that's why he left in such a huff. Nothing like having your lead dancer walk out on you. Leave your sisters holding up the entire show."

Oh, no, she wouldn't get away with that one. "This tough love thing will not work on me."

Starr's face paled. She pushed past Phee and jogged to the bathroom. Retching sounds echoed against the tiles.

Luna and Phee stared at one another. "If she has the flu…" Luna's hand flew to her mouth. "Or…"

"Or if she's pregnant?" The little potential bombshell landed square in the front of her brain probably because it'd be yet another horrible surprise of the day.

"Already? I mean, I thought they wanted to wait." So, Starr and L. had already been talking.

"Is she?" Phoenix glared at her sister. "Pregnant?"

Luna lifted her shoulders in a shrug. "I don't know."

Well, great. It was inevitable, though, wasn't it? One minute their sister was looking at bridal magazines, strewn across every surface of their apartment, and the next thing they knew they'd be picking out onesies and breast pumps.

They both moved to the bathroom. Starr was on her knees, both hands on either side of the toilet seat. Beads of her corset clicked against the porcelain.

"You okay?" Luna scooped hair off Starr's neck.

Starr pushed back onto her heels, her mouth slack, her eyes half-mast. Phee pulled out some paper towels from the wall dispenser and wet them. She handed them to Starr. "Something going on?"

"No. I'm not pregnant. We're not trying. Yeah, I overheard you." She pushed to her feet, dropping the paper towels in a wet plop on the floor. "Though Cherry's going to be disappointed. It would add to her flock." Starr lifted her eyes to Phee. "Sorry for scaring you."

"I'm not scared." The sick knot in her belly twisted anew. What had Phee expected? She or Luna would never have children? Have their own life? Yes, actually. They'd be together forever.

Starr pushed herself to standing. "It was bad Chinese food."

"You had salmon tonight."

"Yeah, with that disgusting truffle sauce you like so much." She chuckled lightly.

Phee wanted to return her laughter—she really, really did but couldn't.

"Do you seriously want to leave Shakedown?" Starr always got right to the point.

"All three of us need to."

"Why? And don't you dare say it's because of what Ruark MacKenna tried to do to me. You're not using him as an excuse to avoid falling in love with Declan. There, I said it."

Her damned eyes pricked. What was wrong with her? She didn't cry—ever.

Starr swallowed. "Sorry. I'm being blunt because I love you and I'm worried you see all men as the enemy."

"The question is why don't you?" Phee's brain had no trouble regularly inventorying all the crap from her life—most of which Starr and Luna had lived through, too. It seemed like she was the only one of the three, though, that had her past rise like inflated balloons at the bottom of a lake every single day of her life.

Finding their father had unearthed all kinds of things she'd buried deep. First, his alcoholic rages would arise in her mind, starting with the slamming of their bedroom door against the wall as he stormed inside and dragged her to the floor for no reason. Next always came the foster home, the image of which she did a reasonable job squishing with a mental fist immediately. If not, she'd have considered a lobotomy to end those memories. Then Maxim's strip club rose again. That one was harder to quash, maybe because it was the most recent set of humiliations the three of them had endured.

Starr shrugged. "I have Nathan now. Life is good."

Which is how you got in that mess to begin with she didn't say, but oh, so wanted to. Her sister's cavalier tone had to be some avoidance technique because the woman had nearly died at the hands of the sociopath Ruark. It was only a matter of time before Ruark was out on parole to exact his thwarted plans. And that would be fine by his family, right? Kill two birds with one stone—get rid of Nathan, rattle the owner of Shakedown until he sold to them. Then? They'd be slaves to a mob family that refused to let you go.

"You don't hate Declan." Starr smirked. "Ya know what Gabrielle called him? Declicious. It fits, don't you think?"

"Of course, I don't hate him." Her sisters had never understood her feelings about Declan Phillips, the man who would not stop mooning over her. Yes, that's what he did. He *mooned*. She didn't hate it or him. He wanted her in all the ways a man wanted a woman, and she could not go there. Letting herself fall for Declan was simply futile.

She turned away. Her makeup needed re-arranging. The lipsticks were not in the proper order. "And that's a ridiculous name, Declicious." Ick. It was juvenile and undignified—especially for him. He'd be a Sir Declan if anything.

In her periphery, Starr and Luna glanced at one another, then back at her, both sporting wide smiles. Ever since her sister got engaged to Nathan, Starr couldn't stop pushing everyone around her into romantic *whatevers*.

Phee cocked her head toward them. "I see you're feeling better, Starr."

Starr shrugged, staring into the mirror, swiping under her eyes. "I bounce back pretty easily."

Of the three of them, she had. That's where she differed from her sisters. They all had scars inside and outside, but hers were etched in her DNA.

"Tell you what." Phee squared herself to them. "If I find a

place for the three of us to dance, consider it. Sisters forever, friends always, remember?" She wasn't above pulling out their mantra. Starr and Luna had many times over the last few months.

Starr crossed her arms. "Consider, yes. Believe it'd ever be better than what Declan offers?"

"Unlikely." Luna sang.

Phee turned back to her mirror. "Good," she said to her reflection. It was a start. "See you both at home."

"You seriously aren't going on?" Luna's mouth dropped to an *O*.

"Seriously. I'm headed home and will feed Moonlight." The cat Nathan had brought home was the only good thing that came out of that union, as far as she was concerned. Good thing she'd adopted the little one out from under them. Starr's ability to hold a routine was nil.

"Well, let's hope we don't get fired first," Starr whispered under her breath.

7

———

"How?" Declan didn't stop to take off his coat when he posed the simple question to Trick and Max. As soon as he'd stepped outside of Henry's, one glance at his phone and a nightmare stared back at him.

<<Two guys. Guns. Gone now.>>

The two men followed Declan to his office because his face had to be wearing everything he felt about that message. Exposed. Provoked. But most of all? Fury. Phoenix spotting two men with guns was unacceptable. It should have been him. Instead, he'd been nursing a bruised ego at Henry's and pussyfooting around with Carragh in a goddamned limo.

Max cracked his knuckles. "Their IDs didn't read MacKenna, so we're not sure."

"I didn't ask what their names were. I asked how the ever-loving fuck they got inside packing."

"Unless I frisk every man and woman who comes in…"

"You can find flasks, you can find guns." Declan stared down his most trusted doorman and bouncer. The man wasn't sloppy, so this made no sense, especially after what had gone down mere months ago with the MacKenna clan.

Trick chuffed. "The guys likely had hidden their weapons until they could put them on display to the most vulnerable among us." He didn't need to name who—the women on stage. Blinded by floodlights, wearing high heels, few clothes, and expecting happy patrons? They might as well have been wearing targets instead of corsets.

"I want six new men hired by tomorrow."

"Your dime." Max shrugged and walked out. The man had to be pissed at Declan's tone, but shit, they'd targeted Phoenix.

Trick pushed off the wall he'd been holding up. "We always knew they'd be back."

Declan scrubbed his chin. "Carragh MacKenna isn't exactly playing by the rules we set a few months ago. Ran into the man tonight." Which couldn't have been a coincidence. He likely sent those guys into Shakedown because Declan had left. That meant they watched him. "Every employee gets an escort to their car. And don't spare the show of weapons."

Trick nodded. "Anything else?"

Declan threw down *The Baltimore Sun* newspaper and pointed. "Real estate section. That warehouse down the street went for $6 million in a bidding war. Anonymous buyer."

Trick picked up the paper. "Curious."

"That family is up to something, as usual."

"So much for the truce. They were to leave us alone and we leave them alone." Trick dropped the paper. "But they haven't made a move here…" He stopped his words, likely from the look Declan was searing into his skin with his eyes. They'd been moving alright. Two guys with guns showing up when he was absent? It'd been planned.

That family operated under one tenant—strategic takeovers. First, the MacKennas would shake up the environment by sending in people to merely appear menacing. Next, minor accidents would arise, like being run off the road. Then? A body would be found floating in the river right outside Shakedown.

Declan wouldn't wait for things to happen. "Where's Phoenix? Dressing room?"

Trick pursed his lips and shrugged. "Where she always is?"

The woman would stick close to her sisters or Cherry, the only people she got near. He glanced at his watch. Everyone might have already gone home.

He stormed to the dressing room wearing the wrong mood and the wrong words swimming on his tongue, wanting out. But there was no way he was letting any of his dancers near the parking lot without someone escorting them. Knowing her, she'd balk every step of the way. Tough.

"She's left already," L. reported once he made his way down there. "She texted."

He'd send someone to watch the apartment, pronto. "I suppose she told you what happened tonight."

Luna nodded.

"I'm handling it."

"We know." A kind smile spread across her face.

"Please make sure Phoenix knows that."

She sucked in air. "I'll do my best."

"Now, let's get you and Starr to your cars."

Luna's forehead bunched in concern, but she didn't balk. At least one of the O'Malley sisters was reasonable. He'd made a promise years ago he'd take care of the three of them, and he intended on fulfilling it to his dying day.

He drew out his phone and sent Phoenix a quick text. He debated whether to say something about the guys she'd encountered. What could he say, though?

<<You get home alright?>>

Three cascading dots appeared and then vanished. Words escaped her, too?

They were at an impasse—as usual.

8

Phee didn't cry—ever. That sting behind her eyelids, a rising sentimentality at confronting Maxim's sign over the red door, wouldn't shift into actual tears. Or perhaps all this sudden emotion was because she'd taken the initial step for her and her sisters to move on, and they'd balked so resolutely. Or perhaps it was seeing that young girl standing on the curb, hugging the backs of her arms, stomping her feet in those ridiculous high heels as if trying to keep warm. Six years ago, Phee had been that girl.

Phee should be back at her apartment. Her sisters would be pissed she wasn't home and for being out so late by herself. She'd needed to go for a drive to clear her head. Instead, she'd found herself parked in her VW on South Haven Street.

The *Girls Girls Girls* sign blinked a pink hue onto the slick pavement. She hated this street, hated the Maxim strip club, hated her memories of her time spent here, but tonight, she'd had to counter the men-measuring-the-size-of their-balls energy by doing something useful. A peek at what Maxim's spit out at the end of the night was harmless. If she came across someone who required help, she'd help. If not, her actions were a harmless drive-by.

The girl hopped a little to the left as she lost her balance. Jones didn't allow his strippers to turn down a drink with a customer—ever. She teetered on her heels, her face a slack mask. The women who stripped here often stumbled out of the club drunk and sloppy. The girl didn't look around once —not a single time—to see if any of the strip club's clients might be lingering in the shadows of the alley a mere six feet from her. Yeah, she was either young or brand new to this scene. The new girls were the stupidest girls.

Phee glanced at her dashboard clock. It read 3:52. If no one swung by to scoop her up by 3:55, Phee would swing her car around and offer her a lift.

Rain tapped on the roof and windshield. The weather that week had pivoted—as so many things in life did. One minute they enjoyed a beautiful fall. The next? The Baltimore skies turned gray and unforgiving. One day you're dancing in a swanky burlesque club, the next you're dancing in a swanky burlesque club that is owned by a MacKenna.

She curled her fingers tight around the steering wheel and mentally drew X's across the images of Declan in her mind—a trick to remove negative thoughts. Rachel, who used to work at the club, had shared the tip with her. They both had a need to constantly wipe their minds clean from memories pulling them down into a sinkhole. It was one of the very few things they had in common. Unlike Phee, however, Rachel was back at school getting her degree and about to have her first baby, two things Phoenix would never get to do.

A cab turned the corner at the bottom of the street, the triangle sign on its hood lit up. The stupid girl turned her face away from the approaching taxi, cupping her palms around a cigarette to light it. The cab whizzed by. Her face shot up and her arm flailed, attempting to hail him. She mouthed a curse and hitched her purse strap higher onto her shoulder. Hurried glances up the street told Phee no one was coming for this woman.

Phee had to move before Jones stepped out of the club and onto the concrete stoop, no doubt flanked by his two ponytail-sporting bodyguards. It was his pattern, anyway. The man couldn't resist an opportunity to abuse a damsel in distress.

Phoenix shifted into first gear and swung her car around to stop in front of the girl just as the front door of Maxim's cracked open. Jones' porky frame filled the doorway. A shudder coursed through her limbs—which truly annoyed her. The man dramatically drew in a lungful of air and stepped onto the concrete stoop. His guys, both in black T-shirts topped with cheap sports coats, did the same.

Phee couldn't stop now. She'd have to risk Jones noticing her—or worse, recognizing her. She leaned over and cranked the window down, the glass stuttering as it lowered. "Hey, need a ride?"

"Lady, whoever you are…" The girl raised her hand. "But I don't swing that way." She furiously marched up the sidewalk, swiping water off her forehead. At least the girl had some sense of self-preservation. Not all of them did.

Phee let the car drift and follow her up the road. "I'm not picking you up. I'm offering to drop you off at your house. I, uh, used to dance for Jones there." She cocked her head backward toward Maxim's.

The girl stopped and nervously looked around as if weighing her options—which Phee knew weren't many. She and her sisters had been where this young woman was too many times to count.

She came over and settled her forearms on the doorframe, now wet with rain. "Who'd you say you were?" She was pretty with long blond hair, but she would be. Jones didn't hire women unless he was sure his patrons would be desperate to stuff dollar bills into their G-strings—and ejaculate in their pants on sight.

Phee held out her hand. "Phoenix. I'm a dancer at Shakedown." Or was, until tonight.

"Never heard of it." She ignored Phee's offered handshake.

Phee picked out her business card, ones she had made up for these occasions, and held it out. The girl took the card and eyed it suspiciously. "Huh." She scanned Phoenix's name and phone number. "You one of those religious types who go around trying to save people or something?"

"No. I can't save anyone or anything. You want that ride?" Jesus, girl, make up your mind and fast.

The girl eyed her and shrugged. "Okay." She got in and Phoenix pulled away before the girl even had clicked the door shut. In her rear-view mirror, the reflection of Jones' black Cadillac pulling up to the front of the club made her shudder.

With every few feet between her and Maxim's, more adrenaline fanned out through her limbs until a giddiness thrummed through her whole body. Score one for her, one loss for Jones because she was going to make certain this girl never returned.

"So, Uber not working for you?" Phee ignored the water seeping into her seats. The girl was soaked from head to foot.

"No credit card."

"So, where to then?"

The girl dumped her bag between her feet. "Oh, I gotta wait a while. I'm crashing at this friend's house and she let me know she's got company. You can drop me off at the Motel 6 up there." She pointed up the street. "Or..." She swiveled her head. "...it's back that way?" She hitched her thumb to the back. "I dunno. Man, my head is messed up tonight." The girl slurred her words.

Phee tried not to stare at the bruises coloring the girl's neck. "What's your name?"

"Desha-biller."

"I mean your actual name."

The girl rolled her head to the side, wet strands of hair sticking to her cheek. "Does it matter?"

Honestly, it didn't. "Tell you what. How about I show you my club? It's a nice place and no one will bother you if you want to crash. We have laundry services and you can at least get your clothes dry." Every office had a couch at Shakedown and she could get the girl out before anyone arrived. None of the staff showed until noon anyway, and she still had her keys. "There's food, too."

The girl chewed her fingernail again. "Can't. Jones says I gotta lose weight before I can have another night."

Yet a stiff wind could blow this girl over. "Okay, there's a bar." Where she'd brew coffee for her. "And the owner is nice. He won't care." She wasn't lying about either.

Her face swung in Phee's direction. "They looking for new dancers?"

Now she had the girl's interest. "Maybe." It wasn't a total lie, but it'd keep her off the streets, at least for a few hours. Plus, once she saw Shakedown, perhaps she'd see there was more to life than stripping. At least, that was the first thing Phee had thought when Declan gave her and her sisters a tour of the warehouse he was turning into a club. He'd been passionate about his vision, waxing on about real velvet curtains and stage lights. She'd bought into the entire vision, his words on how Shakedown could be their sanctuary. Now? She needed to find new shelter—once this girl was cleaned up.

9

———

Phee shoved the door open with her shoulder. Damn back door always stuck.

"You sure you work here?" Naomi gave her the side-eye. It hadn't taken Phee long to find out her real name and that she'd been crashing on one of Maxim's bartender's couches for the last three weeks, not yet finding her own place—one that dealt in cash only and didn't mind dealing with an unemancipated seventeen-year-old.

"Positive. You'll see, come on." She hadn't brought any of the girls she'd pulled from Maxim's street to Shakedown or to her home before, but this girl was in rougher shape than expected. She wasn't only drunk. She was high on something and needed water at least. Crashing for a few hours on the cot in the staff lounge would do her well. Phee couldn't take her back to her apartment, not with her sisters there.

Once the door unjammed, she flicked on lights in the long hallway and urged the girl to follow. Hesitation crossed the girl's eyes but she followed.

Concrete dust, cinnamon, and lemon furniture polish grew stronger as they approached the black curtain separating the unimpressive cinder-block hallway and the main floor. She swiped the curtain back, gestured for Naomi to enter.

"Wow." Naomi stopped short. Her eyes widened. "You weren't shittin' me."

"Look." She pointed at the long row of oil paintings along the back handicapped ramp. "The owner used to deal in antiques, so he commissioned portraits of all his lead dancers. That's Cherry. Aspen. Cortelana. Nicholas-slash-Nikki. And that one is me." Declan and his romantic notions. "Those are my sisters."

"They look like you."

"My sisters and I are triplets."

"Get out." The girl jutted her chin back. "I've never met a triplet before."

"Most people haven't." She turned to face the stage. "That's where we dance." Now that she really looked, Shakedown *was* impressive with its heavy red curtains, velvet booths, white tablecloths, and high-end lighting. When had she lost her awe?

"Where are the poles?"

"No poles. We dance more like cabaret and burlesque."

"Oh, great movie. That Christina chick can belt them out. So, you sing?"

"I don't, but Cherry, the emcee does, and some of the other performers, too. Come on, I got coffee, soda, whatever you want." She headed to the bar, clicking on the espresso machine.

Naomi slid onto a barstool. "I'll have Jack." She pointed to a bottle of Jack Daniels.

"No." Declan's voice rang in the air.

Phee's nerves crackled at his sharp bark. Of all the times, the man was pulling an all-nighter. The tiniest tremble ran through her fingers as she gripped the bar edge. A dose of adrenaline from the male intrusion, that was all.

Naomi swiveled around and held up her hands in surrender. "Look man, she made me come here." She stood. "I don't want no trouble."

Phee pulled out two espresso cups from under the counter. "Don't worry. He's just the owner."

Terror crossed Naomi's face. "Fuck, what did you get me into?" She would be scared. Jones, as an owner, was the polar opposite of Declan. In fact, those bruises on the girl's neck had deepened over the last forty-five minutes. Phee brushed her fingertips over her own throat, the small muscles there remembering the grip of a hand wrapping around it.

The coffee machine hissed, snapping her back to reality. "Want an espresso?" She glared at Declan.

One side of his mouth inched up. "Don't mind if I do." He sauntered over, swinging his cane. The young girl eyed the thing as if it were a taser.

He held out his hand. "Hello, I'm Declan Phillips. I run Shakedown. And you are?"

She didn't return the gesture—another familiar sign. Naomi wasn't about to be yanked toward him and groped, though Declan would never do such a thing.

He dropped his arm, seemingly unbothered by Naomi's suspicions.

"He's not going to hurt you," Phee said over the hiss of steam. "I would know. I've been here for six years."

The muscles around Naomi's eyes relaxed. "I'm happy to audition. My name's Desha-biller." She inched closer, ran her eyes up and down his torso.

He smiled down at her. "Well, Desha-biller—"

"Her name is Naomi."

The ungrateful woman sliced her eyes toward Phee. The girl would learn Phee was not her enemy—eventually.

"Naomi." He cleared his throat and grasped her wrists before her hands landed on his chest. "We don't audition acts like that here. Our dancers do their work on stage—and only on the stage. Here, take a seat. You look like you could use that coffee." He helped her up on a stool. "Hungry?"

"Shit, Phoenix here was right. You are a gentleman."

He cut his eyes to Phee. "Is that what she said about me?"

Damn his smug smile. "Don't let it get to you." She set a small espresso in front of him. "I still meant what I wrote."

"Ah, yes, the napkin." He pulled it out of his suit coat pocket and placed it on the bar.

The girl glanced at the tiny espresso cup. "How much you charge for these tiny things?"

Declan chuckled. "A lot."

She took a sip and wrinkled her nose a little but gulped the whole thing down.

Phoenix inclined her head to the end of the bar. "Got a second, Declan?"

He pocketed her napkin note, took his espresso, and followed her to the end of the bar, his gaze trained on her face over the rim of the cup as he took a leisurely sip. "Decent espresso. A second calling, perhaps?"

"Perhaps."

He set it down, his eyes never leaving hers. "Let me guess where you found her."

Declan knew very well where she had found Naomi. When Phee first worked for Declan, she often urged girls from Maxim's to audition at Shakedown. "It doesn't matter."

"I told you never to go back there."

Jesus, could the man look any more stern? "You don't get to tell me what to do. I don't work here anymore."

He glanced over at Naomi, who had laid her head on the bar, and then back at Phee. "Tell you what." He reached into his suit jacket, pulling out the napkin. "If you do work here, she can stay."

Blackmail? Over her dead body. "To serve espressos?"

"To dance."

They both glanced over at Naomi, who'd let out a slight moan as she settled into dozing, her face pressed against the bar. Jesus.

He laid her resignation on the bar before her. "Where else is she going to go? Back to Maxim's? You know that place better than anyone."

She scowled. "You would bring that up." He'd once brought a girl back here before—three of them actually: her, Starr, and Luna, two days after they'd met Declan. Back then, Shakedown didn't look like this—it had been more like an abandoned warehouse filled with Declan's dreams of turning it into the swankiest music hall in Baltimore.

"You put yourself in danger like that again and—"

"And what, you don't bring danger?" It felt good to spit that out.

His jaw tensed. He lifted the napkin again. "I burn this. She can stay."

A string of expletives waiting to be unleashed sat on her tongue. She choked them back. "Fine. But only until I find someplace else for us to go." She could find a better club than this place.

"Come on. I'll put her in my office." Declan moved to the sleeping girl. "Okay, beauty, time for rest." She slipped into his arms so easily, just folded into him. With one hand on his cane, the other arm full of Naomi, he eased her toward the back rooms.

"Mmm, smell good." Naomi murmured against his jacket —a vintage Ralph Lauren if Phee wasn't mistaken. She mentally curled a fist around her desire to take a strong inhale of his scent. Her willpower squeezed the life out of it. Damn Declan and his impeccable taste.

She followed them to his office. Declan laid Naomi on his couch and pulled the blanket that always hung off the end over her. She didn't visit Declan's office often, yet she'd always noticed that worn red and blue plaid blanket. She'd wondered if it was sentimental in some way.

When he straightened, he appraised Phee. She squeezed her heart shut in case that warmth in his eyes reached her. She had to stay the course and keep that blood-pumping organ where it belonged—under lock and key. If she didn't, she'd bleed out.

"I'll fill her in when she wakes. Try to place her."

A stab of sorrow arrowed through her chest anyway at his kindness, his immediate acceptance of responsibility for the lost girl.

He gestured to the hallway. "Now, we talk."

"Tomorrow."

He pointed to his door. "Now."

10

Declan shut his office door, and they faced each other in the corridor.

"Starr or Luna know you've started up again? Trying to save the world one stripper at a time?" For the life of him, he could not figure out why she'd throw herself before the lion's den again. Her self-destructive pattern couldn't solely be because of what was going down at Shakedown.

"Isn't that what you do?"

"Apparently not." He shifted a little, leaning on his cane. "I mean, I'm a mobster, right?"

"Yes, you are, and I'll be back early to get her." Her response wasn't unexpected. If he said the ocean was blue, she'd say it was green.

They both knew the truth. Getting Naomi out of Maxim's was futile. The girl would hear how much money she could make at Shakedown washing dishes or waitressing compared to stripping, and she'd be out the door. That was the problem, wasn't it? The girls were promised a lot of money stripping—and the occupation delivered. What the club owners don't tell you is the price for such a wage. There was a 90 percent chance Naomi would end up back at Maxim's, prostituting herself behind closed doors.

He leaned against the cinderblock wall. Phoenix wasn't running for the exit. Rather, her brow wrinkled in thought as she examined the floor beneath her. The soft *plink-plink* of a dripping pipe echoed from somewhere, each *ting* as loud as a church bell in the thick silence.

He couldn't stand the hush like a calm before a raging storm. "Then I'll see you Tuesday? You'll be back to work?" He might as well throw it out there.

She peeked up at him with nostrils flared, which was adorable. "Why do you care if I work here, Declan?" An exasperated sigh floated between them. "A hundred girls can take my spot. You're worried about Starr and Luna leaving, too? Well, I have news for you. Starr's getting married, so splitting up the act is inevitable anyway."

"Ah." He tapped his cane on the inside of his foot. Now all this ratcheted-up attitude made sense. This woman standing before him was staring down at her worst nightmare. The sisters splitting up had to be terrifying. If only she could see staying here would get her what she wanted—stability. "You told me in no uncertain terms long ago you were a package deal. But now... not so much?"

Her chin rose in bravado. "No one will pull us apart."

"But almost losing Starr to Ruark MacKenna, and now she's getting married, well, it's a lot to handle. And Luna finding your father..." He softened his voice, though he wanted nothing more than to either handcuff her to the first thing he saw to keep her here—or kiss the hell out of her. "You'll always have a home here. All three of you. But don't you think it's time to end the bitchy attitude? I'm not trying to cage you."

She stilled, and her exquisite throat moved in a swallow. "Look, I apologize. I just..."

"Just what? You want me to fire you, don't you? It'd make things so much easier. Then maybe you could walk away from me." Arrogant. But he knew the truth. The minute a man showed interest, she panicked. She only danced with her sisters—primarily for his very male-heavy clientele—because she didn't want to ever be severed from them again as they had been as kids. Of course, Starr getting married would push her over a new ledge. But then this woman had so fucking many ledges to jump off of.

Steel entered her voice though her gaze dropped, defeated. "You can't fire someone who's already quit. I'm sorry for being so strident. But you won't stop, and I don't think of you… that way."

Her lashes, like silk, lifted so slowly he could almost hear the air move. He wanted to kiss them, to lay claim to every last detail of her. Then maybe, just maybe, he could stamp out the anguish of her past with it—the misery that drove her to such self-sabotaging behavior.

Her back went straight. "Stop trying to date me."

He stepped forward, and she blanched. She did that whenever anyone got close. In fact, he'd never seen her touch or hug another person other than her two sisters—and even that was rare. She didn't hate him—not even a little. She was petrified of him and presumably of all men.

"I have no interest in dating you, Phoenix."

The bewilderment on her face was priceless.

"There can't be more for us," she insisted.

Bullshit, but whatever. His plans for Phoenix Rising were so much grander than a date. "Okay, but I won't let you throw your life away based on the past. You don't want to dance for me. Fine. It's a right-to-work state. But whatever you're running from is going to follow you."

"The MacKennas. Great."

"Yourself." She had a heart as big as Canada with no one

other than her sisters to care for it. She'd been abused beyond understanding, and yet she kept getting in her own way—refusing to move forward. Leaving Shakedown wasn't progress. It was fleeing, and the only thing she knew how to do thanks to that loser father—the man Declan would have put in the ground if he'd glanced in her direction.

Declan let a few seconds pass, let her absorb where he was going with this conversation. "Now, ask me what's on the tip of your tongue. Why am I so patient with you? Why do I want you here?"

"You don't get to pity me, Declan Phillips."

"Nothing I do for you or anyone here comes from pity. It comes from an understanding."

"Is this the part where you say because you're an ex-con, you know what it's like? I see all the new bouncers you have working here. And I'm tired of being around people who have the deck stacked against them, who are hunted, who are broken, who are—"

"Like you? Is that why you started going back to Maxim's? To save the broken? I know all about your trips there the first year you danced for me. Girls showing up here, saying there was a red-headed girl talking about a place where they could be safe and dance. I knew it was you from the start."

Her chin lifted. "I thought you were trying to build up the business."

"No, you were trying to end Maxim's. And, in the process, put yourself in danger to help others."

"Those girls deserve more. There's nothing wrong with stripping—provided that's all you're asked to do. It's when the line gets crossed."

"Jones' specialty. I know. He's a front for prostitution. Learned that the first time I walked in. They took one look at me—my leg—and they thought I was an easy mark. Talk about being pitied." He settled both hands on his cane. "They said a certain redhead would do anything I wanted. They were trying to break in—"

"Me." Her delicate throat tensed. "He offered me."

"Their words, not mine." Yes, they should have had this conversation long ago. Instead, they'd glossed over a lot. Years passed so quickly. Now, with the MacKennas breathing down his throat, he had no more room or time for secrets or bullshit.

"I wasn't a hooker," she spat. "I made that clear."

"And they punished you for it, didn't they?" He lifted his hand, hesitated, but then fingered a piece of her hair. Miraculously, she let him—for about three seconds—and then she pulled back.

She crossed her arms. "Is Naomi going to be okay here?"

Phoenix knew this girl for, what? Three hours? Already she worried. "I'd cut a man's arm off of whoever raised a hand to anyone here."

Her throat moved once more in a swallow. "What will it take for that not being necessary? Because you don't need to."

She wanted him to predict other's behaviors? This woman's need for certainty knew no end. "You can't stop people from making foolish decisions, like a woman quitting a job where she is safer than she knows." No matter she wanted to stay in a box only she designed for herself, she had to understand she would not be better off elsewhere.

"You only say that because you feel guilty about what happened… that last night at Maxim's." When she'd been beaten up because she did something kind for Declan. Shit, he wasn't trying to make her relive her past, but there it was.

"I made a promise to you, and I plan on keeping it."

She raised her hands in exasperation. "Keep me safe, keep us all safe."

"Yes, but I'm talking about my first promise. Do you remember it?"

She knew what he referred to. "That last night at Maxim's. You said a man wouldn't raise his hand to me ever again. Shouted it from the street, if I recall."

It was ridiculous, a man in torn jeans and a blue work shirt looking far older than his then-thirty-eight years. Hard times aged a person, and he'd barely recognized himself in the mirror when he got out of prison. "After I got thrown out —literally—on my ass. Not my finest look."

"But you'd come back for us."

"You looked surprised. But not as much as me. Saw that black eye on you from across the club."

She shrugged. "Didn't think I'd ever see you again. Do you have any idea how many men have promised me things? Diamonds if I only gave them that blow job. Trips, a house, all if I did one little—" she pinched her fingers together "— tiny thing for them."

The crude words out of her mouth sent a chill through him. "Those aren't little things. No man should ever believe the favor of your company can be bought."

"Is that why you bought me a car?" She rolled her eyes.

He chuckled. "That wasn't a bribe. If Allegra broke down, you'd be late and I'd have an angry mob on my hands waiting for you to take the stage." Naming her car was cute. The possibility of her breaking down while going through West Baltimore was not.

"No one cares that much."

"You think that little of yourself." His brow pinched.

She drew in a stuttered breath. "No." It came out like a whisper. "And thank you for never asking for a return favor." Her voice grew stronger. "But stop trying to coddle me." She turned away and spoke to the wall. "Six years ago I was the stripper who gave you a free lap dance and then got punched in the face for my generosity. It's time we let each other go."

She couldn't even look at him when she uttered those words. So broken, so beautiful.

An ocean of feelings rose and swamped him. "You did more for me that night, and when you're ready to hear what it was, I'll tell you." She had no idea how much she'd changed his life. He couldn't let her walk away without something in return. Giving her a job was one thing, but he'd hoped to give her a better life. Now, he saw she'd merely been treading water—as if she was waiting out her life, not living it. "Phoenix…" Her hand flew up in a proverbial stop sign. They were getting nowhere. He sighed. "Come on. I'll drive you home."

"No, I have my car."

"Letting you go this late in that old relic?"

"She's vintage, which I thought you loved. Besides, you have to convince sleeping beauty inside your office she is better than what Maxim's has to offer."

"Because that's what I did for you."

She looked so sad at that moment, he'd nearly breached that shield she kept around her just to hold her.

"It's time you stop trying to…" She waved her hand. "…save me. What's done is done."

Yet this woman couldn't stop trying to save others. The irony was almost too much to bear.

11

Declan swiveled in his chair, watching the young girl's chest rise and fall, her face pressed into his Cheshire couch.

He shifted and a long groan from his chair cracked the stillness of the empty building. Not even the usual morning sounds—the *beep, beep, beep* of a backing up trash truck or a far-off ship's horn—could be heard. One quick glance at the clock showed 10 a.m. He'd been staring at paperwork for hours, not getting anything accomplished. Rather, he'd scoured all the waterfront properties on the market and considered making a move of his own. What would that accomplish, though? Nothing.

He stood and moved closer to Naomi. Four slight bruises lined the side of her neck as if fingers had pressed against her flesh there. He recognized the pattern, had seen it many times. The first was on Phoenix Rising six years ago.

It's time you stop trying to save me. What's done is done. Her words formed the saddest declaration he'd ever heard. She didn't think she or her life could change. She was right about one thing, however. She didn't need saving. She needed reassembling.

If she'd started up luring Jones' girls away from him again —she'd gone through a spate a few years ago—she was not okay. Giving her space hadn't worked, so a different tact would be required.

Naomi flopped to her back, her arm dangling off the edge of the couch. A long line of spittle ran down her cheek. The ability to sleep that soundly was wasted on the young. Then again, had he ever slept that hard? He hadn't since his world turned upside down more than a decade ago when he'd been found by Tomas MacKenna himself. His mother's pleas the night she died—"no funeral, no obituary, promise me, promise me"—had been for naught. An obit appeared in the paper anyway, thanks to a zealous reporter. The MacKennas, people he didn't even realize he was related to, showed up next, not three weeks after Declan laid her in the ground.

He hadn't been about to let Tomas direct his life. Instead, a certain redhead had, hadn't she?

She may believe her past damaged her beyond repair, but he wasn't going to let her continue to believe that. He'd started this club to do the opposite, give people a chance at a productive, safe life—and he'd make good on that promise.

A rap on his door frame nearly had him come out of his skin.

"Hey, you pull an all-nighter?" Nathan's eyes glanced toward the sleeping girl.

She stirred. He strode to Nathan, motioned him to the hallway. He closed the door behind him. "That's Naomi in there. It's a long story and not what you think."

"Not thinking anything. Starr had me up half the night worrying about where the hell Phee had gotten to."

So, Phee had lied to her sisters? Things were worse than he realized. "Phoenix get home alright?" She hadn't answered his one text asking.

"Yeah, like 5 a.m."

"She brought Naomi here—" he inclined his head toward his office door "—early this morning. The girl needed a temporary place to crash. She's..." He didn't want to say it.

Nathan held up his hand. "No need to go into it."

Nathan had a sixth sense where trouble lay. He would, however, given his ex-con history. Prison made you hyper-aware of your surroundings.

He debated for a few seconds on whether or not to tell Nathan about Carragh's appearance last night but opted against it. What could the man do? Nathan was finally happy, and this was Declan's situation, not his.

Declan eyed the man, who seemed restless. "You're in early."

"Yeah, want to get a jump on that shipment that came in yesterday. But also..." Nathan rubbed under his chin. "Was, uh, kinda hoping to talk to you before people arrive later. I want to ask you something."

"Sure."

The guy shifted from foot to foot. "So, you know Starr and I, well, we're getting married. It's going to be small, just family and a few friends."

"You want to hold it here at the club?"

"Starr wants us to do it outside somewhere. Like on the water. She's got a thing for boats. In fact, we're thinking of going on a sailing honeymoon. Not my idea, but as long as it makes her happy." The guy flushed and stiffly ran a hand over his chin again. "So, uh, I was hoping maybe you'd stand up with me. I mean, best man stuff. Max already has called dibs on Luna. You know how they have to be walked up the aisle? So, that means..."

"I get it." He'd walk with Phoenix. He didn't mind one bit. "Yes, I'd be honored."

"And… I don't get involved in the sister stuff, but Starr's worried about Phoenix. Said she's been acting weird lately. Thought you should know."

"Since I'll be walking her down the aisle?"

The man wisely just nodded. Everyone knew how he felt about the woman. If Starr was sending out smoke signals through Nathan, he'd been missing other signs with Phoenix. Perhaps she'd been waiting for a reason to quit—and he'd given her one by revealing his family relations with the MacKennas.

"Hey, can I get another one of those shots of coffee again?" Naomi leaned on the doorframe. Mascara lined her eyes, and her hair was tangled.

"Sure." He tipped his head toward Nathan. "This is Nathan. He works here."

"Oh?" Her eyes cleared a little of the sleep. "This who I'm auditioning for?"

"No."

"Shame. I'd do you on the house." Her lips inched up into a lopsided smile.

Nathan eyed Declan and raised his hands. "I don't want to know."

"Naomi, after I get your espresso, we're going to talk about your options. None of which involve you 'doing' anyone."

She rubbed her nose vigorously. "That right?"

Nathan chuckled and shook his head. "See ya, Declan."

Of course, nothing Declan said or offered made a difference to Naomi. She drank her coffee in one shot, bummed forty dollars from him for a cab, and was gone. The entire morning exchange took less than twenty minutes. That meant Phoenix might go through with her napkin threat.

He'd bided his time for six years with that woman—and it

was time to stop. Phee needed more from him than she knew. She needed a friend—the one fucking thing he hadn't tried. To be her friend, however, required a little tough love. He headed to his office. He was going to give her what she asked for—he would let her go. At least in one way.

12

———

Phee inspected the exquisite, painstaking detail on the Victorian coral pin. The filigree casing sparkled in the shop's overhead light.

"It's stunning, isn't it?" Blair smiled at her from the other side of the counter. The owner of Stich-n-Time knew her stuff. The shop burst with women's clothing and accessories from the mid-1940s to the 1970s.

"You have the best eye, Blair. You can't find workmanship like this anymore." Phee held it up to her neck, which is where she'd pair it with her new Hermes scarf snagged from eBay—an elegant pattern depicting a Paris fair.

She could devote hours to trying on the dozens of garments hung like art against the wall—so many pretty dresses with cowl necklines and A-line silhouettes begging for crinolines. Cowboy boots and silk clutch purses lined the far wall shelf while tea partyish hats and gorgeous belts of all colors and eras hung on pegs. She'd once scored a Hermes Kelly bag from the '40s here.

Starr sidled up to her. "What's that?"

"My new purchase. I'll take it." She handed the brooch back to Blair, who winked.

"Readying yourself for a date or something?"

Phee rolled her eyes.

Luna peeked around a rack of high-waisted pants fit for the 1940s. "You have a date? Tell me it's with Declicious."

"If only she'd be that smart," stressed Starr. "You know how many women are after that man? One is going to eventually catch him."

"Leave it, you two." She grinned at the two of them. They never wasted a chance to needle her over Declan's obvious crush on her.

"I saw he texted you yesterday." Starr stared at her hard. "What? You left your phone on the kitchen counter and it kept buzzing. I just peeked. Who is Naomi? He hiring a new act and you're the only one he told?"

"No." Declan's text from yesterday flashed in her mind.

<<Naomi has left, despite my best efforts. Put her in a cab with a little money. See you Tuesday.>>

See? The man was fucking perfect—and presumptuous if he thought she was coming back. She'd only agreed to continue if Naomi stayed.

She'd texted him back immediately. **<<Our deal is void.>>**

<<If that's the way you want it.>>

His response was unexpected and, truth told, nipped at her pride a bit. Yet she'd set up the rules so it was time to abide by them. She still hadn't replied. She'd show up, of course. Until she found a new gig, she couldn't afford to stop cold turkey.

Phee ran her finger along the glass countertop, admiring the cameos lined up like perfect Victorian ladies on their velvet trays. "Naomi was a girl I gave a ride to Saturday night —or Sunday morning, depending on how you look at it."

She could almost hear the dust motes moving in the air from the stillness that came next.

Starr broke the silence first. "And where did you find her?"

"On a street corner when I was out driving around. She was by herself. In the rain. I gave her a ride. End of story."

"How did Declan get involved in this? Was he with you?"

Phee was going to have to tell them, wasn't she? "No, I brought her to Shakedown. She was drunk." And high.

"You found her outside Maxim's." It wasn't a question, and Starr's eyes filled with accusations.

"What? So what if I did?"

"But, that place—"

"Hence, me scooping her up and taking her to Shakedown."

"You took her from a place we never wanted to see again to a place you quit." Starr measured her words carefully as if trying to understand them like she had over breakfast when the three of them had continued to discuss Phee's withdrawal from Shakedown. Why did everything have to be so hard?

Luna moved forward first. "I'm sorry. This is my fault. Finding Dad—"

"What's that got to do with anything?" Phee shook her head as if that would stop the exchange altogether.

"Everything," Starr scoffed.

"I should have never looked for him," Luna exhaled.

"Oh, God, here we go again." Her father could rot in hell. Why did they have to keep resurrecting him? Leave him there where he belonged.

Luna's weepy gaze zeroed in on her. "I just thought being able to say what you needed to say to him would help you move on. I mean Starr—"

"Is moving on?" Phee raised her hand. "Stop. Both of you."

She may have been a splintered mess on the inside but talking only sharpened the edges. They did nothing to stop the cuts.

"We're worried about you." Luna's phone buzzed but she ignored it. "I mean, first, trying to leave Shakedown and then going back to Maxim's?"

"I wasn't going to Maxim's. And for the record, I wasn't trying to quit. I did. And only until I find us a better place. I won't leave you in the lurch. I struck a deal." Sort of. One that was null and void but whatever. Declan would give her at least two weeks. That was a standard notice period, wasn't it? "Once I find a new gig, that's when we all can 'move on', as you say."

"A deal…" Starr repeated and glanced at Luna. "Thought you were sick of those."

Luna eyed her. "Or maybe it's because this deal is with Declan." A smile worthy of a cat spread across her cheeks.

Phee gave her sister a sideways glance. "You really do take 'wishing will make it so' to a new level, L."

"Without dreams, we're lost," she sang.

Phee didn't dream anymore, only the occasional nightmare. Her mind had shut down long ago, and it was better that way. No disappointments were set up.

After paying for her brooch, they headed down the narrow stairs to the street level.

"By the way, Phee." Starr turned to her as soon as they got to Starr's car. "And I'm only telling you so you're not in the dark—but L. and I saw Dad this morning when you were sleeping in."

"Okay." She clamped down the familiar anger that arose at the thought he was anywhere near them.

"He asked about you." Starr immediately raised her hands. "Told him you were fine, and we dropped it."

"Good." The least amount of information given to that

man, the better. She tugged open the car door and climbed in. "Let's go."

Starr put her keys in the ignition. "He's not well."

Jesus, her sisters would not drop the topic of their father already. "Of course, he's not." Abusing one's body for decades with alcohol and ending up in a coma this last time—and God knew what else—would do that to a person.

"Well, it's worse than that." Luna, sitting in the front passenger seat, glanced at Starr. They gave each other an odd look.

"What? Just out with it." Phee was so done with all this heavy talk.

The vinyl squeaked under Luna as she turned to face the windshield. "He's got early-onset Alzheimer's."

How does one prepare themselves for such a revelation? Be shocked? Smug? Angry that he got to forget and she didn't? Phoenix chose her most honest reaction. "I don't care."

Luna pulled out her phone, which had been buzzing incessantly since they left the shop. "You should. Once he succumbs, that's it. No more answers."

The man had no answers for her. He only brought misery.

Luna sucked in a long breath. "Oh, my God." She furiously tapped on her phone. "Oh, wow. Oooooh, God. Remember Sally Mae, that dancer from the charity show?" Luna held up her phone to Starr's face. "She texted me a listing on Backstage." Her mouth fell open, and she swiveled to stare at Phee. "Are we fired?"

Phee leaned forward. "What are you talking about?"

Her sister held up her screen. "It's an ad on the Backstage online portal."

The inside of her throat went dry. "Son of a bitch." So,

Declan was doing exactly what she'd instructed him to do—move on—because the ad was clear: *Auditions at Club Shakedown. Baltimore, Maryland. Tomorrow at noon.*

13

Phoenix eased the car into her designated parking spot. A line of at least thirty men and women snaked from Shakedown's entrance down the front sidewalk and into the parking lot.

"Touché, Declan," she mumbled and killed the ignition.

As soon as they'd arrived home from shopping yesterday, Luna tracked down more Shakedown advertisements for variety and cabaret acts on both CircusTalk and Backstage. It wasn't unexpected people would show up for a chance to join Declan's roster of entertainers. His club's reputation had long ago been established as a premier gig. He offered health care insurance, decent hours, and a decent wage—unheard of in the dance scene. Phoenix hadn't foreseen so many familiar faces showing up, however.

Starr turned to her. "You sure you want to do this?"

"Positive." Phee cracked open the door.

She'd placed calls of her own yesterday to clubs and theatres seeking a new place to land and discovered very few people were hiring. Once they found out her offer didn't involve her sisters, they'd balked altogether. She had to move to Plan B—whatever the hell that was.

She implored her sisters to call Trick instead of Declan to uncover their boss' plans. He reported Shakedown was merely in the market for additional acts and told them "not to worry." Yeah, right. Not telling your headline acts you're hiring more dancers? This move was Declan's cannon shot across the bow.

Her head had filled with imaginary, pointed conversations with him all night.

You bastard.

I want to stay.

I hate you.

I'll help you.

Okay, not conversation. More like things she'd wanted to lob herself.

She'd run every scenario in her head about how to get a handle on this situation until the answer thunked down from the sky. Declan wouldn't intimidate her with this play. She'd remain at Shakedown until she could be replaced, and she'd help him vet the potential new acts. She'd be a professional.

Luna hurried over to some people she knew. "Jezebel, oh, my God, where have you been?"

"Everywhere." The woman in a fake leopard jacket sporting bright orange lipstick jumped out of line and hugged her. "God, you are a sight for sore eyes." She playfully slapped her arm. "Luna, you didn't tell me Shakedown was hiring. I got on the first train here from New York. Oh, to work for Mr. Phillips would be a dream." She flicked her eyes toward Declan and Trick, who stood in the doorway.

"Well, glad to see you here."

Trick's voice rose. "Ladies and gentlemen, can I have your attention, please? We'll start auditions at noon. Please, have your resumés and headshots available. We will take you in the order you lined up."

"Declan," Phoenix skirted by him to get out from the cold and into the entranceway. "Can we talk for a minute?"

He nodded once. "Trick, let everyone in. It's freezing outside. Give them coffee, tea, water, no liquor. I'll be out there in a second."

A sly smile stretched across Trick's lips, which he directed at her. So, perhaps he was in on this reverse psychology move? Well, it wasn't going to work.

Once inside Declan's office, she closed his office door. "So, auditions."

"After Naomi left, your text said our deal was null and void." He glanced at a newspaper on his desk.

"I won't leave a hole in the show. I'll still be here until I can find another place." Phee swallowed. Being honest seemed on point for this fresh development.

He raised his gaze and let a long minute pass between them as he appraised her. "Sure," he finally said. "You can still dance here. I'll allow that."

It was a dick male move to toss that in her face but also fair play. Her intellectual brain told her it was his prerogative to do whatever he wanted. She had quit, after all.

She forced herself to stop picking at her cuticle. "Well, thank you. For trying with Naomi, I mean."

"I didn't think you could say that."

"You think that little of me?"

"I think a lot of you."

He did that with her—started out stern and then softened, almost like dealing with a misbehaving child, which galled her to her bones.

She drew in a long breath. "I can help you audition them. I have a bit of experience, you know. What are you hoping for in a new act?"

Surprise lit in his eyes. Good. It was okay for him to be taken off guard by her.

"It's going to be tough. I need someone as good as you."

She forced a smile, trying to make light of the matter. "Good luck."

"I could say the same to you."

Touché, indeed.

14

Declan held back the black curtain and paused in the archway leading onto the main floor. At least eighty performers, more than he could have hoped for, crowded the space. Bags and coats were strewn about chairs and the floor.

The burlesque scene had shrunk considerably in recent years, and Shakedown was one of the few clubs left on the East Coast that promoted that type of entertainment. Given the size, depth, and breadth of the crowd, perhaps opening up a second club somewhere could work. He had the funding for it, and the MacKennas seemed hell-bent on taking over the waterfront. It might be wise to spread his interests a bit.

Two women nudged each other as they stared at Phoenix talking with another dancer on the other side of the club. He also had the best act in the country—the O'Malley triplets, some of the best-known dancers of their time. Or rather, he'd *had* a triplet act. If he knew anything about those three, they stick together so anything might happen in coming months, like losing Luna and Starr. He'd hoped Phoenix wouldn't make good on her promise to leave, but hope was for fools.

"Well, you move fast." The female voice sounded amused. Declan swiveled to face Starr, who had sidled up to him. She leaned closer and whispered, "I want points for not bombarding you with messages for the last 24 hours asking if we're fired."

"Fired? Of course not. You three are my most popular act, and I'm not losing you to another club despite Phoenix's declaration." He glanced up at Phoenix, who stood about ten feet away chatting with Carina Rose, an old friend of the two of them. Carina pulled Phoenix into a hug.

"Oh, I don't believe she's leaving. Like I always said, her bark is worse than her bite. Still, good move on getting Carina here." Starr winked and moved to join Luna, who sat with Trick, by the looks of it helping him organize the head-shots and resumes.

His "move" had been a stroke of good luck, as Phoenix loved Carina, and the retired dancer was available.

Shakedown's email account had been bombarded with messages yesterday so he'd asked Carina, once the nation's most celebrated burlesque dancer of her day, to help bring some fresh blood to the local scene. He hadn't expected the O'Malley triplets to parachute in to help—certainly not Phoenix.

Carina broke her hug of Phee but held her hands and gazed into her eyes. The woman's forehead wrinkled and she placed a hand alongside Phee's cheek. Phoenix cocked her head, pressing into Carina's hand. That infinitesimal move-ment meant something—something big. Phoenix rarely showed vulnerability. Then again, Carina had a way of bringing out the truth in people. She saw more than most. She'd lost her hearing about the same age Phoenix was now, though thanks to cochlear implants had regained much of it.

Declan made a mental note to ask Carina what she'd seen in Phee. Despite his earlier words about giving Phoenix whatever space she required, he'd ensure her safety and comfort for the rest of his life. For now, however, he had some insurance to hire—as that's what he deemed hiring new acts would mean.

He joined Trick and Luna, who peered up at him immediately. "Declan, I see you've expanded your ideas for the show." She held up a stack of the headshots left with her.

Trick chuckled. "Luna's got some organizational skills. She grouped the acts into type within ten minutes. We've got dancers, an opera singer, a blind juggler, comedians..."

He could see that variety splayed all around him. The dancers were easy to spot as they stretched their legs on the floor and used the brass rail lining the bar as a ballet barre. A few groups appeared fit for a Renaissance festival, a husband and wife acrobat team sported matching, impressive biceps, and a few drag queens and male impersonators chatted up Cherry in the corner.

"By the looks of things, everyone wants to work here." Luna flipped through a series of photographs.

"Unexpected vacancies will do that." He winked at her.

Her mouth twitched upward. "Not everyone. Though you can count on Starr and me being here as long as you want us."

A comfortable warmth spread across his chest at her little white lie. They would never let Phoenix be alone for long. "Given Phoenix and I have reached an understanding, I'm hoping the O'Malley triplets headline Shakedown for many more years to come." He could roll with that fairytale.

Her shoulders rose and fell in a long exhale. "For the record, I don't believe Carragh MacKenna is going to do anything to this club."

What an odd thing to raise, and his gut lurched at hearing the name. "He is not one to ever underestimate, Luna." He stared at her hard.

She didn't break his gaze. "I don't trust him. But I believe there is more to the story of him, isn't there?"

"Who do you want to see first?" Trick interrupted them—a welcomed interference. Declan wasn't discussing with her the depth of sociopath DNA Carragh inherited.

"Comedians. A little humor would do everyone some good." Declan yanked out a chair. At the last minute, he'd checked the box on "Comedy & Improv" on the submission form asking what kind of talent he sought, and he was glad. Laughter would relax the crowd provided the acts were any good.

They listened to the six comedians who showed up, but it was the last man, a tall, thin black man named Delight and sporting an Orioles baseball cap, who had him considering hiring such an act. The man riffed well off the audience—the other acts sitting around the small cocktail rounds waiting their turn.

He labeled the crowd "the playland of misfit toys and boys." He asked one particularly busty blond woman about her act and she answered, "Fire dance." His response? "You ran with scissors as a child, didn't you? And that was a slow day?" Semi-cheesy, but the crowd laughed, which is all that mattered. Maybe it was time to expand Shakedown's offerings. He liked the audience participation angle the man brought.

"Thank you, Delight," Trick called to the comedian now leaving the stage. Trick leaned down to Declan. "Who do you want to see next?"

He picked up the photo on top. "Dancers."

"Mona?"

A Rubenesque brunette with an amazing smile rose from her seat. "Mona Jean Harlow," she purred. She swept off her trench coat and revealed her tight dress cascaded with pearls and fringe. It was two sizes too small and her breasts threatened to burst forth at any minute. "I like to audition in full costume. For the full effect." She winked at him and proceeded to the stage.

Phoenix rose from her seat a few tables away and came over to him. She yanked out the chair next to him and sat. "You have a score sheet set up for the dancers?"

"No."

She let out a thank-God-I'm-here sigh. "Mind if I do?"

"Not at all, Miss O'Malley."

Phoenix reached into her bag and pulled out a notebook. One glance revealed she'd already set up a grid with some categories, the details of which he didn't catch. She'd come prepared. Now that he thought about it, it was a shame they hadn't talked about her helping him audition in advance.

Mona Jean turned out to be an old-timey burlesque dancer—slow, reserved, prancing across the stage, taking ten minutes to remove nothing but gloves and her dress down to a second, more transparent dress. After she was through, the woman looked expectantly at him. He gave her a polite smile. Years ago, he'd have hired her in a heartbeat, but Mona had none of Phoenix's fire or enthusiasm.

Phoenix showed him her pad of paper. She was dead-on in her assessment. *Perfect for Shakedown—ten years ago.* He nodded his agreement. He'd been watching Phoenix and her sisters dance for six years. His bar of what constituted good had elevated to an uncompromising level, and therein lay the problem for today.

No one had what Phoenix had, not even her sisters. Phoenix Rising glided and swayed with a violent passion so unexpected from such a delicate frame. It took people off guard to the point they couldn't rip their gaze from her. He'd seen hundreds of his patrons riveted every night to his stage simply because she flounced across it. She didn't entertain.

She captured... and released. She shut down as fast as she rose up, not unlike a derecho.

He rose. "Thank you, Mona. I'm not sure when we'll need a vintage act."

The woman swallowed, her face a slack mask of disappointment.

Phee tossed him an admonishing look—which was rich—and then turned to Mona. "Bad choice of words. Your act is wonderful and you will be given full consideration. Shakedown is seeking someone to replace me. Isn't that right, Declan?"

The woman's face paled further. "Why?"

Yes, why would she? Oh, perhaps because she was a stubborn, damaged, fleeing ostrich.

"It's time." Phoenix smiled at her.

The woman's eyes darted to Declan and then back to her.

Phee cocked her head as if understanding some secret language the woman conveyed in her body language. "He's a good boss. You'd be happy here."

If he could siphon off the unhappiness in her voice, he would. "Phoenix was made for bigger things."

"Than here? Oh, are you going to Broadway? You could totally do it."

"I might. I might do a lot of things."

"She could." As Mona exited the stage, he texted Phoenix.

<<Even if you leave, you can always come back.>>

She glanced at her phone, then at him. The sadness coating her face was going to kill him. "It's better this way." She turned her eyes to the group of performers. "Sally Mae, you ready?"

He stared at Phoenix's delicate profile, her lashes jutting out like a canopy, her nose a perfect slope, her lips pouting with insolence. Perhaps he'd overplayed his hand with this audition move. It certainly didn't seem to thwart her resolve to run.

It was time to engage Plan C—or was it Z? He only had one move left. He was going to have to stop dancing with her altogether. He'd have to tell her the truth around why he wanted her here so badly—and all of it.

15

Phee's arms and legs vibrated with electricity as she curtsied toward the applauding audience. On a whim, Phee had abandoned choreography in part of her dance and improvised, because why not? It was fun, and her time here was limited.

For the first time in months, she'd locked into the music and glided across the stage as if dancing on air. She grabbed a fistful of dusty velvet curtain and kicked to the ceiling. She shimmied across the stage, arms out and fingers gesturing for the crowd to get louder, clap harder. Then, stood in the center of the stage, she pivoted and unhooked her bra only to model-turn back to the stage and throw it off, revealing her Swarovski crystal pasties.

She sucked in a lungful of cigar-filled air. She felt good.

She'd slept well after yesterday's auditions. Perhaps it was because her involvement with Shakedown and Declan was determined—no more ambivalence, no more dancing around one another. Or perhaps her adrenaline surge was because Declan wasn't telling her who he was thinking about hiring. He said he'd decide by tonight's end.

More women than men sat in the first row of tables. By

the looks of their floral dresses and unabashed clapping, a burlesque club was a new experience for them. Come to think of it, Declan probably imported them to show her the club could be safe and fun. If every night had been like tonight, perhaps she'd have found herself in a different place.

As she split the curtains to exit the stage, she paused and glanced backward at one of the young women near the end of the last table on stage right. Clean-faced with no makeup, she glowed with happiness. Phee winked at the girl when she yelled, "You're amazing!" It was the greatest compliment she could ever get—simple and honest. No, *"You're so fuckable, baby."* No adjusting erections under pants. Not that the latter happened often at Shakedown—at least not until recently.

Regret crept in for one minute. If her life had started out differently, maybe she could have been that woman, sitting in a dance club with girlfriends, never worrying about making it to the parking lot unscathed, or sleeping through the night, or any of the other dozen things normal people never worried about.

Maybe she'd go say hello to those gracious ladies. They seemed harmless, and it was intermission. The crowd wasn't as large as most Saturday nights.

She hurried to the makeup room and grabbed her largest feather boa—a fat, snow-white, pure ostrich feather one that reminded her of all those Busby Berkeley movies she'd loved as a kid—and headed out to the main floor. Unlike Starr and Luna who loved to mix with the patrons, Phee rarely paraded herself through the tables like a cigarette girl wielding her wares—or a stripper trying to sell a lap dance. Too much potential for hands to make their way to her ass.

"Hey, Jackie," she said to the bartender. "Can I get a glass of prosecco?"

"Sure thing. Give me something to do. Man, it's been slow tonight."

"Yeah, growing close to Thanksgiving, I guess?"

"Must be."

It wasn't unusual as business slowed down closer to Thanksgiving, picking up with a vengeance with their annual Christmas show before the holidays. Then there was New Year's Eve, which was a human zoo. While most people got time off, she and her sisters worked most holidays.

Jackie uncorked the bottle and filled a champagne flute halfway. "You're in a good mood."

"It was a good night. Hey, you know where those women in the front row are from?"

"North Carolina and it shows. They're super-nice and big tippers."

Phee took a sip of the prosecco, adjusted her boa, and headed toward them. A man sitting at the far end of the bar closest to the main floor swiveled on the stool and stuck his legs out, barring her progress. She sidestepped his legs and gave him a good-natured smirk as she passed. He wouldn't blow her good mood.

"Ladies." She paused at the middle of the table. "Having a good time?"

"Oh, hi." A woman in a black dress spattered with huge yellow flowers jutted out her hand. "You are something else."

"We could never do what you do," another woman in hot pink said.

"Oh, sure you could. A little glitter, a big boa…"

The lover of yellow flowers laughed. "Maybe if I was ten years younger and twenty pounds thinner."

"Actually, in burlesque, you need something to jiggle." She gave them a shimmy.

"Yeah, and give myself a black eye with these." The woman lifted her boobs.

Phoenix couldn't stop smiling. Their light, happy energy was what she needed.

She let them fondle her boa and answered questions about what keeps pasties in place. She was sure she convinced at least two of them to look for dance classes when they got home. Someone must teach burlesque in Charlotte, North Carolina.

When Cherry took the stage to belt out her parting signature song, Phee excused herself so they could watch the show.

Maybe she'd celebrate her decent night with a second glass of prosecco. There had been no men with guns. Declan was finally understanding she was serious. Progress, at least.

She set her empty glass down at the bar and waited for Jackie to finish up a drink order at the other end. Loud drums kicked up a notch, their beat thrumming through her body. Her boa slipped off her shoulder, and she tugged it back in place—except it didn't go very far. She twisted to face the same pants-adjusting guy from the other night.

So much for her wonderful night. Deflated of any good vibes, that old wariness attached itself to her insides. "Excuse me." She adopted her best glare.

His mitt wrapped around the end of her boa, and it slithered from her arm like a snake releasing its prey.

He tossed a smirk onto his face. "Earn it back."

Fresh anger coursed through her limbs. Her boa was $300 worth of the finest ostrich feathers and she wasn't about to let him fondle it. "Already earned it." A sick chill crept up her spine.

"Oh?" The guy shrugged, his stare drilling a hole into Phee's sternum. She held back a shiver.

She held out her hand to the boa thief, a request for her possession. He rose, a clear erection tenting his slacks. His hand wrapped around her wrist.

She hissed and nearly bit her tongue from her teeth clamping down.

"Let go of her. Now."

The guy lazily swung his head and stared at Declan. "Just appreciating the merchandise." The guy released her wrist, and she yanked her boa to her chest. Her skin prickled as if the air conditioning rained down on her.

Declan jerked his head toward the front entrance. "Outside. Now."

Max pushed the guy toward the exit. Where had he come from?

The guy held up his hands, that lazy smirk still drawn across his face. He then leaned over to her. "Carragh says hello, by the way."

Carragh MacKenna. She sucked in a gasp. The minute they'd learned of Declan's affiliation with that family she should have yanked Starr and Luna out by their hair if that's what it took to get the three of them out of there.

Declan grasped the guy's shoulder. "What did you say to her?"

"Not talking to you. Talking to the pretty little lassie here."

Declan's fist came out of nowhere. The guy had too much muscle to pitch backward very far, and his fist quickly rose to deliver a return punch across Declan's jaw.

Declan righted himself and swiped his mop of silver-flecked hair from his forehead. "That was quite the mistake you just made." He let his cane slide through his fist, the tip landing with a resounding thunk on the carpeting.

She had never seen Declan like this before—eyes fired, lips thinned to a straight line, and a twitch in his jaw. His reserve had slipped. Her heart lurched and clawed inside her rib cage as if trying to break through, and still she remained… frozen.

The guy shrugged his suit coat back into place. "Nice way to greet your family."

Phoenix blinked at the two men in a full-on stand-off. Why wasn't she moving? Running?

"I'm going," the guy said.

Declan followed him out, his cane punching the floor through a stunned crowd. Still, her feet remained cemented in place.

She'd let her guard down. Stupid. Stupid. Worse, she hadn't fought back. When had she forgotten how to do that?

16

Carragh held out a linen handkerchief, which Declan waved off. He reached into his suit coat pocket, retrieved his own, and ran it over his bloodied lip. "Your men ever step foot inside my club again, I'll end them."

Exhaust from the man's idling limo rose in the air. One of his guys filled the passenger seat while the other, the one he'd punched, leaned against the car like he hadn't a care in the world. A brunette woman sat in the back and checked her manicure. A wine glass dripped from her other hand. The scene was casual as if his dancer hadn't been manhandled thanks to their presence.

Phoenix had been having a great night—her smile, her relaxed shoulders, and the way her arms drifted up into the air as if she floated. She'd even come out to the floor, the first time in a year. His guys ruined the evening for her.

"You didn't like meeting your cousins?" Carragh's lazy smile held no warmth. His ice-blue eyes glared down at Declan and his slick black hair shone under the parking lot light, a scene straight out of a 1970s hustler movie.

Declan squared himself to Carragh. "If we'd been outside,

I might have put them in the ground." As it stood, he'd breached a major rule of club ownership—take all disputes outside, no punches inside. The image of that guy's hand wrapped around Phee's tiny wrist rose and he wasn't half sure he might not clock the guy again for good measure.

Carragh tsked. "Ease up, Declan. No harm. No foul."

"See your family is up to their old tricks. Harassing women you think are important to us? I know the drill. First Starr, now Phoenix. Luna next?"

Carragh's face turned to stone. "No one's getting harassed."

"Keep them out, or I'll see they're not able to walk in anywhere again. Or walk period."

"My, my, Sean touched a nerve by approaching Miss O'Malley there, didn't he?" He instantly sobered. "I don't care where you get your dick wet. What I care about right now is turning this family around."

"And you thought putting those two within fifty feet of my stage is turning things around?"

"I was at our mutual friend Henry's. Didn't realize they were here until I got Sean's text to come join him. They aren't used to the finer things in life—yet."

"Never again, Carragh. Don't think for one second I don't mean what I say."

"Oh, I believe you. You are a MacKenna, after all."

Declan huffed. "You don't listen, do you?"

Carragh's gaze flicked up to his man. At least the guy dropped his gaze. A silent admonishment? Declan didn't buy one word Carragh had said about them not being plants.

"Won't happen again, Declan. You have my word."

"No, it won't. Set up a meeting with Tomas."

A muscle twitched under his right eye. "I told you they won't be back."

So, the man didn't like to be one-upped. "Tomas and I will talk business and I'll decide what happens and what will not."

The man reclaimed his cool. "What made you change your mind?"

"Who said I've changed my mind?"

Carragh eyed him. "My father will expect a counteroffer. Be prepared."

"Why are you telling me this?"

"Because—" he glanced over at the Shakedown sign "—contrary to what you may think, we are on the same side."

"I doubt that, but if you insist, tell me what it will take for Tomas and the rest of you to disappear altogether."

"Disappear? Nothing. Back off a little? Accept him."

"Not happening."

"Somehow, I knew you'd say that." Carragh knocked on the top of his limo, and the guy who leaned against the car pushed off and got into the passenger seat up front.

Carragh hesitated a moment and then took a long inhale. He turned back to Declan. "Ruark's parole hearing is coming up. Thought you should know if you didn't already."

The shit show that was the MacKenna family never ceased. He'd have to warn Nathan and Starr. The man nearly killed them both.

Tonight, however? He had to go deal with the woman who'd haunt every second of his dreams tonight like she did every night.

He opened and closed his throbbing fist as he stalked to the club entrance. His leg ached a little, but it sharpened his brain.

He had learned important things in recent days, and probably something even more important in the last twenty minutes.

One, Carragh was working on his own, and Tomas must

know it. The top of the food chain sent those guys, not an eldest son gone rogue.

Two, even if Phoenix was hellbent on leaving Shakedown, he would have to double his protection of her.

Three, his Plan Z concerning her was getting enacted tonight. There was no more time to waste.

17

———

Phoenix gulped down the last of her second prosecco. Her throat resisted the bubbles, their scald making her eyes prick. After Declan and Max threw out Mr. No-Manners, her insides had fired. Too little, too late, however. Anything could have happened with that guy.

Luna took Phee's last dance spot so she didn't have to go back on stage, at least. She was in no shape to face a crowd. Instead, she sat at the end of the bar, Max standing close by but not too close.

Across the floor, Declan relayed orders to Amos and Nathan in that quiet way of his. He was a good club owner, his lip a little swollen from taking a punch. For her.

Gabrielle sidled up to her. "Declicious certainly protects his ladies." The woman winked at her and then continued her mooning at him across the main floor.

Phee turned to the bar where Jackie eyed her. "What?"

Jackie chortled. "Nothing. Gabrielle..." She jerked her eyes to the waitress. "Your car's still broken down, right? Is Declan able to give you a ride home tonight?"

The woman was so transparent. If reverse psychology

didn't work on her, trying to make her jealous wouldn't either.

Gabrielle sighed. "I wish. Max is instead."

Jesus. Phee pushed off to head to the dressing room, but she got stopped in the hallway, of course.

Declan blocked her advance. "We need to talk."

Phoenix crossed her arms, the music distant in the background. "I'm not going on again."

"You don't have to," Declan said. "But we will have a conversation."

"Keep the door open," she said as soon as she stepped inside his office and whirled to face him.

"You want to air all this to anyone who walks by, fine."

"I have nothing to hide. But apparently, you do." How could he have let those guys inside the club after the other night? "Fighting with your family now?"

"They are not my family, and quite frankly, that guy's not good enough to lick the bottom of your shoe. Are you alright?"

She dropped her arms, and her face relaxed a tad. "I'm fine."

That little furrow between his brows, the one he got when he didn't believe her, deepened. "Are you really?"

"Yes. Fine." She was. She had to be.

"I know you will be. I'll make sure of it." He circled his desk and perched his hip on the corner. He fingered his cane and took in a long breath. "I have something to tell you."

"Oh? Want me to be your date at a family reunion?" Jesus, her mouth wouldn't stop lobbing things.

"I love you."

A stupid half laugh-half snort erupted from her.

He didn't flinch. All that cool slate-blue honed in on her, taking away her breath. My God, the man was serious.

Spots formed in her sight. "You what?" She had to push herself to suck in air.

"I love you," he repeated.

"What do you mean… love me? You're replacing me."

"You are irreplaceable. But…" He reached over to his desk and lifted her napkin resignation and waved it at her. "You quit. And besides, one has nothing to do with the other. It doesn't matter if you leave or stay, my feelings won't change." He rose to both feet, planted them in a wide stance. "I love you." There was that serious edge in his voice again.

Her insides grew warm and heavy. This declaration meant something to him, an instinctual sense that Declan was laying it all on the line, and that somehow, they were at the end as if they'd arrived at the destination of something.

"You said that already." Her heart began to punch at her insides. "But… don't."

"I'm afraid you have little choice in the matter." He tried to move forward and she raised her hands—an automatic reaction even with Declan.

"As I don't have a choice," he added. "It is what it is. You've known for some time how I feel about you. I've never hidden it, and now it's time to say it out loud. One day you'll see that you and I are meant for one another."

And just like that, they slammed into a wall. *Of all the arrogant… self-centered…* Her brain sputtered even stronger thoughts. "I'm not meant for you. In fact, I'm not meant for anyone. I'm not…"

"You're not what? Capable of loving or being in love?" Declan's eyes were holding her somehow, squeezing the breath out of her with their intensity.

She spun away. She couldn't look at him anymore but found herself once more frozen in place. She'd been denying his feelings toward her for so long, to have those words tossed at her so plainly and suddenly—it was too much.

Move, she silently screamed at her legs, and something inside her broke free.

He caught her wrist before she got very far. "So, you can leave and upset your career here, not to mention put your sisters between a rock and a hard place—"

She whirled to face him. "You know nothing about me and my sisters." He couldn't do this to her. It was madly unfair, and a fury stronger than she'd ever felt gushed from every pore.

The gall of the man. First, to declare something so heavy and ridiculous. Then, to believe he knew anything that went on between her and her sisters? She glowered down at his hold. His fingers were rougher than she'd expected, more masculine.

"Let go of me." Funny, he'd rarely touched her after that first night at Maxim's—just the occasional brush. She wrenched her arm from him.

"Fair enough. But whether or not you are here or not, it will not stop the fact I'm in love with you."

"Stop. Just… stop it." Jesus, she sounded even ridiculous to herself. "I've given you no reason to love me." None whatsoever. She'd made sure of it—worked hard at it.

"Oh, yes, you have. Just being you. You're strong, beautiful, and despite that spectacular temper of yours, you have a kind heart. You help people. It's in your nature. You do it every day with your sisters. So, stay or go. Don't let me be the reason why you run."

"Sometimes it's smarter to run. Like I said, I wanted to leave because there are too many dangerous people after this place. I'm going to take Starr and Luna with me. I won't leave them."

"Are they as convinced leaving is better, too? They seem to be fine dancing here."

She ground her teeth together. He knew the answer to his

question. She'd failed spectacularly at convincing them to go with her. She had to dangle a bigger and better carrot for them—once she found it. She lifted her chin.

He sobered. "I wouldn't let anything happen to them—or you. I would eviscerate someone before I'd allow them to touch a beautiful hair on your head or anyone here." He widened his stance. "Remember, I'm the man in love with you. You'll be safer here because no one else will feel as strongly about protecting you as I will." His voice softened a shade. "But I get it. You don't love me back, and you want to move on."

Her heart hurt in an odd way, and her throat burned. "I have to."

"Okay. So, consider me your friend. That's what I'll be to you."

Her brows furrowed. Friends? After what he declared?

"Isn't that what you'd rather have?"

They froze for a second—looking at each other. Her mind couldn't conjure up one coherent thought about this strange conversation. It was so… bald. Brutal, in a way.

"Of course," she finally said. "And I'll stay until my sisters don't need me anymore."

"Fair enough." He gently took her by the arm and escorted her to the door.

As soon as she stepped through, a loud click sounded behind her. It was the first time he'd ever shut her out. It was also the second—third?—time he'd touched her in a very, very long time. That couldn't be right, could it? Yes, he didn't get physically close to her often, and now he did it just to shuffle her out to the hallway.

After telling her he loved her.

After he said he'd settle for being her friend.

She should be happy. She really, really should be.

18

Phoenix yanked her car into park and glanced around. Naomi's text had been short and to the point.

<<can you meet me at Duner's at 4? got questions about dansing>>

She hoped that "s" in dancing had been merely a typo, though she'd met plenty of girls who hadn't even finished eighth grade and probably hadn't cracked a book they weren't forced to read in English class.

She tapped the steering wheel. She was a few minutes early, unable to sit still in her apartment anymore. After Declan's "I love you" declaration, her limbs coursed with an odd adrenaline. Then, this morning, Starr announced Ruark MacKenna might get out soon. Naomi's text was a godsend, really. It was like the universe telling her to go out and do something useful, even if it did mean she had to be on this street again.

Of all the places to meet, Naomi had suggested the coffee shop a block from Maxim's. Phee should have suggested a different place, but here she was. A glutton for punishment.

Through the windshield wiper furiously trying to keep

up with the pounding rain outside, she stared so hard at Maxim's front door her blood vessels might have burst in her eyes. In the gray afternoon, the place looked like trash—peeling paint, a ripped awning. How had she ever thought it once looked cool? Because she'd been a stupid eighteen-year-old—that's how.

Her hand reached for her car handle when the tip of an umbrella emerged from the front door of Maxim's. It burst open and one of Jones' henchmen stepped out, holding it over Naomi. She smiled up at him. The guy didn't return the smile but snarled down at her. What the eff was going on?

The guy didn't follow Naomi as she jogged down the steps but rather stood there looking out over the street. Phoenix huddled down behind the steering wheel to avoid being seen.

Naomi glanced up and down the street, then seemed to recognize Phee's car. A vintage VW is easy to spot, she supposed.

She jogged over and rapped on the car window. "Coming out?" she mouthed.

Phee would if the goon who still stood at the top of the landing with his umbrella would go back inside Maxim's. Instead, he stood there. The guy didn't seem to be looking her way—plus, it wasn't like he knew her so, okay then, she'd get out.

Phee grabbed her umbrella and stepped out into a river of water rushing down the street. If they were smart, they'd have stayed inside the car. Instead, she found herself jogging to catch up with Naomi, who ran pretty damned fast in her sparkly Converse sneakers.

She shook the umbrella out as soon as she stepped inside the coffee shop. She glanced around, logging each detail of the room in her mind, an automatic reaction. A couple sat in the corner booth, and two older men sat at stools at the old-fashioned lunch counter sipping coffee. The exit sign cast a red halo. She marked in her mind that it was to the right.

Naomi sat in the back.

Phee scooted into the narrow booth across from Naomi, who was already reading the menu. "Hey, you got any money?" The girl didn't even look up.

"Hungry?"

"Starving. But I can only have a salad. Make sure I don't get the burger, okay?" The girl dramatically slapped her menu shut.

"Still trying to lose weight?" If she did, her ribs would show in her back.

"Aren't we all?"

"So, about dancing. You had questions?"

"You want me to work at Shakedown, right?" Naomi fidgeted with her blouse.

Okay, this girl got straight to the point. "Well, it's a good starting off point. And, if you have an act—"

"Nope. Don't have one of those."

"Well, enroll in classes—"

"I got no money to take classes. Or time. What's the shortcut?"

"There isn't one." Phee glanced through the window toward Maxim's. "You aren't making money at Maxim's?"

"They aren't giving me enough nights. I mean, two nights I can pull…" She pursed her lips. "Maybe $1,000 a week? Jones has doubled up on girls so I'm trying… but…" She shrugged one shoulder and pulled out some napkins.

She knew the drill. Make the girls compete for their marks and still take sixty percent of the night's earnings. Still, for working two nights a week, she looked haggard. She had dark circles under her eyes and her skin had a gray tinge.

"But isn't that enough to get into a community college or something?"

"College? Why would I do that?" Naomi spat her gum in one of the napkins. "So I can spend ten years making a thousand a week after logging sixty hours a week? I work two nights and make that."

"What can I get you ladies?" A waitress had magically appeared.

"She's paying." Naomi pointed at Phee.

Phoenix smiled up at her. "I'll take a Diet Coke. Naomi here wants a salad… and what else?" She eyed the girl.

"Diet Coke. And add a side of fries."

Phee leaned back and tamped down a little laugh. "Look, if you really want to dance—"

"I want to make money." Naomi crossed her arms. "So, this cabaret stuff you do? It looks like it might be working. You look like you're doing alright. The Coach purse and all."

It had been a gift from Declan last Christmas, but something told her she shouldn't reveal that tidbit to Naomi, who didn't look above attempting to turn any man into a sugar daddy for herself.

"There's more to life than money. Like self-respect. If you waitress for Declan—"

"I'm not doing that shit."

"Why not?"

The girl dropped her chin and glared. "You don't."

"I have before. Now, I don't."

The bell over the door sounded, and out of habit, Phee glanced up. A large man shook out an umbrella and then swiped a mop of black hair off his forehead. He looked so familiar, but he was across the room and had turned away before she could get a good look.

"How are you dancing at Maxim's if you're only 17, Naomi?"

The girl stilled. "Maybe I'm really twenty-one."

"You got ID?"

The girl then turned to stone. "Look. You know and I know how this game is played—"

"Oh? And how is that?" Phoenix slipped the paper off her straw as the waitress set a Diet Coke before both of them. Naomi reached into her purse, and without a single glance around pulled out a small flask, uncapped it, and poured the liquid into her soft drink.

"Hair of the dog?" Phee asked.

"Hair of what?" The girl capped her flask and put it back into her oversized hobo bag.

"Never mind. Let me ask you something. How did you end up at Maxim's, anyway?"

A cold stillness settled into her features. Her jaw slackened, her eyes grew distant. "The usual way. You said you used to work for Jones. How did you end up there?"

"The usual way." When she and her sisters been released from the state, they had few choices. They waitressed. They tried to get office jobs. They had no money, no real skills, and no one suggested community college to them, though how could they have afforded that back then? They still couldn't scrape up enough to live together. Even a one-bedroom and one bath in a safe neighborhood was close to three grand a month in Baltimore, and going somewhere else would just cost more money they didn't have. They just knew they had to go together, and then a chance encounter with one of Jones' strippers led them to Maxim's.

Phee sat back, fiddling with a spoon that had a tiny morsel encrusted on it. She dropped it. "Where's your family?"

Naomi scoffed. "Not going back there."

"Why not?"

Naomi raised her eyebrows "Guess."

She didn't have to. That's the thing about being abused. It made you hyper-aware of others who'd been as well.

The food arrived and Naomi polished off her french fries in record time. The salad went untouched. As soon as the last fry was gobbled up, Naomi took a long sip of her Diet Coke.

"So, about your club. I guess it's not happening?"

"We have actual acts. You'd have to—"

"Forget it. I get it." Naomi slid across the seat and headed toward the ladies' room.

She felt bad for the girl, she really did. But what else she could do for her? Why was she trying to convince this girl to try waitressing at Shakedown? Why was she here at all? Declan may have been right to let her go her own way.

Phee paid the bill, and when Naomi hadn't returned after ten minutes, she went looking for her.

She wasn't in the ladies' room or anywhere else she could find. Phee moved to the front of the coffee shop, glanced out the window, and caught Naomi slipping into the front entrance of Maxim's. The guy still stood out there with an umbrella as if he was waiting for someone.

Naomi hadn't even said thank you or good-bye. But then, when no one gave you anything in life but grief, perhaps she didn't realize it was necessary when someone was trying to be kind to you.

On the tip of her brain, something lined up—something about Declan. He was kind, always trying to do things for people.

It's not the same she told herself, grabbing her umbrella from the stand. She stepped out into the late afternoon. At least the rain had stopped, though the streets still resembled a creek. She stepped into the street, and by the grace of God, managed to look up at the entrance of Maxim's again. Jones was getting out of a black Cadillac, the goon holding the umbrella over him. Jones caught her eyes. She froze. He cocked his head in recognition, his eyes squinching as if trying to place her.

Shit. Shit. Shit.

Her car was between them, about 100 yards away. She popped open her umbrella to shield herself, and if she hurried could get there before he did, couldn't she? Stupid her, she peeked around her umbrella, and Jones was gesturing to the bodyguard, who glanced her way. Was he coming for her?

She began to run. Jones had recognized her. Holy fuck. Her heart might give out at that possibility.

Phee instantly cursed wearing suede heels. They were already ruined and didn't make good running shoes—which they proved when she lost her balance and found herself on her ass on the wet concrete, a torrent of dirty rainwater rushing by her as the sidewalk slanted downhill.

A huge form lorded over her, holding an enormous golf umbrella. "You okay?"

She looked up into the face of Carragh MacKenna.

19

———

"Now, you wait here, honey." The nurse clicked on the brake of the wheelchair. They needn't make such a fuss over a sprained ankle.

Phee's sister, Luna, crossed her arms. "Not your best look."

"It's this godawful, light blue-green scrub thing." Phoenix pulled at the top the nurse had given her. Her clothes had been soaked from the rain, and the nurse insisted she change into the horrible hospital top.

Luna glanced at Declan and then back to her. "He's taking care of the paperwork."

His broad back stood at the half-moon-shaped information desk.

"Probably charming the pants off those nurses," she scoffed. They smiled and that petite blond kept cocking her head as if hanging on his every word. A distinguished middle-aged man with no ring on his finger? He might as well roll in catnip and lie down on the nurse's station desk in offering.

She rubbed her head. Drugs messed with her brain. "You called him, huh?"

"No," Luna leaned down and whispered. "I think Carragh did." The smile on her face was ridiculous. "It was nice of him to bring you—in a limo! He was in the waiting room when I arrived."

Phee adjusted the ice strapped to her sprained ankle, now wrapped in white gauze. "Don't be so easy. He's just trying to get under Declan's skin." Not to mention pushy as hell.

Carragh had lifted her up from the rain and she'd nearly come out of her skin. She must have gone into shock because somehow, she ended up inside his limo, shrunk into a ball in a corner of the enormous vehicle. She recalled nodding when the words *Emergency Room* floated in the air because that was a public place. He'd pulled up, she'd scrambled her way out, and tumbled right into an orderly.

Phee's head throbbed. Did she hit it, too? "And don't tell Starr I ran into him, L."

"But—"

"I mean it. She has enough on her plate." Picking out high heels for her wedding dress but whatever.

"I won't, but what were you doing anyway—running in heels in the rain? And on that street?" She cocked an eyebrow.

"Shopping. For Rachel's baby shower." *Liar, liar, ass on fire.*

"Well, good thing he was there."

"Luna, you're being too calm about Carragh coincidentally showing up." And Declan's family ties. And the fact Ruark was hitting the streets again—soon.

She shrugged. "If it was such a big deal, wouldn't things be a lot worse? And I thought we were going to go shopping together. I know the best baby store." She clasped her hands together in enthusiasm.

She ignored her sister's enthusiasm. "Calm before the storm."

"Well, Carragh's left, and Declan is driving us home." She rose.

"Okay." She lifted her ruined heel that had been resting in her lap. "Because this won't get me home."

"Do I detect a sense of humor?"

"It's the muscle relaxants."

"Whatever it is, let's get a year's supply."

"Ready to go, ladies?' Declan's voice broke into their conversation. "Insurance should cover everything, but if not, don't worry. I've got it covered."

Phee sighed and was about to protest—because she and her sisters would never again owe any man money—but her lips snapped shut as her wheelchair lurched forward. Declan had released the brakes and took control—as he always did.

He leaned down to her ear. "And on the way home, you can tell me how Carragh MacKenna ended up landing you in an ER."

"Oh, he didn't do anything," Luna chimed in. She grasped the heel from Phee's lap. "These did."

Declan's chuckle annoyed her.

On the way home, Phee fought her eyelids that tried to sink to the floor. She shifted in the seat, her cheek against the soft leather, and fixed her gaze on Declan's profile. His temples had grown gray in recent years. She tried to roll to sitting up straight and failed. The drugs made her all rubbery and warm and, quite frankly, they raised up an odd melancholy inside her.

"Declan?" Her throat could only form a whisper.

"Hmm?" he murmured, never taking his eyes off the road.

"Don't tell Starr, okay? About who dropped me off."

Declan gave her a sideways glance. "I won't, but Luna probably will."

"About Luna, make sure she's never alone, okay? She's being too cavalier about things." Talking made her so tired. She might sleep all day tomorrow.

"I promise."

Her eyelashes were made of lead, but she forced them to open. "And send me the ER bills."

"There won't be any."

"I'm sure there will be." She managed to roll her head to face out the windshield. It took a supreme effort.

"Now, you want to tell me why you were back at Maxim's? Or do you want to wait until tomorrow to tell me?"

So, Carragh had told him what street she'd landed ass first on. Did this mean Luna knew, too? She didn't say so, did she? Her head hurt too much to puzzle it out.

"It's not what you think." Her breath fogged the window.

"What do I think?"

"That I make bad choices sometimes." There, she'd said it. Drugs were truth serum.

"Not exactly."

"Well, I do." What else could it be? Her going back to Maxim's like a fool? Trying to help a girl who didn't understand the first thing about life? "Even more reason to stop trying with me."

"You're just scared."

A jolt of energy coursed through her limbs and her head rolled back to face him. "Don't say that. It pisses me off."

The corners of his mouth inched up. "You're scared, and I won't let you stay that way, or at least stay there alone. That's what friends do for one another. They keep each other company, even in the dark." He reached over and took her hand. She glanced down, his large hand engulfing hers. It was now the third time he'd touched her in a week. His fingers were so tan against hers—and warm and strong.

While his temples had begun to gray, his skin was almost

perfect, and his eyes were framed in those dark lashes too thick to be wasted on a man. He was handsome, so she supposed the name Declicious fit. God, whatever drugs they gave her unearthed unwanted observations from her.

She pulled her hand free. "You could be friends with anyone."

"So could you."

"No, I don't think I can. My sisters are enough."

In her periphery she caught him studying her—glancing back and forth between the road and her. "Are you sure about that?"

"I have to be."

He reached over and grasped her hand again. She didn't have the strength to pull back this time. Her eyelids gave up and closed.

20

Declan hooked his cane on the edge of the counter's lip and settled himself on the stool. "She's asleep." He brushed cat hair off his trousers.

Phoenix had conked out the second he'd laid her in her bed, Moonlight curled up next to her. He'd spent half an hour sitting in that rocking chair—a surprise to find in her bedroom—watching her chest rise and fall, all that red hair spilled over the silk pillowcase.

At one point her cat jumped off and stalked toward him only to brush back and forth up against his pants, sending her one good yellow eye accusingly up at him as if trying to send him a message. As soon as he reached down to pet her, she bristled. Phoenix and this cat were well matched—both needing love and refusing it.

He only rose from his sentinel post when Luna came to him with an offer of eggplant parmesan. Now, Starr and Nathan had long gone back to his place, and only he and Luna remained awake. Perhaps now he'd get some answers, like what the ever-loving hell Phoenix was doing on that street again.

Luna wiped a bowl with a rag. "Thanks for getting her home and for handling all the paperwork."

"Least I can do. Thanks for dinner."

"Dinner was the least *I* could do."

"So, Carragh MacKenna. Want to tell me how that happened?"

She shrugged, set the bowl inside a cabinet, and closed its door. "Not sure. He said he'd found her on South Haven street. That's near Maxim's." Luna sighed. "She's started up again."

Weren't those his exact words to Phoenix the other night? "Yes."

"We have to stop it. It's not helpful." Luna shook her head slowly. "And if Jones caught her…"

"I know." His forehead pinched. "And Carragh being conveniently by? Nothing that man does is a coincidence. Tell me if you see him again, okay?"

She twisted her mouth back and forth. "He doesn't seem that dangerous."

He studied Luna—really looked into her wide eyes. Phoenix was right. She was being too calm. "He is. Please, be careful." He glanced toward the hallway that led to the girls' rooms. "For your sister's sake if nothing else."

She leaned against the countertop. "I'd never take a chance there. None of us would."

"Good, especially now that Ruark might get out."

"Emphasis on might." She fiddled with the salt shaker. "You know, Declan, I've been wondering why you're so enamored of a woman who isn't returning your…" She trailed off.

"My affections?" He chuffed. "I owe Phoenix."

"Like you owed Nathan?"

Well, that was an entirely different matter, wasn't it? "Not exactly." He owed Nathan, of course. Nathan had interfered in a fight between Declan and Daniel MacKenna, that clan's golden boy, and went to prison for nine years for accidentally killing him. If Declan had only handled the MacKennas himself, then maybe Nathan wouldn't have felt it necessary to step up and rescue him. If Daniel had tried to take a swing at Declan today he'd have landed the fatal blow himself. Then again, he'd have gone to jail—or been killed for his act.

Luna set her chin in the palm of her hand. "I don't mean to pry, but maybe I can help. If I know more."

Ah, so she knew there was a story. "In order to tell you more, I'd have to bring up bad memories for you."

"It has something to do with Maxim's, the strip club you found us in, doesn't it? I wasn't there that night things went down."

"I'm glad you weren't." Once more, he caught himself staring at her. Like Phoenix, an intelligence shone in her eyes, something he hadn't really studied before. While Starr charged forward, reckless, and Phoenix was as stubborn as a feral cat, Luna always appeared as the Pollyanna of the triplets. Perhaps she wasn't so blindly optimistic, however.

He sucked in a long breath. "Okay. But I have to start further back than that evening I met Phoenix." Where should he begin?

She circled the island and took the stool next to him.

"You know I am related to the MacKennas. I found out rather late in life my mother was Tomas MacKenna's sister, and when she died, they found me."

She nodded once.

"You also know that I went to prison for vehicular manslaughter. An interesting development shortly after my refusal to be folded into the family."

"Misdemeanor." She flushed suddenly, perhaps at his reaction. "I mean, so I heard."

Of course, she had. Nothing was secret long at Shakedown.

"Criminal negligence resulting in another's death. Got two years."

She didn't flinch at a single word he spoke.

"I'd made a huge mistake, getting behind the wheel of a car with three glasses of wine in my system. Enough to be over the line. Of course, the failed brake lines didn't help. The fact I didn't even try to stop when that pedestrian stepped into the crosswalk helped get me the conviction."

"What?" Her eyes widened.

So, she hadn't heard everything about him.

"I suspect tampering with my car was a shot over the bow by Tomas MacKenna. For not being willing to jump at the chance to work with him. After he felt I learned my lesson or perhaps toughened up from such an experience, I was inexplicably released ahead of schedule."

"And you came back to Baltimore."

"Where else was I going to go? They'd have found me either way and at least here I had friends. So, to the night I met Phoenix. I was out for a few days, trying to get used to walking through a door without someone telling me I could. Not my proudest moment, but I ended up at Maxim's."

There—a visible shudder ran through her whole body.

"Like I said. Bad memories for everyone." Except it held his most treasured one. "Maybe I'll tell this story another time."

"No, please." She laid her hand on his forearm, stopping him from rising.

He glanced down at her small hand against his suit jacket. "That. That's what she did for me."

She lifted her hand. "What?"

"She touched me when no one else would. She smiled at me. Talked softly to me. Made me feel like a person again."

He resettled on the stool. "Seems like such a small, silly thing when I say it aloud like that." He shook his head, studied his shoes. "It's the truth though. Prison can break a man in a thousand ways. Nathan was beaten within an inch of his life."

She shuddered at that.

"For me, it was different. I wasn't touched—not that I'd cozy up to another man and certainly not one of them. But after a year of being completely, utterly left alone… Anyway, this leg never healed properly after the accident and then suffered more damage later in prison…. Well, when I got out? Well, let's say no one was interested in touching me then, either." He tapped his leg with his cane. "So, I had this notion, go to a strip club. Pay for someone to. And then there she was." He had to pause, just like he had the first time he laid eyes on her. "Sure, I hadn't been with women in a couple of years, but Phoenix…" He slowly shook his head. "She had a catastrophic beauty." To this day, his mind could call up her image.

Some men admired breasts, legs, hair, but for him, it'd always been the eyes. He couldn't stop staring into hers—all that sea-blue full of secrets, intelligence, and pain. His heart lurched recalling it.

He scratched at his chin. "There she was, all porcelain skin and delicate bones hovering over a lunk like me, and all I could think was the world was fucking unfair. What was she doing there? How did she get to that place? And what was I doing there? Then she offered me—"

"A second dance on the house. Phee told us that much," she added quickly.

"Having a record, little money, and this…" He tapped his leg again. "My limp was more severe then. I believe she took pity on me."

"Or maybe it was because she was on probation for hitting a customer and saw you were a gentleman—for once."

Luna smirked a little at that. "I was shocked she hadn't been fired by then."

"Yeah, well, it was that second lap dance that got her in trouble. It was on the house, she'd said, to celebrate my being released. She'd gotten me to reveal that, amazingly. Anyway, Jones found out immediately."

"She got punched by him. I remember."

"So do I, and it was more than once." He should have intervened more but instead ended up being thrown out on his ass. "What you don't know is that night I was planning on getting a few lap dances, getting loaded, and maybe walking into the river. I'd lost my business, my life. And then to discover I was a MacKenna, and they'd never let me run? Would send me to prison if they had to? Well, she gave me a reason to fight. Anyone who could give kindness like that under her circumstances? Well, she deserved the second chance I was about to throw away."

Luna sat back. "Wow, Declan. That's…"

"A lot? She saved me and now I won't stop until she's okay. And she's not okay, Luna."

"Yeah."

Of course, Luna would be the sister to understand. A few months ago she'd tried to help Phee make peace with her father, albeit failing spectacularly.

"But if Phoenix doesn't turn around, you wouldn't—"

"No. I have no plans on offing myself with or without Phoenix."

"That's good to hear. Things were that bad?"

He nodded slowly, clamping down the memories of what ultimately drove him to consider such an act.

Luna looked at him expectantly. She was kind. All three of the O'Malley sisters were, in their own way. Even Phoenix, the firebrand.

"I mean…" she began and stopped. "The MacKennas, they—"

"Are that bad, Luna." He was going to have to tell her all of it. "My mother kept diaries. After she died, I read them and finally understood why she would stare at the window sometimes, tears in her eyes for no reason whatsoever. She had no one to help her." He had to stop for a second and catch his breath. "I asked her on her deathbed, did she get enough? She responded with, 'What is enough, anyway? Someday you'll find someone to help. Help her instead.' I remember it distinctly."

"So, Phoenix is that someone."

"Phoenix keeps me awake… if that makes sense. Fighting." He chuffed. "Not very romantic, is it?

"I don't think Phee believes in romance. It's a shame, really."

"Oh, I think you have enough of that to cover her." He winked.

She flushed a little but then recovered. "Can I give you some advice? Don't tell her any of this yet. She's…"

"Burdened. Still." He could see it in her face every time he looked at her. She wore her past like some women wore makeup.

Every time she rebuked him, it only made him love her more. It raised up a primal urge to take out those who'd hurt her and then haul her into his arms once revenge had been meted. He fought it every goddamn second of his life, knowing instinctively she would not respond to that. It was his own brand of hell, the desire to act but being unable to.

He stood and stretched. "So, that's the story. When I first met Phoenix, I thought I could be her savior—and she's been breaking my heart ever since."

"And yet you've been helping us ever since."

"Or not. Maybe continuing on isn't in her best interest. If you didn't dance at Shakedown, what would you do?"

Her lips thinned and she slowly shook her head. "Dance somewhere else? We'd probably end up travelling around. Not many clubs exist like Shakedown."

"How about doing something other than dancing?"

"We don't know how to do anything else. We'd probably work in a coffee shop or retail. Ick. And I think that's why Phee is so angry. I don't think her life is enough for her."

Like his mother. He could see Phee's potential. She snuck books from his library—mostly the classics. He'd moved his entire collection of them to his office just so she could keep doing it. He liked the idea of her touching his things.

"Well." He rose. "We have to make sure she never goes back to Maxim's."

"Declan… what are you going to do now? Sit in that rocking chair and watch her all night?"

Of course, he would.

21

Phee rolled to her back, the sheet catching on her ankle. It was so stiff. She rubbed the bandage with her other foot. Oh, yeah, she'd stupidly fallen on her ass in the rain on South Haven Street. She shuddered—recalling the black rage that had filled Jones' eyes at seeing her made her shudder under the sheets. Then that other guy? He was a new bodyguard, and he'd begun to move for her. She could have so easily been dragged into his car, the alley, or back into Maxim's.

"Phoenix."

Her body seized. *Move, move, move,* her brain screamed, and still nothing except her eyes that furiously searched the shadows could. Movement came to shape in her rocking chair. That was all it took for her body's paralysis to break. She kicked at the sheet, shrank back to her headboard, and managed to rise to standing, her ankle giving out a sharp pain, her palms flat against the wall.

"Get the fuck out!" Her scream made her head pound like someone was punching her forehead from the inside. Moonlight. Where was she?

"It's me," a male voice sounded calmly. Declan. It was Declan.

Soft footfalls padded in the hallway and then Luna was in the doorway. She immediately dropped to the bed and held out her hand. "Bad dream?"

"I'm fine." Phee lowered herself to the bed, careful not to step on her sprained ankle. Her heart slapped against her rib cage and she gulped air.

Something ticked in Declan's jaw. He needed to stop staring at her that way.

"Sorry." She'd screamed like a lunatic. Moonlight was probably cowering in her closet.

"No, I'm sorry. I scared you." His eyes fixed on her. "Luna, I've got this."

Luna glanced at him. "No, I'm—"

"I'm okay," Phee swiped at the sheets, grabbing fistfuls and raising the edge to her chest. "Go back to bed, L. Really. Or better still, find Moonlight."

Luna kept her eyes on Declan as she softly closed the door.

Phee eased herself against the headboard. "How long have you been there?" She rubbed her sternum as if that was going to stop the rushing of her blood.

"Not long."

She glanced at the clock. Not long, huh? It was 3 a.m. She swiped at her cheek and it came away wet. Great. "I won't be going back to Maxim's if that's what you're worried about." Hovering over her like a jailor. "So you can stop staring at me."

He took in a long breath and kept staring. "Do you know the first time I saw you at Maxim's, I thought your hair reminded me of a sunset?"

What was he talking about? "That right?"

"Yes. That was something I'd missed being in prison—seeing the night sky turn colors."

She rubbed her forehead. "Funny you should say that about my hair. The first time I saw my father in years he was at a place called Sunset Home."

"But he's not there anymore. Now he's at a halfway house, right?"

She didn't answer. Starr and L. had shared that news with her and she'd tried hard to forget it.

"He won't get near you again."

Oh, Jesus. Is that what this is all about? She threw off the sheets, heat building in her body as if someone lit a fire within her. She wore sweatpants and a T-shirt. She'd have ripped both off if she was alone.

"No one will ever enter your bedroom without permission ever again."

Fuck him for raising that topic. "You did."

He huffed. "Yes, I suppose so, but I had witnesses. Luna was with me."

"Declan, you can go. I'm fine."

The rocking chair creaked as he pushed himself to standing. "If you say so."

"Leave that light on, please." She pointed to the lamp on the table next to the rocking chair—one of the earliest mini-cocktail lamps from Shakedown before they'd most recently renovated. It reminded her of better days when she and her sisters danced and there were no men with guns hanging around or before she knew Declan was really a MacKenna.

Declan fingered his cane. "One more thing. You don't have to worry about Carragh MacKenna, either. Seeing him standing there in the ER waiting room..." His lips firmed. "That won't happen again."

"I can get with that program."

He smiled. "Well, look at us. Agreeing on something."

Truth was they agreed on many things. His love of vintage cars and antique furniture and reading classics would have made him a perfect friend if they'd met in another lifetime.

"The doctor says I have to take two weeks off." Though what she'd do during that time frame, she had no idea. Maybe find that new dancing gig. The air seemed to grow heavier even thinking of doing such a thing.

"No problem. We'll adjust. What will you do with your time off? And please, tell me you won't be looking for Naomi during that time."

She stared at the ceiling. "I won't. I'm tired now, Declan." She rolled to her side to face the far wall. She couldn't look at his handsome face anymore—seeing all the hope and desire for her that, quite frankly, she didn't deserve. She had nothing to give a man like Declan.

"But promise me something?" she asked the wall. "No matter what, you'll see Ruark can't get to Starr ever again. Or to Luna."

"I'll be in my own grave before I let that happen. Anyone who hurts you hurts me. You have my loyalty, not them. Remember that."

Her throat clogged, but with some effort, she managed to swallow down the choke. "For the record, I meant what I told Naomi about you being a gentleman."

"Well, that's something." He chuckled softly, and his foot-falls told her he was finally moving to the door, the soft punch of his cane accenting every step. It suddenly stopped. She could feel him staring at her, but then the soft click of the door opening and shutting told her she was alone.

She rolled to her back again. Why was it so hard for her to admit the truth to herself? She admired Declan Philips. He was a fool to be in love with her, but he was a good man. Therein lay the problem. She didn't know what to do with a good man. She only knew how to avoid them, and as much as he believed his loyalty lay with her, she knew never to trust words.

I'd never hurt you was the phrase spoken before they did.

I love you was the phrase uttered before they didn't.

22

Declan pulled into his parking space at Shakedown and turned off the ignition. He spent a few moments tuning into the rain punching at his roof. He hadn't slept well, but then any man worth his salt wouldn't after wheeling the woman he loved out from the emergency room. Then, to watch her continue to torture herself by reliving the past?

He knew last night words weren't going to win Phoenix. The woman needed actions, and he knew which ones—starting with ridding himself of the MacKennas for good. It was time to visit the head of the snake. He was calling Tomas MacKenna first thing. Enough waiting around for his errand boy son to make it happen.

He cracked open the door and stepped out. He cursed when his foot landed in a small river coursing toward the gutter. He dashed toward the entrance, his cane slipping on the slick asphalt. Once under Shakedown's awning, a small figure huddled by the door turned. Thin, bare legs peeked out of a tattered jean miniskirt.

He raised his voice above the rain lashing the awning. "Hello, Naomi."

She turned, dropped her cigarette, and ground it out underneath her boot. "Hey, can we go inside? My clothes are sticking to me." Her hair hung in thick, wet strands and she stomped her feet as if trying to get warm.

If he guessed correctly, she'd walked the entire way from Maxim's to Shakedown. At least now, he wouldn't have to hunt the girl down himself—something else he knew he'd have to do. Otherwise, Phoenix would. He knew her too well. She didn't like loose ends either.

He drew out his keys and unlocked the front door. "Been out here long?"

She shrugged and popped her gum. "A bit."

He gently pulled open his custom-made glass door, which thankfully had arrived and been placed during a lull in their recent storms. He couldn't look at that red wooden eyesore another day.

"Wait here." He shrugged off his coat and hung it in the coatroom. He brought out a hanger to find Naomi had disappeared. It wasn't hard to find her. He followed the small wet puddles she left all the way to the main floor. Her gaze fixed on the stage as her jaw worked her gum.

"Naomi, your coat." He held out his hand.

She turned. "Nah, that's okay."

"You're soaked."

She huffed and slipped off her coat—a pink turkey feather monstrosity he'd seen on hookers down at East Baltimore Street. "It's vintage, so I want it back."

"Of course."

After hanging the hideous thing over a barstool, he turned to her. She was back to staring at the stage.

She pointed toward the red velvet curtains. "So. That's where your girls dance."

"We have shows Tuesday through Saturday nights. Closed on Sundays and Mondays."

Her eyebrows shot up. "You close?"

He supposed that would come as a surprise to her given most strip clubs in the city were open seven nights a week. "What can I do for you? Coffee?" He slipped behind the bar and turned on the coffee machine.

She strode over and put both forearms on the bar. "I want a job." Red welts marked both wrists.

He inclined his chin toward the damage. "Jones do that to you?"

She quickly slipped her arms to her lap. "So, you once said I could work here."

The coffee machine gave off its distinctive hum. He pulled out a bag of coffee grounds from under the counter. "I said I might have an opening for a waitress, but you made it clear you didn't want to do that."

"I don't. What will it take for me to dance here?" She glanced around. "Looks like we're alone here. I could show you a lot of things." She leaned the top half of her body on the bar again.

"I'll bet you can. But we don't do those kinds of dances here. We hire actual acts." He placed two white cups on the bar top.

"Yeah, Phoenix said."

"She's right." And when the hell did that conversation happen? Perhaps that's what she was doing on South Haven.

"Well, how do I get an act together? You seem to be the kind of guy who likes to give advice."

He studied her. "How old are you?"

"Twenty-one."

"Mmmhhh. Tell you what, you come by tomorrow and I'll have Gabrielle show you the ropes. She's our head waitress."

"If I had an act, would you at least lemme audition?"

The coffee machine gurgled behind him. He placed one of

the cups under the spigot. "You sure you don't want that coffee?"

"Nope. Just a job."

"Okay. Come back here with a dance, and I'll audition you." An idea skirted his mind around that. "Better yet, I'll have Phoenix do it."

Why hadn't he thought before of having her vet some of the people who inevitably ended up here with the same request as Naomi? His thoughts didn't get far because Nathan strode in. The guy took one look at him and one look at Naomi and chuckled. He was gone through the curtains in a flash, and Naomi was already pulling on her soaking wet coat and headed for the door.

"You got a ride, Naomi?" Declan asked.

One of her eyebrows arched up. "You're kidding me, right?"

"Come on, I'll drive you to wherever you want to go."

"How about you give me some money for a cab? Take it out of my first paycheck."

The woman had some attitude, but then he'd been putting up with Phee's snark for years.

He sighed. She'd end up back at Maxim's whether she walked or he drove her. He could at least spare her the hassle of marching twenty blocks through pouring rain.

After securing her in the back seat of a reputable cab company vehicle, he paused under the awning, the sky gray as ash as the heavens spit down on them.

Tires splashed and a vehicle thunked over the pothole at the entrance—something else he needed to fix soon. He lowered his gaze and cursed at the slick asphalt under his feet. As if adding yet another insult to the day, Carragh MacKenna's pretentious limo pulled into his parking lot. Perhaps he didn't need to call Tomas after all. And while

Carragh wasn't the part of the snake he wanted, it was the part he would deal with first.

23

Now that he thought about it, Declan shouldn't have let Carragh inside. He should have let him stand in the rain. Instead, he stood in front of Declan's desk, a glass of his finest Scotch in his hand as if they were old friends.

Carragh slowly turned the glass in his hand as if studying the deep cut pattern. "Why not?"

"Because it's a bullshit proposal." Expanding Shakedown with the MacKennas as the lead investor? Over his dead body. He'd wasted the last ten minutes listening to something they couldn't seriously believe he'd take. He'd demanded a meeting with Tomas, not an offer to lose control of his business.

The man put down the glass and then knocked both sets of knuckles down on his desk. Declan leaned back in his chair, flicked his gaze to the guy's hands and then back up to Carragh's face. He rather enjoyed the man's frustration—displayed in *his* office, in *his* club that *he* solely owned. And it would stay that way.

Carragh righted himself and shrugged his coat back into place. With a casual scratch across his chin, he slowly shook his head. "My father doesn't make these offers lightly. To get back in the game is an honor."

"So now it's an honor to split my profits?"

"It takes money to expand. You could have a string of clubs up and down the East Coast. Why not jump on it?"

"I rather like going it alone."

Carragh took in a dramatic intake of breath and huffed it out. "You know what it means to turn away now?"

He gripped the top of his cane tighter and let the bird head dig into his palm. "I was never in… Cousin." It was a familial bond he did not relish, but this game of sometimes-you're-family-and-sometimes-you're-not was officially old.

"That your final answer?" he half-laughed.

Declan's chair thunked forward. "I only give final answers."

"Jesus, Declan, just say you'll consider it so I can go report back to my father and then maybe we'll both get to end this stand-off."

"No." Declan rose from his chair. "No in-person meeting. No more discussion." He rounded his desk.

A muscle around Carragh's right eye twitched. To the unobservant, one might not have caught it. Prison taught Declan many things, and the tiniest facial tick could foretell a great many things—restrained anger, surprise, or in Carragh's case, frustration he didn't want anyone to see.

The man sighed. "Whaler's Waterfront Bar. Tuesday. 12 noon. Don't be late." He spun and headed to the door.

Ah, so Tomas had agreed to meet. Declan's thoughts of Carragh going out on his own moved from being a mere suspicion to a real likelihood. Had Tomas even come up with this proposal? Or was this all Carragh's doing? And if so, what did he want with a burlesque club? Perhaps he wanted to take over his father's drug business.

"And take in your entertainment elsewhere from now on." The man's presence was unwanted.

Carragh paused, put his face into profile. "Good thing I was around when Phoenix fell. You may want me around more."

Declan wouldn't take that obvious bait.

When he didn't answer, Carragh peered over his shoulder. "Dangerous business, burlesque."

The man yanked open Declan's office door and strutted out.

24

———

Declan stood on the riverbank, the lapels of his suit coat lifting from the breeze coming off the water. The river shone with oil and tiny whitecaps glinted in the twilight. Some might even call it romantic the way the gray water seemed to darken and grow a deep indigo blue as night threatened to fall. That thought was all it took for Phoenix's blue eyes to rise in his mind.

Jesus, he couldn't get over that woman if he tried.

Gravel crunched under tires behind him. Amos' car pulled up near him. Trick eased himself out with Max and Amos following. Good, they'd come together as he'd asked—and not in Trick's car. Too recognizable.

He turned to them. "Gentlemen. Thanks for coming."

"Waiting on Nathan?" Trick asked.

Declan settled his cane between his feet. "No, only the four of us for now." Nathan had enough. It was time for him to enjoy his newfound happiness with Starr, even if they did have a parole hearing hanging over their heads.

"We still trying to keep him out of most things?" Max

leaned against the car, stretched out his legs. "The groom in his enchanted bubble or something?"

"Or something."

Trick scratched the side of his beard. "There a reason why we're meeting in an abandoned parking lot a mile from Shakedown?"

"Yes. Amos, scan Shakedown for bugs. Can you do that before the show opens tomorrow?" He was taking no chances. His "cousins" had been hanging around a little too much for his taste.

The man nodded, his eyes narrowing with unasked questions.

It was enough of a surprise that Tomas agreed to meet, but in public? Not like the man, which meant he was up to something. No matter. He'd been biding his time with the MacKennas, and it was time to stop. He wasn't about to be played with any longer.

"I realize doors open soon, so let me get to the point. Ruark MacKenna will likely be on parole soon. Carragh MacKenna is showing up too often, this time with a bullshit business proposal, and it won't be long before more of them slither out of the woodwork." Declan drew out three folders from a briefcase by his leg. "These are photos and important information on every MacKenna member I could drum up."

Trick took the stack and handed one folder each to the other two men.

As the men flipped through the pages of photographs and basic information, Declan began the speech he was hoping he'd never had to give. "You're going to see these men show up—often. It's their next play. I'm convinced of it. But none of them steps foot inside this club again. Be ready for them to try to force their way inside. Don't let them by any means necessary."

Trick glanced up from the paper he was studying. "Not

even Carragh? He seemed to be the only man who could make the others stand down."

"Not betting on the ability to hold that power. I asked Carragh to do something he didn't want to and he balked. Then he came to see me this morning—offered to invest in Shakedown."

Trick cursed under his breath. "You said he balked at something. What?"

"To set up a meeting with Tomas, his father. But he did it."

Heads swiveled and hard glances were exchanged among the men.

Trick shifted on his feet. "You're kidding, right?"

"Not in the slightest. I'm convinced Carragh is operating on his own, wants to stay under Papa's radar. If his father gets wind of that, Carragh's wings will be clipped within the hour—before he attempts to overthrow Tomas."

"Thought Carragh was being groomed to be next in line."

"Tomas doesn't share power. I suspect—" and until recently it was just suspicion "—Tomas has no idea what his boys have been up to. All the real estate being bought up and down the waterfront lately might have been Ruark's way of breaking out from under Daddy's shadow—until he landed in prison. Carragh may be picking up on the idea. I don't know, but I'm going to find out."

"We'll be ready. Say when." Those were Max's first words.

"You're not coming."

All three men's eyes darted around to each other. Trick, of course, was the first to speak up with the expected response. "You can't."

"I go in there with any of you and Tomas will have thought he'd cowed me a little. Needing protection. Well, I'm not, and I don't. The man isn't going to kill me or rough me up. One mark on me and he knows I'd burn the place down. I'll shut it down, split up the entertainment and get them gigs elsewhere, fully financed. Then Shakedown is just a building with overpriced drinks to offer, if even that."

"Maybe that's what he wants."

"No, he wants to own me and everything I've ever built. I won't give him anything."

"He could be looking for businesses to launder money, then it doesn't matter what Shakedown turns into."

"Eventually it would. There has to be some business for even that to work. Carragh gave me a lot of valuable information the other night. Like how I should show up with a counteroffer—blackmail money. That's not a money launderer talking. No, he wants the waterfront to boom. Easier to hide drug runners coming and going via waterfront in a crowd. Leashing me is a bonus."

Amos cursed under his breath. "Man, I'll stick around until this is sorted, but I can't get mixed up in that shit."

"Not asking you to. And if you need to go—"

"No, man. I'm here, but if shit really hits the fan…"

"You go when you need to. Just tell me. If you disappear I'll wonder what happened." If he was at the bottom of the river. "Trick. You need time off? I mean, with Rachel being pregnant…"

"No. Maybe."

"I'm shocked she hasn't ordered you to quit yet."

"Oh, she has. But you don't abandon people so I'm not about to. Plus, we haven't seen any real violence. I mean, other than Ruark, and I understand he was a wild card. One false move and he's back in prison."

"I wouldn't consider you leaving abandonment. I also don't get a violent vibe from Carragh."

Trick cracked his knuckles. "But you sure he'll stay that way?"

"No."

Trick quirked his lips and nodded his head a little. "Well, I get now that Phoenix has quit we needed more dancers. But the new hires—"

"She's not quitting. We have come to an agreement. At least for the time being. We'll see how long it holds." Because with her nothing was certain. She was shifting sand, but sand he'd bottle before letting her loose and therefore vulnerable to a mob family seeking someone to make an example of.

"The two new acts will need to be reassured. Move them from probation to permanent. I'm not letting Tomas think I'm folding even a little bit. Quite the opposite."

Max shook his head. "Need more of us?" Shakedown already employed 20 of "them."

Trick smirked. "We have a bouncer for every other person we employ. How many do we need?"

No one wanted to answer that question because the truth was the MacKennas would always have more.

25

Phoenix tucked a crutch under each arm and swung her way to the front door. The last person she expected on her doorstep in the middle of the day was Cherry, out of drag—mostly—wearing a women's business suit with heels and heavy eyeliner.

"You know I don't gossip, but this girl has something to tell you." She pushed her way inside.

Phee awkwardly turned on her crutches. "You love gossip."

"Hmm." Cherry swiveled her head around the room. She pointed. "Nice new chair. Wayfair or Pottery Barn?"

"Cherry."

She straightened. "Of course, I don't have time to compare decorating tips. I only have three hours before this —" she swirled her hand in front of her face "—has to be full-on. I had to come by, though."

"You have my phone number, right?" She laughed. It was so good to see her. A maudlin sentimentality had been creeping up on her all morning for no particular reason.

"Some things are delivered better in person, like how I

overheard Declan say he was meeting with Tomas MacKenna tomorrow at noon at Whaler's Waterfront by himself and you have to stop him," she said in a rush.

Whoa. That was a lot of information.

"Someone has to talk that man out of it. And that someone is you." She pointed at Phoenix. "You're the only one he listens to."

Ha! "Where did you get that idea and how did you hear this, anyway?"

"I stopped by the club to pick up my paycheck so I could finally go pick up those vintage cowboy boots… the ones I've been dying for?"

"Did you get them?"

She snapped her fingers. "They're in the car," she sang.

"And Declan happened to shout out he was meeting with Tomas MacKenna?"

"I might have been hovering a little longer than I normally do in the hallway outside Declan's office when I heard Max louder than I have ever heard that man, and you know that's saying something. The boys had some man-meeting this afternoon, and Max kept saying, *"You_can't."* Well, that's all this girl needed to hear—and I mean *needed*—to hear more about what Declan could. Not. Do." She slapped her palms on the last three words.

"But meeting with the head of the family he's been trying to get away from? It makes no sense." Or did it? The man was one of them. They could be planning a family reunion for all she knew.

"Exactly. And it's dangerous. So come on." She gestured her toward the door. "We're going."

"He's a grown man. He can choose what he wants."

Cherry turned dramatically. "What if something happened to Declan? What if he was gone from this earth? And you could have done something about it?'

Her words stung. "That is not fair…"

Cherry raised her eyebrows. "All is fair in love and war. And you, my girl, are in both."

Both? Love. War. What the hell was Cherry going on about? That love thing was one-sided, and she hadn't declared war on anyone except for one strip club owner.

Cherry swung open the door and stood there. "You know I'm right."

A thousand denials should have risen up, but her belly twisted and held them inside her. Declan gone? That hot truth blazed inside her, got under her skin, and jolted her into a realization. So many people counted on him, including her. She'd been able to hold it together because of his unwavering presence. She did owe him, after all.

Time to even the score. "I'll get my purse."

26

———

Declan fingered the gun. So seductive, so lethal. And, unfortunately, more necessary in his life than ever before.

"You're really doing it?" Trick stood in the doorway of Declan's office. "You're actually considering going alone?"

"Stop worrying like a mother hen." He slipped the gun back into his top desk drawer. "Shouldn't you be out on the floor? Full house."

"Nathan and Max are there. Amos and Charlie on the front door. And Dex and Trace in the alley. A lot of muscle for a reason, and all the more reason for you to take one of us with you tomorrow."

"Not happening." He rounded his desk and jogged his stiff leg a little. It had been feeling pretty good lately. Guess all that physical therapy was finally paying off.

"And no one can convince you otherwise?"

"No."

A waft of cinnamon blew into the room. "Not even me?"

Trick turned to face Phoenix looming in the doorway, propped up by crutches.

Goddamnit. Declan had planned on keeping this meeting

from her for a reason.

Trick sighed, stared down at the floor for a brief second, then looked back up at her. "Give it your best shot." He skirted past her, giving her a slight smile as he passed.

She hobbled inside and Trick closed the door behind her.

"Don't go." Phoenix limped forward, her blue eyes ablaze. "Why are you doing this? It's dangerous. People count on you." A sheen of wet coated her eyes.

Well, he'd be damned.

He crossed his arms and bent toward her. "People." He would make her say it.

"My sisters count on you." She hopped to his couch and lowered herself to the leather seat.

He took her crutches from her and leaned them against the wall. "Ankle hurting?"

"I'm fine."

If he heard "fine" from her one more time… This woman hadn't been "fine" even once in her entire life.

A drink would be really good right now. After pouring two fingers of bourbon for each of them, he brought them over. Her forehead bunched and the corners of her mouth turned down. She still was the only woman he'd known who could make a frown sexy.

He handed her a glass and fell down next to her.

She took a sip. "I usually don't drink." She angrily swiped her jacket off her shoulders. He grasped the shoulder to help her, which only caused her lips to screw into yet another pout, the kind seen in the old French movies. His own mouth ached to kiss that irritated mood right off her lips.

Instead, once freed, he slung her jacket over the arm of the couch. "Not taking anything for your sprain?"

"I don't like to take anything. Ever." She took another sip of the bourbon. "Except this. Sometimes." She squared herself to him. "Declan, what are you doing?"

"Enjoying a drink with you."

"You know what I mean."

"I do." He smiled and sighed. "Tomas isn't going to do anything to me. Or you or anyone else for that matter."

"Then why meet with him?" She lowered her chin and peered up at him as if he was trying to pull something over on her—as if he could ever.

Thoughts crammed his brain for a minute. He then rose. One drink wasn't enough to numb the pain of all the things he needed to tell her. "You hungry?"

She shook her head a little. "Food? Now?"

"I'll take you to dinner. Trick's got things covered here, and—" he glanced down at her foot and back up at her "—you appear to have time. I'll explain everything at Trovino's."

She chewed on her lip. "Not exactly dressed for it."

It wasn't a refusal. "You're perfect." The woman could be wearing a flour sack and still doors would still open for her. "Besides, *'She's beautiful and therefore to be wooed.'*"

Amazingly, he earned a smile with that one.

"'She is a woman, therefore to be won?'" She pushed herself to standing with his help. "You do love to quote Shakespeare. But wooing and winning are not on the menu, even at Trovino's."

At least she seemed to agree to dinner. Perhaps it was a sign that Phoenix was open to hearing his story tonight. It was something he'd been waiting to tell her for six long years. With any luck, he'd not end up with a lap full of lasagna but rather the opening he sought.

Despite the fortress she'd put up between him and her, she was a woman to be wooed, just not in the way any other woman might need. The only time he'd ever gotten inside her was with brutal honesty. Time for a bit more, like opening up his past to her and what it means.

27

Phoenix lifted her wine glass and clinked it against Declan's. The privacy of their small dining alcove comforted them. The heavy, thick velvet drapes half-hid them from other patrons, and they reminded her of the stage curtains.

"You come here often?" she asked.

"Friends with the owner, though I'm not usually here this early on a Thursday."

"I can't remember a time when I went to dinner at a normal hour." Taking the stage by 8 p.m. most nights pretty much excluded any nighttime activities for her and her sisters.

"Other than now, when's the last time you've taken any time off?"

"I don't need time off. I like to stay busy." Her leg began to jog at the mere thought of having to sit around anymore.

He twirled his glass by the stem. "You're welcome to come to the club and—"

"Hang out?"

"Or perhaps do other things." He adjusted his jacket. "Naomi came to see me this morning."

Phee straightened in her chair. "And?"

"She's going to come back with an act. Told her I'd audition her. Or perhaps you can." He took a sip of his wine.

Her eyelids grew tight as they instinctively narrowed. "What kind of act?"

"Don't know. But she seems determined, and now you don't have to go back and try to rescue her."

"I wasn't trying—"

"Oh, yes, you were." He poured her more wine, though she'd barely touched it.

He himself took a long swallow of wine. "And I admire your tenacity. My mother was not unsimilar to you. She always wanted to be a dancer but she never was."

Her hands relaxed. She hadn't realized they'd been twisting her napkin. "She danced? Is that why you own a burlesque club?" Now, *this* was an interesting development. She really knew so little about the man she'd worked for. But she'd kept it that way, hadn't she? She hadn't trusted herself to learn more and still not care.

"Not exactly. My mother was born and bred for one thing —to be offered up as a wife someday."

"Offered up..."

"There was a tight-knit group of families who did business together. Their children were expected to marry one another. And my mother? Well, she was a beauty. Considered an asset. Black hair and blue eyes."

"Like Carragh. And Ruark." She nearly spat out the latter name.

"Yes. But that's where the similarities end. She didn't have the stomach for her family's business. She knew all along what her brother did, and Tomas was a hard sibling. He believed the more she knew early, the better. But she threw a major monkey wrench in his plans to arrange for her to marry the son of a business partner. She was seventeen when she ran away, pregnant, and with a purse full of stolen money out of her father's safe."

Anxious pinpricks danced along her spine. "Pregnant with…"

"Me. Some neighborhood boy. She wouldn't tell me. And she, ever the rebel, went by a different name, though not changed legally. She had me alone in Kansas City. Stayed hidden until she died. That's when they found me."

"How?" A slice of anger cut through her. Was there no end to the unwanted advances?

"Obituary. Apparently, Tomas never stopped looking for her. Thought he could right one of his father's life's greatest disappointments."

"To lose a daughter? Or sister?" She knew one man who'd have loved to have "lost" three of them—and did.

"No, to not *own* a daughter. Or, in Tomas' case, being unable to turn a sister into a bargaining chip to seal the deal with that other family. To prove he was worthy of running the family business." He took a large swallow of wine. "My mother refused the men in her family control. And now? Having me run around doing whatever I want? It's considered the worst kind of loose end."

"Then why help him tie it up? I mean, don't meet with him." Her heart hitched at the thought he was going to meet with the MacKennas, a family that probably rode about in cars with trunks full of ropes and duct tape—just in case. His family didn't care about him as her own father hadn't cared about her and her sisters.

"He enjoys toying with people. I'm not going to be in reaction to him any longer. If I did, I'd lose my own power. I prefer offense to defense." He rested his elbows on the table as if he was confiding in her. "There are three things Tomas values. Family, being in control, and courage. Not necessarily all in one person, however. He wants everyone who is family under his thumb. He only demands courage from his opponents."

Oddly, she could see that. People who craved power over others felt a need to exercise it—often. "Makes it a more interesting game. Gives him something to play against."

He cocked his head. "Well put and accurate. I learned that from my mother's diaries. How both he and his father loved to slap their competitors around, see who would rise to the occasion. Tomas loved to fight." He took a final swallow of his wine. "I want no part of that family." He dropped his glass to the table—harshly.

She jumped a little at that gesture. Declan's composure didn't slip easily.

A woman wearing a white shirt and black apron approached, her arms laden with dishes. Her smile widened. "Ah, here we are. The spaghetti carbonara for the lady and the lasagna for you, Declan."

The woman's eyes fired as if saying his name was a turn-on.

"I'll have some of the parmesan." Phee nodded at the cheese grater the woman held under her arm.

"Oh, of course," as if she'd forgotten her role for a second. Declan really did have that effect on women, didn't he?

"I will as well, Mary." He winked at her and the woman flushed.

Heat rushed through Phoenix's cheeks at the exchange. Any woman with any understanding of quality could see Declan was a man of taste. The man invited flirting with his beautiful tweed coat and mahogany cane nestled against the curtain, but did *Mary* have to do it in front of her?

A garlicky, cheesy scent rose up and lured her to study her plate. "Wow, that's a lot of carbs." It looked and smelled delicious, but without her dancing, she was going to have to watch it.

"Helps with healing."

"You made that up." A smile floated to her lips, though she tried to stop it.

"Yes, I did, but trust me, this spaghetti and meatballs will be worth it. No one makes meatballs like Rosalina."

"That's true." Mary beamed down at her but finally turned away to leave them in peace.

Phoenix swirled her fork in the pasta and rose it to her lips. The tomato laced with cheese hit her tongue and she nearly groaned in pleasure.

"I see you like it."

She nodded and took a big mouthful of spaghetti. Too much. Declan hadn't yet dug into his lasagna, instead studying her face. She must resemble a squirrel with fat cheeks stuffing its nuts in its mouth. He didn't hide his amusement.

She put her fork down and dabbed her mouth with the napkin. "Declan, I have a favor to ask..." She took a sip of wine.

He searched her face. "Anything."

"It makes me uncomfortable that you notice so much about me." Uncomfortable didn't come close to it. He was just so much. Remarking on her appearance. Complimenting her. Tracking her moods. *Telling her he loved her.*

"Luna warned me not to tell you too much." His smile didn't waver. "Clearly, I failed at that warning."

"Why would she do that? I hate being pitied." She cut a meatball in half and stabbed the portion with her fork. They really were fantastic.

"I don't pity you, Phoenix Rising. I love you, and love has no room for pity."

Her fork clattered to her plate. After choking down the incredible meatball, she wiped her mouth with a napkin once more. She gripped the sides of the booth and leaned forward. "You don't want to be just friends, do you?"

"No, but it's what I'll settle for."

She slowly shook her head, twirled more pasta on her fork. "You should never settle for anything, Declan."

"You do."

She sat back. She should have never gone to dinner with him. He must have understood he'd crossed a line as his hand rose up.

"I apologize. Friends care for one another so you can't ask me to not worry."

"There's nothing to worry about."

"Oh, yes, there is. You avoid being loved and that is no way to live."

"I'm living fine. I just prefer things to be uncomplicated. So, stop seeing me as the one who needs to be rescued." She nearly gasped the words.

"I don't see you that way at all. I see you as a survivor."

The air was so still, not even the sound of traffic or sirens so common in this part of town sounded.

"I thought I was the resident bitch," she spat. That's what she was, wasn't it? The one who couldn't stop being angry if she tried. It was like a beast out of control inside her.

"I have never called you that. And if you are angry, you have good reason for it. Next to my mother, you're the strongest woman I've ever met. You had to be. When you were young, your bed was closest to your bedroom door, wasn't it? And you made sure of it to spare your sisters. You stepped between your father and them."

Words were potent weapons that could stop a heart—like hers did at that moment. In three seconds, she'd been catapulted back, like being yanked through a wormhole to the past. How would he have known? And how dare he bring that up? Did Luna tell him?

For a minute she'd been lost in the scent and taste of parsley and oregano, and now a bitter black truth coated her tongue. She was damaged goods—and he reveled in it? Why else bring it up?

Where were her crutches? She glanced around frantically.

Mary approached their table. "Anything else I can get you?"

Damnit. In her periphery, Declan's stare might as well carry X-ray vision as he drank her in, took her in. Through an ocean of blood running through her ears, she heard his rumbling voice. "I think we're okay, Thank you."

Okay? They weren't okay by a long shot. Her hands found the table edge and then the velvet curtains. She yanked herself up and a stab of pain through her ankle brought her back to the present. She was panting.

Declan was standing and handing her crutches. She clutched at them, positioned them under her arms, and began to move.

Declan Philips could wrestle with hell, but he wasn't taking her with him. She'd already been there and back.

28

"Forgetting something?" Declan's voice rumbled behind her. She knew he was there. She could tell his footfalls from anyone's, anywhere, at any time.

She kept her face held up to the sky. Kept her eyes closed despite the fact she stood on a public sidewalk. The damp cold cooled the fire raging under her skin.

She'd overreacted. He shouldn't have brought it up. Both were true. Therein lay yet another problem between her and Declan—neither was right, neither was wrong in their stance about each other.

She had placed herself between her father and her sisters —repeatedly. And between Jones and them at Maxim's. But they didn't need that anymore. Starr had Nathan, and Luna would soon find someone, too. Then what would she do? Keep deflecting Declan?

Go somewhere else, her brain screamed. For the love of God, why hadn't she just left when she announced it last week? Her limbs felt heavy even thinking about starting over.

Ever the gentleman, Declan laid her coat over her shoulders.

She took in a long breath. "Thank you."

"I'm sorry. I shouldn't have—"

"No, you shouldn't have." When his hands fell to her shoulders, she yanked herself free and nearly toppled, but he grabbed her arms.

She turned awkwardly, given her crutches and the slick concrete. He dropped his arms, stuffing his hands into his coat.

She might leave Shakedown for good, but Declan might follow her, still not give up. So, she had to end this, and she knew how.

He thought she was damaged? How about beyond it? "You don't know me. Not really. But, whatever. Want to fuck? Let's go fuck. Then maybe you can get me out of your system."

His face hardened. "You don't mean that. It's not what you want."

"Who cares what I want? When has it ever mattered? You want what you want and—"

"Enough." His bark made her seal her lips. "A man has limits. You're trying to reach mine, force me to do something. But you haven't even touched my limits, sweetheart. And you will never be out of my system." His gaze raked over her.

"I'm just the unattainable one. The one you could never have."

"Once more, thinking so little of yourself. Not a single woman in the world compares to you. I'm not talking about your looks, which are spectacular, by the way. It's your spirit. So what if you have some damage? We all do. It's what makes us interesting." He inched closer. "I'm going to risk this next bit because you're worth it and I want you to consider it, really think about it. No knee jerk reaction. What would you do if I kissed you?"

This man did not play by the rules. He was to take her up on fucking, not kissing. "What do you mean… kiss me?" She scoffed.

"Exactly what I said. And I'll stop the second you tell me to."

Her throat moved in a swallow. "I won't have children." Her words came out in a rush. "I… I won't do that."

"Who says I want them? A kiss would suffice."

She sniffed and huffed. "Sure, you don't. Doesn't every man want to make sure his name goes on?"

"Not necessarily. I'd rather be the man to make sure you don't ever have to be closest to the door to save someone else ever again." He was so close to her she could smell the wet wool of his coat. "And I promise you that you never have to do anything like that again. Kiss or no kiss."

She swallowed hard at that statement.

"Because I won't let it."

Her crutches nearly slipped as she'd been leaning toward him. His coat brushed her nipples as he righted her. His hands were so large they wrapped around her biceps. With his cane hooked over his elbow, he held her there, gazing down with those silvery-blue eyes, as determined as she'd ever seen him. "No. I will make sure you are never presented with that choice again."

She grasped one of his hands and brought it over her breastbone. "You need to stop trying to save me, Declan." This man was good. He deserved someone *good*.

"Not trying to save you. I'm trying to love you." His hot breath moved over her face, and a tingle cascaded through her entire body.

Then he doesn't know what love is. But then again, did she? "Why?"

"Do I need a reason?"

"Most people would."

He rested his forehead against hers, his large hand held between hers, keeping space between them. "I'm not most people."

No, he wasn't. He was remarkable and infuriating and as stubborn as her cat. "I've given you nothing."

"You've given me everything." Now he held both of her hands in his between them.

He must not want much then. The cool breeze kicked up, a sharp contrast to the warmth of his skin. Insects droned in the trees around them and sirens were going off in the distance. But his eyes glittered in the dark, and that's when her resolve slithered to the concrete like a sail deflating in dying wind. He had always looked at her like that—like she was someone to him. Like she mattered.

His thumbs moved over her knuckles. "You and I are the same in many ways. But your strength makes me stronger. Makes me want to fight harder." He pulled her closer. One of the crutches clattered to the concrete. Neither of them moved to get it. "You make me want to be worthy of you."

Worthy? Her eyes pricked. "I don't deserve that." God, could she hear herself?

His cane slipped down his arm and dropped over his wrist to land in one hand. His other hand—the rogue— moved up to cradle her cheek. "Oh, yes, you do. I'd say we deserve each other—and the world that doesn't want us to be happy? It can go to hell."

She glanced at his lips. "You want to kiss me." It wasn't a question or a statement. More like utter disbelief this man would settle for just a kiss—from her.

"I do. But I won't. You have to kiss me now." One side of his mouth inched upward. "For making me wait six years."

A slight laugh cut through her chest and up her throat. "You wish."

He sobered. "I do wish."

Her hands made their way to his pecs, the cashmere of his overcoat soft under her palms, his muscle hard underneath. "There can't be more."

He nodded once.

So, she rose up on her one good foot and placed her lips on his. Her hand curled around his lapels as his arms banded around her and crushed him to her. His lips moved, slow and strong, for a long minute. And then his tongue dipped inside. He wasn't polite or urgent—just one hundred percent in control. She got the sense he enjoyed her mouth, exploring with his tongue, slow and sure yet not fully devouring her.

She pulled back, shocked at herself and the kiss. It wasn't bad. On the contrary, it was great. She stared into his eyes, and good thing for him he didn't adopt a smug I-told-you face. Rather, he was unreadable.

He held out his elbow. "Now, let me get you home."

Maybe it wasn't perfect for him? Maybe that really was all he wanted? Turns out she was wrong on all accounts.

At her front door, he kissed her again. The second time, it was even better. There was no gentleman in that second kiss —dead opposite. His lips took over her mouth—sure and strong and better than she'd expected. It was not like any kiss she'd ever been subjected to. His whole body pressed her against her front door, and they'd fit like two puzzle pieces designed for one another. She lost herself—everything around her and inside her fell away.

When he broke contact, his eyes locked on hers. "'Love sought is good, but given unsought, is better,'" he rasped.

"Olivia. *Twelfth Night*," she whispered back.

"And like her, you were meant for great things, Phoenix Rising. Take it."

He then freed himself from her arms that had wrapped around his body—the only man she'd willingly touched in years. After kissing the back of her hand, he opened her front door and gestured for her to step inside.

She backed herself inside. He pulled the door closed, separating them. She pressed her ear to her side of the door and listened until his footfalls and that telltale punch of his cane faded away.

Her mind couldn't get a lock on anything. *Huh.* This is what bewilderment felt like.

It wasn't until three in the morning, as she studied the long crack in her ceiling, that she knew what was different about Declan and his desire for her. There was no subjecting herself to anything. He didn't want her to change or do anything different. He'd just wanted her to stay. He'd fought for her—and somehow, she'd won.

Love sought, love unsought. They'd collided tonight.

29

Tomas wasn't hard to pick out. Hair a deep silver gray with no trace of his natural-born black. The casual way he sat in his chair, his hand resting around a coffee cup, the other lazily draped over the back of the empty chair beside him. The scars on his neck.

The fact his back was to the parking lot and he gazed over the water wasn't lost on Declan. The man showed all the signs of someone whose worries were far behind him. Declan knew otherwise. Inside, the man must be strung tighter than a drum if he was still attempting to control every molecule that swam around him at age seventy.

"You're late." Tomas hadn't turned to see who approached.

Declan scraped back a chair and set his cane against the table. "Oh?"

Tomas' eyes slid his way. "Yes."

"I suppose this is the part where you tell me that's not a good way to start off a meeting."

"Is that what this is? A meeting?"

"Two men, sitting by the waterfront for a talk?" Declan gazed over the metallic gray water. "I'd say that constitutes."

Tomas murmured and took a sip of his coffee.

They sat like that—two men staring out over the waterfront.

"What do you think, Declan?" He inched his chin up toward the water. "My son tells me this waterfront and all these properties that line it are a good investment. Do you agree?"

"No. I do not."

Tomas chuffed. "Is that because your club is one of them? Or do you honestly believe that?"

"I honestly believe that."

Tomas finally twisted in his chair, set both forearms on the table. "I don't believe you. But it doesn't really matter. I don't think developing this land is a good idea, either. All that Chesapeake Bay watershed nonsense. So, let's get to it. Why did you want to meet? You seemed hellbent on staying away."

"That hasn't changed. Under no circumstances am I going into business with you or anyone else in your family." Phoenix had softened toward him, to say the least. Now, with a shot at something real with her? Nothing mattered more than ridding himself of the MacKennas' interest for good.

The man gave off a familiar patronizing sigh. "Tell me, Declan. Why do you think I've been so successful?"

"I'd say we have different definitions of success."

"Family doesn't matter to you?"

Declan gritted his teeth but didn't say anything. He wouldn't take any chum this man threw down.

"To me, success is ensuring my progeny are taken care of and kept close. I've built quite an empire, but if there isn't anyone to take it, well, one day no one will even remember I was alive."

Ah, so the man craved immortality. "That so important to you?"

"It's not to you?"

"I hadn't really thought about it. I understand your son is seeking to buy real estate up and down the waterfront without you."

The man flinched. Yet another suspicion nailed into reality. Carragh was most definitely operating without his father.

"My son has many interests, as do I." Tomas took a sip of his coffee.

"And Ruark? What are his interests? I mean, now that you've arranged for his early release." It was the only explanation for him coming up for parole a year early. Declan might as well push the man's law-bending antics into the light. "Make sure you have a strong leash handy for him."

The man chuffed. "Ruark has made his bed. I'm afraid he's breached enough family etiquette that I am no longer interested."

So, the man was going to let his rogue son re-enter the world to seek any revenge he might have planned? "You want me to kill him for you, don't you? Let him try something again and have me do your dirty work? Not happening. And you can call off Carragh."

"Ah, Carragh." Tomas twisted his cup in the saucer.

Interesting how the man skipped right over Declan's words about Ruark. He was getting damned tired of his suspicions turning out to be the real deal.

"My eldest son is another matter altogether. He seems hell-bent on hanging around you for some reason. And he wants to make his own way. I can respect that. So, I'll let him think he is for a while longer, but then arrangements will need to be made."

This man would harm his own son? Why did Declan think time would change this man? Losing Daniel, his wife—which rumor has it was a revenge killing—none of that made him rethink his choices over the years? The family was rife with sociopaths.

"You want me to kill both your sons for you." Jesus. It made sense. Remove any obstacle at any cost.

"No." The man dramatically sighed. "Family is important, Declan, and my family will always be safe. But if you have no stake in the family, what's to say you won't work against us? Something tells me you have a moral righteousness that, quite frankly, could be… inconvenient."

"The fact I have a moral compass at all threatens you? The fact I know what you do and you can't control me makes me a liability? You'd have to take down the better part of this city. *Most* people wouldn't agree with what you do."

Tomas swung his gaze to Declan, his ice-blue eyes boring down on him. "Always jumping to conclusions. Just like your mother."

"I don't have to jump to anything. I have my mother's diaries. She kept a lot of them."

The man's nostrils flared. "Writings of a dead woman don't count for much."

"You'd be surprised how much they count when presented to people who've wanted to nail you for years."

"Anything my sister may have written down is merely the musings of an overly romantic girl. The law is the law, my friend."

Declan had had enough. He came and said his piece, and he'd warned Tomas, which felt damned good after being on the receiving end of so many threats. "You would do well to remember the law, Tomas."

"What? No Uncle honorific?" he laughed.

Declan rose. "Stay out of my business and I'll stay out of yours. Keep Ruark, Carragh, and the rest of your damned progeny away from me and my staff, and I'll keep those diaries to myself."

The man's face stilled. His eyes fired, however. Tomas had enjoyed this exchange, which chilled Declan to the bone.

Declan may have unwittingly started a war.

He left. What was done was done. But he'd be damned if he'd go down without a fight.

30

"Why do all baby stores look like candy stores?" Luna held up a baby blanket covered in pastel rainbows. "So we can't resist?"

"Maybe mothers are afraid of bright colors?" Phoenix had never been surrounded with as many pastels as inside Bloom and Blossom Babies. Pink, baby blue, soft yellow, and don't get her started on the ugly organic section with all its unbleached tan cotton.

Luna checked the price on the blanket. "Well, my children are each going to get a signature color that isn't so…"

"Predictable?"

Luna pointed at her. "Bingo."

Phee knew her sister well. She touched a pair of yellow crocheted booties. They were adorable but did little to distract the bizarre anxiety she felt. Or perhaps her heart jitters were from the fact she couldn't stop herself from looking at her phone for the hundredth time. Declan would be meeting with Tomas MacKenna right about now. Her ears strained for sounds of sirens—as if they meant anything about Declan's current scenario.

She'd stewed all day at his pure stupidity—and fought the urge to call him to find out what happened even though she was justified in knowing the outcome. Her sisters' welfare was at stake.

Why did he have to admit he loved her? They were doing just fine dancing around that not-so-secret secret. And then there were those kisses. That damnable, fabulous kissing. Sure, at 3 a.m. her heart did funny dancing things inside her chest, but the light of day had sobered her right up.

"Are you looking for something for a boy or a girl?" the clerk asked.

"Boy. Shower gift." Phee lifted the price tag of the onesie. Twenty-five dollars for something the kid was going to poop in or throw up on?

Luna held up a frothy pink dress with tiny rosebuds floating inside the tulle of the layers. "Look how tiny! It's like a doll's dress." She ran her fingers through the hundred-or-so layers with so much glee on her face Phoenix was concerned her sister got pregnant just holding it.

"The baby would be lost in all that," Phee laughed. "I think Rachel's little boy would rather be wearing a pair of overalls. Look at these." She held up a tiny pair of dungarees with a train applique across the chest.

Luna cocked her head. "That could work." She abandoned the dress fit for a Quinceañera and took the miniature overalls from Phee. "Oh, it's on sale, too. Only $50."

Only? All these miniature clothes with designer price tags were making Phoenix rethink her career choice.

Luna sighed. "Starr should be here."

Their sister really did have the flu, which hopefully, they wouldn't get.

Luna's eyes widened. "Don't you wish she really had been pregnant?"

"No," Phoenix scoffed.

"Why not? Babies are cute."

"Who do nothing but throw up, scream, and poop."

She peeked inside the overalls. "It's machine washable, not hand wash. And all that diaper stuff is only the first two years or so."

Again with the only? "Now who's being naïve?"

"Well, I think it'd be nice for the three of us to have kids—at the same time so they can grow up together."

Luna and her romantic notions. It would be nice for a tight-knit group, but her having kids? Not in the cards, which Luna well knew about her.

"So, about Thanksgiving. It's coming up." Luna picked up a pair of tiny cowboy boots and handed them to the clerk. "We need to get these, too."

Of course, they did.

"Mmhhmmm. Cherry's coming, right?" The queen insisted she make the turkey with stuffing. She really did have a mother complex, which Phee hoped she never dropped.

"Yeah, so, since we now have so many of us coming—Nathan, Cherry, Max—I think we should invite Amos, too."

"Sure. More the merrier. If we can fit them all in our apartment."

"Good, because I invited Declan."

Phee sighed. Of course, she had. "We've never done holidays together before."

"And it's time we did. I mean, you did go to dinner with him the other night, right?"

"It wasn't a big deal." A thought occurred. She turned to her sister. "You didn't invite Robert?"

Luna wouldn't look at her.

"L. Tell me you didn't." If their father attended, she'd eat at Howard Johnson's.

"No, I didn't. But you may want to—"

"To what, L.? I'm through with him. I told you that already."

The bell over the shop door rang and a male voice murmured at the front of the store. As usual, Phee's radar went up. There was something familiar about this voice. Luna took the dungarees up to the counter just as Carragh MacKenna rounded the corner of a shelf holding stuffed kittens and puppies.

Carragh was in a *baby clothes* store.

"Following us?" Her words blurted out of her mouth. Twice he'd mysteriously shown up, and not exactly in the likeliest places.

Luna's eyes grew wide and gaped at her.

"What?" she mouthed to her sister. Carragh stood in front of them in a black trench coat, a sharp contrast to the sea of pastels, and L. was worried about manners?

The man smiled down at Luna. "Yes, actually I was. I saw you both go into the store and—" his eyes darted over Luna "—I wondered if I had congratulations to deliver."

Luna smiled—actually smiled at that. "Oh, not us. Rachel. Trick's wife."

Phee glared at her with a why-are-you-telling-this-man-anything message.

"I see. Please, pass on my best wishes." He nodded down to Phee's arms wrapped tight around her waist. "And how is the ankle?"

She was finally off crutches, though it wasn't fully healed yet.

"Fine." She dropped her arms to her sides and turned away, keeping one eye on the man in case he got any ideas.

Luna stepped forward. "Thank you again. For rescuing her."

"For the ride," Phee clarified. "Yeah, thanks."

Carragh eyed the dungarees Luna held. "Trains, huh?"

She held it up to him. "Too much?" She wrinkled her nose.

"Couldn't say. I haven't dived into fatherhood yet." A phone rang inside his jacket. "Ladies." He dipped his chin once to both of them, turned on his heel, and drew out his phone as he exited the store.

"He's stalking us. Not good." Phee mock shuddered a bit.

"He's not so scary. I mean, he did—"

"Don't you dare say 'rescue' again. He's a MacKenna."

"Who seems different than his brother. Plus, I'm sure Declan's got it covered. And now that he's family…"

"Oh, really? Is that why two guys were sitting at the stage with guns the other night? Good thing Starr wasn't around." Their sister had been through enough, and Luna's Pollyanna attitude around everything couldn't stand right now. "Please, tell me you'll be careful if you see him again."

"Why would we see him again?" Luna shrugged and handed over the dungarees to the girl behind the counter.

The clerk picked up the price tag and scanned it. "He was rather handsome."

Luna's flush returned, which only pinged Phee's radar again. As soon as they'd paid for their items, Phee steered Luna to the front.

"L., tell me you are not interested in Carragh MacKenna."

"Are you kidding me? No way."

Phee's chest filled with oxygen. "Good. Because I kind of always thought you'd end up with Max."

Luna gasped and then let out a giggle. "I don't think I'm his type. We're just friends. He said I remind him of his late sister."

Oh. Her radar was clearly only good for one thing—citing danger and little else. "Well, be careful."

They stepped outside and huddled under the small awning in front of the store. Sheets of water fell from the sky and a small river poured off the fabric over their heads to the concrete below, splashing their ankles.

"Oh, great. No umbrella." Luna lifted the bag holding the gift-wrapped items. "I paid extra for the wrapping. I don't want it to get wet."

Phee didn't want to bust her ass again. What was up with these storms that came out of nowhere? "It's what November does in the Mid-Atlantic. We can wait it out."

The door of the black limo parked in front cracked open. "Can I give you ladies a lift?" Of course, it was Carragh, with a rather gorgeous brunette in the back, too.

"We have a car," Phee said.

The man got out and dramatically cracked open that huge, familiar golf umbrella. His driver did the same. "Well, at least let us get you to your car without getting soaked."

"Carragh, we'll be late." The brunette gave them a fake smile as if the entire group was inconveniencing the hell out of her.

Carragh didn't respond to the woman—rather, he held the umbrella out.

Luna smiled at him—again—and stepped under his huge umbrella. Phee had no choice but to step under the driver's since he held it out. *Hand to God, if I so much as sense a gun on either of them...*

After they were settled into Luna's car, the doors had clicked shut, and Carragh and his driver had turned to go back to their limo, Phee faced her sister. "Don't even think about it."

Luna started up the car. "I don't know what you're talking about."

Phoenix knew her sister—knew every facial expression, every tone of voice. They were in bigger trouble than they knew. Luna wouldn't watch out for herself.

31

___

Phoenix pushed against Shakedown's front door and stepped into the swell of Hey Big Spender and shouts and hollers. The familiar scent of the club rose up. Oranges and furniture polish would forever remind Phoenix of Shakedown. Putting in a fancy filtration system that scented the air was yet another thing Declan had done when she'd complained about the cigar smoke.

Oh, man, her mind couldn't stop connecting him to everything now. This is why women get swallowed whole by the male species—women's brains couldn't stop making men the center of everything.

No, that would not be her. She'd come tonight only because there was nowhere else to go and sitting in her apartment alone wasn't happening. She hated that Starr and Luna were still going on tonight and she wasn't going to be a part of it. Plus, she needed to see everything was still okay there, then—maybe—that uncomfortable restlessness that had taken over her limbs could stand down.

Max looked positively cheery standing outside on guard. Perhaps Declan's meeting with Tomas wasn't the harbinger of the end of the world. Otherwise, the place would feel different.

She gingerly made her way to the bar. Her foot was feeling so much better. A few more days and she'd go back to work. For now, she'd have one drink and go home once she was assured things had returned to normal—or as normal as a burlesque club could be.

She glanced at the stage. Sally Mae had taken Phee's part in the Big Spender number and was flanked by Starr and Luna. Sally's black hair was such a sharp contrast to her sisters' flaming red it made her stand out like she was the star.

Her leg bent and then rose up to the ceiling in an impressive high kick. The woman had some flexibility and her super-white teeth gleamed under the spotlight. Oh, yeah, that woman had "star" written all over her.

Wow. Phee really had been replaced. A kernel of remorse arose, which she squashed immediately.

Phoenix slid onto a stool at the far end of the bar near the waitress stand. "Hey, Jackie, have you seen Declan?" She needed to tell him they'd run into Carragh. She could have texted it, but she needed to see him in the flesh for such news. The man would just show up at her apartment otherwise and then the kissing business was in danger of arising.

"He's in back."

The amount of relief at hearing that pissed her off royally. She wanted him to be okay, but there was no reason to hang all her emotions on him. They'd kissed—that was all.

"Want a drink?" Jackie asked.

"A vodka gimlet?"

"Sure thing. You okay, honey?"

"I'm fine."

A guy slid into the stool next to her. "Put that on my tab."

"That's nice of you, but no thanks." That's the one thing

she'd never do again. Be forced to drink with patrons like at Maxim's.

"Caught your dancing last week. You been doing it long?"

Of course, he wanted to talk. "You could say that."

He raised a hand. "Don't want to be bothered, I get it."

Shit, he was a customer. "Sorry. It's just..."

"Yeah, I saw that guy reach for you the other week. What an ass." He raised his drink to his lips and drained the last bit. He threw a $50 down on the bar. "Thanks, Jackie. Have a good night, Miss Phoenix."

Shit, she really was a bitch, wasn't she? Why? Because she'd been replaced so resolutely? Because Declan was in love with her? Even on her blindest day, she could tell she'd crossed some ungrateful, spoiled-ass line.

She swiveled in her chair and touched the man's arm. "Thank you for the offer, anyway."

He nodded once and strode away.

"That guy was harmless, ya know," Jackie said. "He's a regular."

"Yeah." But she didn't know, did she? Maybe she was permanently screwed up on the inside, not ferreting who was good, who wasn't anymore. She had no radar where before she had honed it to a fine point. Then Declan had to go and kiss her and screw up her resolve.

Sally Mae whirled in a series of turns, perfect posture, perfect foot placement.

Oh, and he had to replace her with someone amazingly great.

Jackie put a drink in front of her and then set her elbows on the bar, putting her hand on her chin. "So. Want to make me a thorough cliché and confide in me?"

"I wouldn't know what to say. My brain is a little... lost right now." That was an understatement. She couldn't gain any mental footing.

Jackie eased up at seeing someone at the far end wave at her. "That's okay. Sometimes you gotta get lost to be found." She winked at Phee.

Phee picked up her glass and gulped down half, the vodka burning a trail down her throat. She didn't drink often and an involuntary shudder racked her body. See what Declan was making her do? *Drink.*

She eased off the stool. She'd wait for her sisters in the dressing room, maybe not talk to Declan after all. She managed to slip inside the room just as his office door was cracking open.

32

Declan's neck ached from too many hours bent over paper-work. The fact he'd been alerted by Jackie that Phoenix was at the bar was a perfect excuse to take a break. However, the first person Declan made out in the crowd wasn't her.

He turned to Trick, his manager, the man who was supposed to closely monitor his floor. "What is Carragh MacKenna doing here?"

"Slipped by the new guy at the door." Trick turned hardened eyes his way. "With so many new employees around here, they're clearly not as bought into the cause. Makes it real hard to follow your orders. There's bound to be mistakes, okay?" Lines deepened around his eyes. The man didn't look like he'd slept in a year.

"Everything okay at home?"

He lifted his chin once. "Rachel's been having some early contractions. The doctor said it's nothing to worry about, but first baby and all…"

He sucked in a long breath. "Sorry, man. I'll handle Carragh. You go home. Get some rest."

Trick nodded. "Thanks."

Tempers were shortening and nerves were fraying, probably in large part to Carragh leaning against the bar. He watched the stage with extreme interest—too much interest for Declan's taste.

"Carragh, it's time for you to leave."

The man turned his attention to him for a brief second and then he was back to drinking in the sights onstage—namely, Luna Belle.

He lifted a beer bottle to his lips. His drink of choice was unexpected. "Checking on how your meeting went."

"Papa didn't tell you?"

"No." The man straightened and set his beer bottle down on the bar. "Anything you care to share?"

"No."

He nodded slowly. "By the way, I saw Luna Belle and Phoenix Rising out shopping. I hear congratulations are in order to your manager."

Declan's nostrils flared. "What do you mean?"

"Of course, it was pure coincidence, but it was not unwelcome. Perhaps if you were as friendly as…"

The man wisely shut his mouth. He looked down at Declan's chest, which was one inch from his. He'd strode up to him, ready to haul him out if he had to. Carragh had the gall to appear nonplussed.

"Stay away, Carragh. Or you may have more trouble than you can fathom."

Well, that got the man's attention. His face shifted—into what, Declan couldn't have said. But he clearly wasn't happy with the mystery of Declan's statement. Carragh's happiness wasn't high on Declan's list, however. Phoenix and Luna had encountered a MacKenna. Coincidence, his ass.

"See you around, Declan." The man strode to the door—suddenly and inexplicably.

Declan had touched a nerve, alright. He swiped the black

curtain that led to the back room and ran smack into Cherry and Starr. "Phoenix? Heard she came in."

Starr blinked. "No, she's hanging out in the dressing room."

Hanging out. Isn't that what he'd encouraged her to do?

"Good. Mind giving us a minute?"

Cherry's lips inched up. "Sure thing."

"Starr, you feeling better, by the way?"

She shrugged. "Just the flu. I'm okay now. And Phee's ankle seems loads better. She wants to start back tomorrow night."

"We'll see about that." Who cared if his statement was arrogant? He was glad she'd be back in Shakedown's orbit, but she had some explaining to do, starting with why he was hearing about her run-in with Carragh from the man himself and not her.

She irked him. Drove him crazy. Made him want to tear his hair out. Damnit, he still fucking loved this red-headed, angry, damaged, gorgeous creature who had kissed him back —twice. She didn't slap him. Which was all it took for his resolve to fill to the brim, even if she had uttered those useful, meaningless words again. *There can't be more.*

He knocked on the dressing room door.

33

"Come in." Phoenix sat at her makeup table, toying with her makeup, stacking and rearranging the little pots by size.

"Why didn't you tell me you ran into Carragh?"

She startled. "Declan." She blinked at him. He closed the door behind him and leaned against it, tapping his cane on the inside of his foot.

"Your meeting not go well?" She swiveled to give him a view of her back. Her emotions were all over the map, and dealing with him right now… She couldn't.

"You need to tell me if you ever encounter a MacKenna. Remember?" His voice was strung tight as if holding in his own emotion. *Well, join the club.*

She shrugged. "Okay. We encountered a MacKenna. Carragh. In a baby store, which was surreal enough." More than.

"And you didn't call me right away."

"I'm here, aren't I?"

"Phoenix—"

She faced him when she heard that tone. "Declan," she

gritted out. "You're the one who said he'd never get near us again, and funny how he keeps showing up in our orbit."

"Like you do at Maxim's? Which you will never step foot near again." He pushed off the door.

Unbelievable. "Excuse me? You keep telling us not to worry, so right back at you." Truth was, she was worried—a lot. She'd come to tell him, but his anger would not stand. She swiveled her stool and stared into her mirror. She fluffed her hair a little for a reason she couldn't fathom. The man made her do such stupid things—like let him kiss her, perfectly and wonderfully.

"If anything happened to you…"

"Nothing is going to happen to me." She rubbed lotion on her hands and finally turned his way again. "You won't let it."

He took two steps forward. "You playing games with me?"

"No, Declan. Why would you think—" Jesus, maybe he was reaching a breaking point with her. "I-I'm sorry." God, he was too close. She stood and moved to the garment rack, absently running her fingers over hangers. "Well, if it makes you feel better, I warned Luna away from Carragh. I don't trust him. He's up to something."

"Yes, he is."

"Then there's nothing to talk about unless you're going to let me in on your meeting."

"I'm handling things."

Handling it. Handling it. That's all she got from him. Well, that and *kissing.* "How?" She raised her hands and let them fall to her lap. "You have to stop him. They're all I have."

"They're important to you… and me. But they're not all you have."

No, she guessed they weren't. Damn his lips.

Remembering their conversation about how she'd protected her sisters… it made her raw inside. Like now he knew some of her secrets. But to be understood so completely wasn't something she was used to beyond Starr and Luna. She'd never had a man talk to her like he had recently—not ever.

And then his kiss! *Gah.*

He studied her eyes. "Had I known that would make you cry…"

"It's not you." She waved her hand in the air.

"Who then? I told you, I'll manage Carragh."

"It's not only that. When I can't work, my mind…" She twirled her finger near her temple. "Conjures up all kinds of things." Like how she didn't hate him kissing her.

"You were worried about me today."

"Of course, you're my boss." She swiped under her eyes.

"Is that all?"

She nodded.

His gaze trailed her body. "How's the ankle?"

She lifted her leg and moved her foot in circles. "Almost good as new. I'm going to test it tomorrow. One dance."

"Only one?"

"Pushing me to do more?"

"I've learned not to push you."

"Well… I… appreciate that." Now, if he'd only stop staring at her. "Now that that's settled."

"What's settled?"

"Us." She waggled a finger between them. "You. Me. Not…" She chewed on her lip. "You not kissing me again." She stared at his mouth, caught herself, and turned away.

"I didn't say anything about kissing."

No, she guessed he hadn't. A prickly heat bloomed across her cheeks.

"But you liked it."

Her body did what it always did in these moments—it seized like someone cranked on a series of vises. "I didn't say I didn't. That's not the same as a 'yes.'"

"Of course. I was rather shocked you didn't slap me when I did."

That smugness irritated her. "I have a strict policy not to slap my boss."

"So, I can burn that napkin?"

"No."

"Want me to kiss you again then?"

Her heart began to pound—such a silly reaction in the face of something so simple as a kiss. But with Declan, nothing was simple. In all these years she'd not known much about this man. Oh, but she'd done that on purpose, hadn't she? It was easier to keep him labeled as their boss.

One of the constants in her life was Declan. But he made things *unfurl* inside her that had no business being let out. It was like knots that were tied so tight—on purpose—were coming loose. She could go adrift at any minute.

"I'm not suggesting a trip to the gallows." He smiled, and her gaze landed on his lips again.

Damnit, the taste of his lips and what his hand felt like wrapped around the back of her neck was *right there* in her memory. Swear to God, if he had some magical power that made her crave them, she'd... do what? Suddenly not want him to lean in, take her mouth ever again?

He drew closer. *God, he smells good.*

He swept some hair off her face. "I like it that you wear your hair down so much."

Warmth spread throughout her body at his statement. This is what women talked about, how they got all squishy on the inside when the man they loved noticed things about them. How had the tables turned so suddenly? And over a few lip-locks?

"What are you doing?" she asked.

"Waiting for you to kiss me again."

She scoffed. "Oh, really?"

He nodded once. So, she pecked him, harshly. "There."

"Was that enough for you?"

Damn him. So, she went for it. Deep, hard, and then somehow, she ended up melting because his cane fell to the floor and she was flattened against his body. Only this time, her crotch pressed into the granite-hard length of him. It did insane things to her body, like make her crave to spread her legs wide and get taken. But no one *took* her.

Only in that second, he could have.

She broke the kiss and pressed her fingers to her lips. Her chest was heaving like she'd been starved of oxygen.

He was smiling at her. "And you may do that anytime you wish."

She nodded once, her mind unable to form words.

"The club is closing soon. Let me get you home."

"I have a car." Okay, she had at least those words.

"Which only means I'll be following you home."

"And then what?"

"Whatever you want."

34

———

Phoenix's shoe scraped on the dirty stage floor as she tried the swivel turn again. Her ankle was holding up but her balance was all off. She sucked in a long breath, found a spot on the side wall, and tried again. It was better. And it felt so damned good. A few more hours of practice and she might regain her sure footing that she'd lost during her forced sabbatical.

She'd wanted to see how her ankle held up. If it was good, she'd go on and do something simple—easy, like rejoining the Hey Big Spender act, a sure crowd pleaser and an act she could do in her sleep. Sally Mae could take a rest now that Phee was back.

This morning, she'd woken up feeling great despite the fact Declan had proven his mouth talent again last night. He didn't force himself on her or try to get inside. But once more, after pressing his whole body into hers against her door for long minutes in a drawn-out assault on her mouth, she found herself inside her apartment with her ear pressed to the door to hear him stride away.

She'd let him kiss her now—how many times? She shook

her head, raised her arms, and tried the three-point turns necessary for tonight. Not too bad.

Loud clapping startled her. She walked to the end of the stage and peered out into the dark. Her eyes could only make out one shape from the bright lights she'd turned on to help her stay warm.

Naomi stepped into the light. "That was cool." She plunked her bag down on a table. "I was hoping I'd find you here."

Fresh bruises colored the girl's face. "What happened to your eye?"

"Oh, it's nothing."

Phee came down the side steps and drew closer to her. "Oh, yes, it is." She angled the girl's face, and Naomi wrenched her neck to get free.

"Don't worry about it, *Mom*. I came to get your help. I need an act. I started to practice but…" She shrugged.

"Not coming together?"

"Something like that." Naomi's eyes roamed the stage from one end to the other. "You dance alone up here? During the day?"

"Sometimes."

"A lot of space to cover."

"Tell you what, it's just us here. Why don't you come up on stage? See what it's like."

Instead of taking the side stairs, the girl hopped up onto the stage in an ungraceful leap. She turned and faced where the audience would sit. "Wow, it's different. Bright."

Phee pointed to the rafters where the theatrical lights hung. "Depends. Okay. What song are you choreographing to?"

She shrugged again. "Does it matter?"

"It's everything. What do you like? Your favorite?"

"I like country."

Not exactly burlesque material, but Phee could figure something out. "Okay. How about this?" She strode over to where her phone lay on the edge of the stage and scrolled through her songs. She had a hunch and pulled up "Old Town Road."

"Oh, my God, I love this song!" Naomi started bouncing around.

"Good," Phee called. "Keep going. Do what you feel like."

"It'd be better if I had a pole."

"Use your imagination. That's half of what we do here." Phee crossed her arms.

"I wish I could bring a horse on. I've always wanted one."

"Then pretend you're riding one. The crowd loves that kind of stuff. We could get you one of those child stick ponies to use."

"Oh, yeah," Naomi snorted. "And have them try to impale me with it."

Wow, this girl really did expect the worst. "Not at Shakedown."

They spent some time dancing and moving on the stage, playing around. It was fun, actually. She hadn't danced with anyone but herself and her sisters in years. The girl had rhythm at least, though her "moves" were limited to hip undulations. After twenty minutes and a few pointers, Phee turned off the fifth time the song played.

"Okay, work with that."

Naomi rolled her eyes. "Oh, yeah, it's so easy for you."

"Nothing is easy. But you have good rhythm, and just be sure to not duplicate movements too often. Mix it up."

"So, I can audition now?"

"Come back in two days. With the song finished."

The girl beamed at her, then rushed up to her and threw her arms around her. *Oh, a hug. Awkward.* She tried not to flinch. She'd been touched by more people in the last few weeks than she had in years.

She removed the girl's arms from around her neck. "Okay, get out your calendar. We're booking a time. And get the stick pony and a cowboy hat. Trust me. Costume is half of it."

"Oh, and a little cowgirl outfit. What do I wear underneath?"

"Anything you want because you're not taking it off."

Naomi raised her eyebrows. "Seriously? How do you get tips?"

"You don't. You get paid a salary here. Benefits, too."

"Get. Out." Her eyes widened. She jumped off the stage and pivoted back to her. "How much?"

"You have to get the gig first. See you in a few days, Naomi."

The girl grabbed her bag and jogged to the entrance. "Thank you!" she called before disappearing through the curtain.

"Wasn't sure you could say that," she said to the empty space and moved to the very center of the stage.

She tuned into the quiet whoosh of the ventilation system and the warmth of the lights overhead. Her limbs felt loose, light. Declan's club did more than give second chances. It was more like a home, wasn't it?

"Thank you, Shakedown." She meant it, too.

35

—————

Amos widened his stance at the doorway. "You're not going to like this." He dropped a white, brick-sized block wrapped in cellophane and a few rubber bands. "Found under your Jag."

So, the MacKennas were now planting drugs on him. "You sweep all the cars in the parking lot? Of my employees?"

"First thing I did. No bombs found. Nothing suspicious except that." He inclined his chin toward the cocaine. "What do you want me to do with it?"

"Leave it to me."

The man shifted on his feet. "I'm headed back south."

"Understood."

"I mean, I'm sorry I can't stay."

"Amos. It's okay. You can't afford to get mixed up in all this." Before the man could turn away, Declan felt compelled to add a point. "You do know this isn't mine?"

"Of course, Declan. But this is just the beginning, right?"

"Oh, they began some time ago." He dropped himself into

his chair, stared at the big brick on his desk. "Tell your wife I said thank you."

The man inclined his head and strode out.

So, another shot over the bow. But did this latest nuisance come from Tomas or Carragh? He was convinced more than ever that the two of them were no longer working together. The problem was the mystery around who was more dangerous—and who had the gall to plant drugs on him.

He fingered his phone.

He should call Henry to warn him. After that? He had a visit to pay to show a certain long-lost relative he wasn't afraid. He wasn't. He was pissed.

After advising Henry to double up on security measures, he called up the address of the MacKenna complex in Roland Park. It was an old, upper-class streetcar suburb of beautiful historic homes framed by miles of concrete sidewalks, majestic oak and poplar trees, and hundred-year-old boxwoods edged to perfection. Such a beautiful street that Tomas MacKenna raised his family on. Too bad it produced such ugly outcomes.

An elderly gentleman opened the front door that looked so new Declan could make out his own silhouette on the black high-gloss paint. He stated his business and was left standing on the stoop as his arrival was "announced." His being left outside was a message, but one Declan couldn't care less about. He wasn't about to enter any place his mother escaped from to save him.

Five minutes later, Tomas MacKenna appeared, shirt sleeves rolled up, a white cloth napkin in his hand. Carragh stood behind him, a good foot taller than his father. Both wore grave faces as if Declan was the grim reaper finally coming to get them. If only Declan was that lucky.

He dropped the brick at Tomas' feet. "You or your men

ever pull a stunt like this again with me, I will drop a dime on you so fast…"

Tomas eyed him from the doorway. He glanced down at the coke and back up at him. "With what? Suspicions? That isn't mine. Now, if you'll excuse me, I was in the middle of dinner." Tomas' frame was replaced by two men who folded their hands in front of them and blocked the doorway.

Declan stared between the guys and got an eyeful of Tomas' back. He squeezed Carragh's shoulder as if the two men were having a jovial dinner and weren't plotting to raise the stakes on him.

"You think I'm stupid?"

Both men turned. Tomas arched one eyebrow. "I didn't until you made these ridiculous accusations."

Carragh hadn't said a word, just stood behind his father like the good little soldier he was.

Declan narrowed his eyes at Tomas' eldest son. "Never again, Carragh. You'll never set foot in my club again."

Tomas' mouth thinned. He glanced over at his son. "Still taking in the entertainment?"

So, Tomas was unaware of his son's late-night visits to Shakedown. Score one for Declan—and he'd amassed so few points lately.

Carragh gave a delicate shrug. "I frequent all the water-side establishments. I like the atmosphere."

"Like grit, do you, Son?" Tomas chuckled.

"I like the absence of bullshit."

Tomas shook his head and strutted back to ostensibly where the dining room sat. Carragh stared at Declan for a few minutes but then finally broke the eye contact. He strode over to him, the two men parting for his frame to fill the doorway. He gripped the frame, peered down at the cocaine brick. "You need to start thinking, Declan. Who would have access—real access—to…" He cocked his chin as if studying the thing. "A million at least? For what? A warning?"

"Sounds exactly like your father."

"He doesn't waste money." He glanced up at him. "By the way, Ruark's parole has been moved up. It's next week." He pushed off. "See you around, Declan. Don't be a stranger."

"But you be." Declan turned and eased himself down the walkway. His leg was killing him, more from doubling up his physical therapy. He didn't have time for a single faculty to be compromised.

36

Phee took a swig of wine. At least baby showers served alcohol. A strange confusion had crept up on her, and her roller-coaster of emotions was only getting worse.

It didn't help that every night Declan followed her home. Kissed her for long minutes and then… left. Now that was all she could think of when she'd had years—frickin' years—of resisting that man.

Plus, he'd told her, just *announced,* they'd be seeing a car sitting outside her apartment every night. Security! Which didn't make her feel secure at all.

To boot, Naomi hadn't shown up for her audition that morning. Literally stood her up. She was sorry she'd wasted her time with the girl who wasn't serious about getting out of Maxim's.

Luna squealed and held up a tiny jeans jacket. *What would a baby require such a thing for?* "Oh, promise me, Rachel, you won't ever let this one go. We can pass it around to each of us."

"Luna," Starr laughed. "I'm sure Rachel can do whatever she wants with her own baby clothes."

"Oh, don't you worry." Rachel patted her huge belly. "I'm saving everything for when you three have children."

Starr flushed. "Here's one from the three of us."

Rachel made grabby hands. "Oh, wow, I can't wait to have a girl next because the three of you—" she waggled her index finger at them "—are in charge of her wardrobe. For now, let's see what the burlesque queens want for my little boy."

As soon as the overalls came out with trains on them, Rachel and half a dozen other women whooped. Phoenix was so over the squealing, and the oohing and aahing over a stack of diapers arranged to resemble a wedding cake, and a thing called a "diaper genie" that took dirty diapers and made sausages out of them. Babies were exactly like she thought. Everything centered around poop.

Luna clapped her hands. "I promise to find the tiniest tiara for your little girl. In the meantime, your son will also be on the best-dressed list." Luna handed over the second package, which Phee knew held the tiny cowboy boots.

Phee gulped down the last swallow of her wine.

Starr cocked her head at her. "I've not seen you drink so much in a while, Phee. You okay?"

"Fine." Damn, her wine glass was empty again. "We should be more worried about L. She might get pregnant just for the wardrobe." She rose to go see what she could munch on at the table.

Trick's mother, a tidy older woman with bottle-dyed hair, sidled up to her. "We haven't had the pleasure of meeting. I'm Catherine Masters, Trick's mother."

"Nice to meet you. I used to work with Rachel."

"Oh, at the college?"

"No, Shakedown."

The woman's smile tightened ever so slightly. "Oh, that's nice. At first, I wasn't sure. Rachel and Trick had a... rocky beginning."

Phee smiled and lifted her chin in an acknowledgement. Gossip wasn't her style, but it must have been Catherine's. She leaned her head closer conspiratorially. "You've known Rachel long? I confess we don't."

"Not long." Phee looked over at the smiling pregnant woman. "But she and Trick seem very happy together."

"Oh, they are. I expect those two to have many children together. You have children?"

"Oh, no. Not married. No kids."

"Well, a pretty little thing like you I am sure won't be single for long. But don't let your boyfriend linger too long." She waggled her eyebrows.

"Don't have one of those either. And it's fine."

"Well, don't wait forever." The way the woman kept twisting her pearls between her fingers, Phee chalked up her advice as supportive talk from a different era. "Remember, dear, God's delays are not God's denials."

What was up with everyone telling her not to wait too long? She was 28, not 78. And what was up with women's worth still being tied to their relationship status? Hadn't they gotten past that? "God and I haven't always been on the best terms."

"Oh." The woman flushed.

"Sorry." She refilled her glass with champagne. It was the closest bottle to her. "It's been a long week."

"Well, try the mini red velvet cupcakes. They're divine." She lifted a tray of small, white-frosted confections. "Freshly baked this morning."

The woman was trying to be friendly, and she'd promised herself she'd try to stop thinking the worst at these such moments. "Your family from here?" Catherine asked.

"No. Just my two sisters and I."

"Hang on to them." She swiped at Phee's arm. "Family is important."

She pulled back at the touch.

"Oh, Mrs. Grant," Rachel called and held up a basket filled with small stuffed teddy bears, bunnies, and elephants. "I love them!"

"Oh, dear, it's Mom to you." The woman scooted closer to the gaggle of women.

Phee bit down on the red velvet cupcake.

Cherry moved to her. She was dressed in a men's suit with minimal makeup, her closely cropped hair making her look like an androgynous Egyptian queen. She crossed her arms, a wine glass dangling from one hand. "How's the momsy-in-law?" she whispered out of the side of her mouth. "Do we like her? Is she good enough for our Rachel there?"

"She'll be fine. I mean, Rachel got the high-end, stainless steel diaper genie out of her. She can bake, too." She lifted what was left of her cupcake.

They both burst out laughing. "Oh, girl, it's good to see you laughing." Cherry circled her shoulders and brought her closer. "Baby showers are a fascinating study in a certain subculture, don't you think?"

"How so?"

"It makes me better understand Grimm's fairy tales."

Phee slipped her hand into Cherry's—a hand that was rough like Declan's but so comforting because it was Cherry. "You should have a hundred children."

"Oh, I do. You're at least two with that split personality of yours. Just don't let it get in the way of love."

Oh, Jesus. Baby showers really did bring out the mother in everyone. "You worry too much."

"I worry about *you*, girl child, though I'm glad to see you and Declan seem to be getting along better."

Cherry did love her gossip. "I'm not a child anymore."

"You never were."

"Please, tell me we're not going down that road."

Cherry waved her hand. "There's not enough wine at this party for *that* road." Cherry reached into her jacket and pulled out her phone that had begun to vibrate. Her eyes widened at seeing the screen. She frowned.

Starr also reached down to her purse about the same time and drew out her phone. She looked up at Phee and mouthed *What?*

Phoenix retrieved her cell from her bag.

<<Ladies, take the night off. We're not opening this evening.>>

Starr fixed her eyes on Phee. Luna also stared at her phone screen. Something was up.

"If another Crown Vic smashed Declan's new door, I'm going to have some words to say." Cherry pocketed her phone. "I was the inspiration for that dancer etched in the glass."

"One second. I'll find out what's up." Phee wasn't waiting. She excused herself to the balcony.

She dialed Declan's number. He didn't answer. She texted him back, privately.

<<Everything okay?>>

When she got nothing but radio silence, she grew antsy. She texted again.

<<The MacKennas did something, didn't they?>>

Again, no reply came. Maybe he *had* lost another door. A few months ago, Ruark MacKenna had blackmailed someone to drive a car into the entranceway. If only it could be that simple—which was ridiculous, given how a car smashing into Shakedown didn't sound *that bad* to her right now.

Starr and Luna joined her on the balcony. "What'd he say?"

"Not answering his phone."

"I'm sure it's fine. It could be a gas leak," Luna offered.

"He'd have said as much."

"Let's go by," Phee said.

"He said to stay away."

"No, he said to take the night off."

"I'm with Miss Phoenix, ladies. It couldn't hurt to do a drive-by. I'll drive Phee's car." Cherry slipped through the sliding glass door. "What? I am no good in the dark."

But when they went by Shakedown, no one was there. It was as much of a ghost town as they'd ever seen. *So, this is what it would be like if Shakedown didn't exist.* Then what would she be left with? Another of God's denials. *Fuck delays.*

"Do any of you know where Declan lives?" How had she not known? All this time?

Cherry raised her hand and waggled her fingers. "I do. I make a point to know *everything*."

37

———

Carragh's words rang in Declan's head. The man was right about one thing. He needed to think more, react less. Maybe he'd take a drive, clear his head. He found himself heading back to his home instead, and he was glad. Two cars idled in his driveway—the Mustang he'd bought Phoenix that Starr now drove, and a vintage VW. So much for telling his stubborn O'Malley sisters to stay away.

Cherry unfolded herself from Phoenix's VW—the driver's side, he noted. "Cherry, ladies, what can I do for you?"

"Oh, we're doing a drive-by, seeing if there's anything we can do to help." Cherry then got into the back seat of the Mustang—not an easy feat for the six-foot-tall drag queen. Starr smiled at him from the windshield and then drove off after giving him a wave.

Phoenix stood by her car, a grimace painted across her face. "You didn't answer your text messages." She held up her phone. The woman was pissed at him for not answering his phone? This woman had ignored him for six fucking years.

He drew closer. She wobbled on her feet as if she'd been drinking.

"What's wrong?" He took her by the arm and led her toward his house. "Rachel's baby shower was today, wasn't it?" His keys jangled against his front door.

"I didn't know where you were."

He pushed open the door. "You were worried about me again."

The woman had most definitely had her share of alcohol. Her limbs were loose and floppy—plus, she was allowing him to handle her too easily.

She stepped inside and her usual attitude instantly pounced on him. "You should have never kissed me!"

Here they went again. "You look like you could use some coffee."

She peered around the entranceway. "Nice house. More books." She pointed to his first edition classics lined up on a side table under the hall mirror. They should be under glass somewhere, but he rather liked seeing them every time he crossed his threshold.

"You want to talk books?"

"No. I want you to stop filling my head up with mystery."

"Like how it would be for me to kiss you right now?"

The tiny flare of her nostrils was adorable. "Like why we're closed when there's a mob family on your tail and you don't answer your phone. You didn't want to have to tell me anything, did you? And Naomi didn't show this morning for her audition. Why doesn't anyone do what they say they're going to do anymore?"

She'd most definitely been drinking as he'd never heard her ramble so much. "Come. Coffee." She also needed to be kissed more often.

38

Declan had the audacity to chortle—fucking *laugh* at her—when she spilled some coffee on herself. Jesus, her white shirt was never going to be the same.

"So, that's it?" she asked. "You're not going to tell me why we're closed tonight?"

"I like that you said 'we.'" He poured her another cup.

"Coffee does little to counter the effect of alcohol, ya know. It only makes one a more wired and awake drunk." She and her sisters had tried the caffeine trick with their father—and lost.

He leaned back in the kitchen chair. "You're not *a* drunk. You're also drinking decaf right now."

"Well, that's a waste," she said into her cup.

"Let's go into the living room." He held out his hand, which she stupidly took.

They cut through a dining room that was lined with shelves filled with glass and ceramic pieces that were lit up behind the glass doors. A pastoral painting hung over a polished walnut credenza with tiny brass handles adorning each cupboard and drawer. In the living area, an old, cast iron Singer sewing machine in a dark walnut stand sat in one corner, and small·Dutch paintings mixed with larger oil paintings of sea battles on the walls.

The man did love his antiques. She made a 360-degree turn in the large room and took in the vintage farmhouse pieces living alongside Victorian English furniture. Somehow, it all worked, not unlike the various paradoxes of Declan himself.

"Oh." Her feet moved her to a Sheraton lamp table. "I haven't seen a turntable in forever."

"There's no sound like the analog of vinyl."

She cocked her head. "Let me guess. Classical?" She arched an eyebrow on purpose.

"You know me so well." He leaned down and ran his finger over the spines of a dozen vinyl records standing side-by-side under the table and selected one. He slipped it out and dropped it on the center spindle.

The static-y drop of the needle onto the record raised up a memory. She and her sisters would sit for hours listening to her mother's old records from the 1970s, especially Fleetwood Mac and Tom Petty and the Heartbreakers.

Phee stared at the spinning disk. The first horn sounds rose in a familiar tune.

"Tchaikovsky. 'Waltz of the Flowers' from *The Nutcracker*. I loved that ballet." She closed her eyes for a second and got lost in the harp cascades.

Declan gripped her arm. Crap, she'd almost fallen over. *Note to self—do not shut one's eyes when a little tipsy.*

"You've seen it," he said.

"One of our foster mothers, the one who owned the dance studio, took us one Christmas." She swayed to the oboe part playing with the French horns.

"I have tickets, December 18, Baltimore Ballet. Come with me."

She stared at him. "You're kidding."

'Until then," he took her palm in his, "teach me how to dance."

"What?"

"Show me something."

"Always wanted to learn to shimmy?"

He placed her hand on his shoulder. "I never took the time to learn the basic waltz."

"No one waltzes anymore. I mean, where would you? It's mostly West Coast swing or salsa these days."

"That's a pity. The waltz is so beautiful."

"It is." His other hand had made its way around her waist. He grasped the hand dangling by her side and lifted it high. He then stepped forward and she had no choice but to follow his lead.

Oh, come on. *Teach him the waltz?* His dance ability was apparent as he spun her.

"You know how to waltz, don't you?"

He shrugged. "A tiny lie. Don't hold it against me."

He moved her forward and back and then another sudden twirl. Within minutes, they had moved down the hallway and back into the kitchen. The swing, rise, and fall of the music pulled at her belly. It was bold and big and elegant. Like Declan. Her eyes filled and his face grew wavy.

He had her back through another entranceway, through the dining area, and then back into the living room. The man was an incredible dancer.

She snuffed up her nose, and her eyes cleared.

If only men knew that a man who could dance impressed the hell out of most women. It was like their version of a home-cooked meal or lingerie. Total foreplay material.

This man, with his impeccable lead, moved her around

furniture as the music swelled in that great, rolling way she'd always loved. She'd wanted to dance ballet a long time ago, hadn't she? Starr had wanted them to pull together a burlesque routine—more money and an immediate placement opportunity with Shakedown had her go along with her sister's plans. Six years flew by so fast. So many years.

"Le Lac des Cygnes" from *Swan Lake*, the Black Swan, her absolute favorite, began next. And then she was crying again. She stopped him. "I… I… ", she stammered.

"It is beautiful, isn't it?" His eyes never left her face.

She gave him a series of tight little nods. She couldn't talk. Her throat had closed up. It was the music's fault.

"You're beautiful." He cupped her cheek.

And wouldn't you know it, his mouth captured hers. This time, as he kissed her, his hands didn't stay still. They roamed her shoulders and her back as if exploring. Chills ran over her skin. She should pull back, not allow this… touching. She leaned into him instead.

Time passed. His clock on his wall chimed. The needle on the record player sounded a tick-tick-tick against the center of the record. He finally broke the kiss—after his hands had been over every inch of her.

"Can I hear more?" She needed more music.

He led her over to the turntable. Without letting her go, he flipped the record with one hand and played the other side. "My Sweet and Tender Beast" by Eugen Doga played. His lips found hers once more, but this time he moved slower as if mirroring the music. They stood like that in front of an old-fashioned turntable listening to the music, their lips and tongues moving with each other.

At some point, the music ended again. Without a single word, he scooped her up, and with halted, limping steps, took her upstairs to a large sleigh bed—his bed. He laid her down, pulled an old quilt over her, and set himself in the corner wing chair. "Sleep."

"Sleep with me."

"Are you sure?"

No, she wasn't. But could she do it? Would it be possible to let Declan lie next to her? She didn't know. For now, she knew only one thing. She wasn't leaving Shakedown.

39

———

Declan leaned against the bar in his usual spot, enthralled by what was unfolding on the stage.

Phoenix raised both arms high and the sold-out audience roared. She was doing his favorite act, The Matador, with Carina Rose's old mechanical bull lifting its head, tendrils of dried ice smoke snaking from the nostrils. Such fire. Her red hair glinting under lights. Her blue eyes squinted in that confident air only someone as talented as she could adopt.

They had locked eyes once, but now she only cast those sparkling blue eyes over the crowd.

It'd been a fantastic day thanks to last night's developments, which elevated his mood to unprecedented levels. Perhaps it had been good for her as well.

Phoenix had slept in his bed—with him. She'd stayed fully clothed, as did he, and nothing could have pleased him more. He'd curled his body around hers, his nose buried in her hair, inhaling all that warm, cinnamon scent.

In the very early morning, even before the sun rose, Declan heard Phoenix leave his house, a soft, far-away click of his front door echoing in his hallway. Waking in rumpled clothes from the night before wasn't usual for him, but he'd have had it no other way.

Of course, he'd texted her about an hour after making sure she got home okay.

He'd included a simple note. **<<Foxtrot next?>>**

She'd responded immediately. **<<How about a rhumba? >>**

<<What? No paso doble?>>

<<No one does that outside a competition... but then I do enjoy being the matador>>

Holy hell, they'd bantered. Their relationship most definitely had taken a turn.

He'd arranged for a bouquet to be placed on her makeup stand when she arrived tonight. He'd spent a ridiculous amount of time discussing the options with the owner of Hedge and Rose flower shop, trying to find the right ones. Long-stemmed red roses would be too much, yet carnations and freeshia would be too ordinary. He'd settled on an arrangement of white hydrangeas, white roses tipped in pink, and peonies. The shop owner called it extravagantly elegant, which was exactly what he was going for. This woman made him do so many things he never thought he would—like wait years for a kiss.

Then tonight? She'd nodded at him in the hallway as she took to the stage, no traces of her earlier sprained ankle and no acknowledgment that they'd had a breakthrough in their relationship.

The music died in a crash of cymbals. Phoenix split the curtains in a dramatic flourish and was off the stage in record time. If he hurried, he'd conveniently run into her in the hallway where he'd extend an invitation to a late dinner.

Nathan stopped him. "Declan, sorry to spring this on you, but Ruark's parole hearing? It's tomorrow. Not next week."

So much for Carragh and him being on the same side. "They didn't give you much notice, did they?"

"No. Could use the day off—" he scrubbed his hair "—and maybe the night, depending on how it goes."

He slapped the man on the shoulder. "Take the time you need but tell me it's not only going to be you and Starr."

"No, Max agreed to at least go to the hearing. Starr didn't like the idea of walking in and Ruark seeing she felt she needed protection, but that's the way it's going down. I want him to see he's outnumbered."

He was glad his friend was taking things seriously. He would scratch off worrying about Starr.

"And the other two sisters?"

Nathan shrugged. "I never get in between those three."

Declan smirked. "Wise man." He, however, needed to know if Phoenix and Luna were also planning to go. If he had to shut down the club so he could escort Phee, he'd do it.

He was headed to the back rooms when his phone rang with a familiar number.

"Henry."

"Guess you heard the news."

"No, what?"

"Someone tried to torch my club last night."

All air died in his lungs. "Tell me—"

"Caught it before it took the whole place down, but I'll be out of commission for a while. With any luck, I don't have to tear it all down."

"What can I do?"

"Nothing. Just watch your back because those warnings you gave me? They were on point."

So, someone was playing hardball. Now, to figure out which of his relatives—God, his gut roiled on that word— was responsible. The more he thought about it, Ruark may still be behind bars, but that didn't mean he couldn't pull some strings, make shit happen on the outside.

And right there sat a thought worse than a crime family trying to get him into their folds. How about a family breaking apart, trying to outdo one another?

That dinner he'd planned with Phee would have to wait.

40

––––––

Declan spent half the next day with Henry and his family. He'd left word at the club he had an errand to run and might not make it in. No reason to give any other details that would worry them unnecessarily, especially Phee. He wouldn't risk dinging her trust in him.

Still, he had a shit ton of people who did need to worry, like other friends in the industry, and then some to keep out of the growing mess. Like Trick with his very pregnant wife. And Max, who had to be fresh for the parole hearing babysitting job. Nathan and Starr? They had enough emotional turmoil going on with Ruark's sudden hearing. At least Nathan texted him with the only good news of the day—Phoenix was not attending Ruark's hearing, which was nothing more than a political sham. He had his hands full with one potentially emotional woman in Starr.

A few hours on the phone and one visit to Henry, who refused his help in some misguided attempt to keep Declan free from trouble—if only the man knew—Declan was finally free to see Phee. He darted home for a quick shower and then decided to just show up at her place.

He grabbed his keys off the side console and his rain jacket because the storms showed no sign of letting up and swung open his front door.

Phoenix's blue eyes stared up at him, her thin arms wrapped around her body. Water streamed off the stonework around his door frame.

"Phoenix, how long have you been out here?" He swung his gaze to his doorbell to make sure the small light glowed indicating it worked.

"Not long. A minute. Maybe."

Phee's hair hung heavy with water, her eyes bloodshot as if she'd been crying. Damnit, he'd seen those blue eyes rimmed in red far too often of late.

He waved at the security guy who'd probably followed her here. The man would get a raise for that bit of extra attention. He pulled her inside, an instant puddle forming under her feet.

"She's going without me. She didn't want me to go, she said. Just Nathan." She huffed and dropped her purse. "And Max. Jesus. If you need Max, you need me." She punched her chest with her index finger. "God, that sounded stupid."

"Not at all. Come on, let's go." If she needed to attend so badly, he'd escort her. "If we hurry—"

"No." She shook her head violently. "She asked me not to, and I have to…" Her lips turned down in a grimace and a choked sound came from her throat. "She's really moving on. Really doing it."

Interesting choice of words, given Phoenix was going to quit Shakedown at one point. "And you were leaving Shakedown, weren't you?"

Her eyes grew wide. "I was never leaving without them. Never." She launched herself into him. He held the shivering, wet woman until his shirt and pants were soaked, too.

"Where's Luna?" he asked into her hair.

Phee sniffed. "She said she had to… go out. By the way, your other security guy followed her, too."

Ah, so she had noticed the extra precautions. At least she wasn't fuming angry about them. But shit. Luna was likely headed to the hearing. Well, at least Max was there. Nathan, too, who'd go back to prison for a third time if it meant any of his family were hurt.

He grabbed two towels from the powder room and dried off her hair. She hadn't moved, staring down at the floor as if her mind was whirling.

"Come on, let's get you some dry clothes."

She raised her face to him. "Have a bunch of women's clothes lying around?"

He chuckled. "One of my T-shirts will fit like a dress on you and it'll give me a chance to throw those in the dryer." He pointed at her sopping wet jeans.

He found her the largest T-shirt he could find—an old sports jersey. After slipping it on, she insisted on being shown the laundry room where she handled her clothes. The woman was impeccable—setting the dryer to low for her jeans and socks and hanging her top and jacket on hangers. He left her in peace, but not before he caught a glimpse of her laying an ivory satin bra on top of the dryer. He thickened at the sight because he was a man, after all.

She joined him in the living room, her arms crossed over her in an odd modesty. There was no need—his shirt swallowed her. Was he really that much larger than she was? She seemed so formidable when really she was a delicate thing. His body lit up remembering how well she fit inside his arms last night.

"What can I get you? Something to drink?"

"No, I'm fine. I wanted you to know I'm staying. I mean, if you'll have me."

Not running? Progress, indeed. "That's good news."

"So, need another waltz lesson?" she asked nervously.

"Always."

"Maybe again to 'My Sweet and Tender Beast'. I'll play the part of the beast."

"You could never be that."

She scoffed. "Sure."

"Neither of us are." He sucked in a long breath. "If the world was ending, your face is the last one I would want to see. Even with that look you are giving me. You didn't know you have different looks, did you?" He rose from his chair. "There's the one when you're watching your sisters." He took a step forward. "There's the one when someone gets too close to the stage." He closed the final distance between them. "And then there's the one when you see me."

Her lips parted. "What do you see when I look at you?"

"Fear." Her eyes held all her imagination, all the things that could happen to her that would hurt.

"I'm sorry. I really am." She stared at his chest.

"What would it take for you to look at me differently?"

Her lashes lifted. "I wish I knew."

Oh, but he did. "I do. Say your piece to your father."

Every muscle in her body froze.

"And before you balk, know that I will kill him before I let him get within ten feet of you. You need to say everything you've ever wanted to say to that man—from a safe distance but to his face. If you don't want to do it, fine. But if you do, I'll stand right next to you the whole time."

The resignation in her eyes held strong. She lifted her arms. "Dance with me instead."

He circled her waist and took her outstretched right hand. "Always." She wasn't ready to do something so drastic as confront her father.

"Good, because I have a question." Her arm shook a little as he lifted it high in the traditional ballroom stance.

"What, Sunset?"

She smiled a little at his nickname for her. She peered up at him, the blue there as clear as a spring morning. "Can we start over?"

"We already have." He twirled her to some imaginary music. He didn't want to stop to put on a record.

"But I mean really start over."

"Not afraid of me?"

She swallowed. "You may be the only man I'm not afraid of."

No more dancing. He took her back to his bed.

41

————

He hovered over her. She meant what she'd said about him. She wasn't exactly fearful, even if her heartbeat ran as fast as a hummingbird's. Could he feel it? His whole body pressed down on her, still in his shirt and trousers, and she only half-clothed in panties and his jersey. This adrenaline surge may have come from someplace else—something just out of her grasp. She understood why she reacted the way she did to such intimate moments. Perhaps Declan would help her get it under control.

His hands rested on either side of her face. "I want to say your real name. Out loud."

Seriously? She hadn't heard her legal name in so long her mind had to adjust for a second, to really think. Damn tax records that revealed her true identity.

"I've never liked it." She'd have never used that name again if it wasn't ridiculous to legally change it to Phoenix Rising.

"I've always found your name—both of them—uncommonly beautiful. Your real name means ancient. Humane. Sensitive. May I?"

Time for her to prove her new bravery. She nodded once.

"Elizaveta." He spoke in a hushed whisper, both tender and nearly reverent in its tone.

A scoff flew from her throat. "My mom and her Russian fantasies."

"Is that why you enjoy so many Russian composers?"

She'd never thought of the reason like that, but her mother had a proclivity for Tchaikovsky and Stravinsky. The only music she couldn't listen to was Gnossiere. Too sad, she'd said.

His hips rolled a little and he nestled his length between her legs, though they stayed mostly closed.

"I haven't… much." She flushed. Her lack of sexual experience was embarrassing.

"Or at all?"

"Oh, no, I have but wished I hadn't."

"I see." His eyes hardened. "Is there someone I need to kill?"

She laughed. "No. You can just imagine killing him like I do." She swallowed. "I mean, I consented. It wasn't fun. He was rougher than I expected."

His eyes slanted. "Or wanted." He took her mouth, strongly but not with a scary edge.

His kiss loosened, but his lips didn't disconnect fully. Warm breath mixed with hers, and her heart rate slowed. "I only desire you to want me, Elizaveta. And then I'll give you anything *you* want."

He'd give to her? That's all he did when it came to her. His generosity was baffling and seductive. Perhaps that's why resisting him was beyond futile. Staying angry around him proved difficult at best. He raised up something she hadn't indulged in years—hope for feeling different, maybe *being* different, all because he believed she could.

More possibility floated to the surface—to feel the skin of

another man on hers after all these years. There went her heartbeat again. She could have propelled them to the moon with its power. "I'm not sure what I want."

"I can imagine enough for both of us."

"You imagine me..." She flushed anew at the thought she was the center of his fantasy. Another irony given her choice of profession. She sold fantasies five nights a week. But they were to strangers. Declan was no stranger.

"All the time. I breathe you in my dreams, Sunset."

The man was poetry incarnate. "Can we go slow?"

"I plan on it. Do you know where I'd like to start?"

She did want to know. "Where?"

His lips inched up, wickedly. He then crawled down her legs, split open her thighs, and pressed his mouth over the fabric of her panties. The contact was warm and so sudden, she sucked in air that was let out in a long moan.

She eased up on her elbows and peered down at him.

"I want to taste you. That's all for tonight."

That was all? This man could not be for real. She found herself nodding anyway, and he whisked her panties down her legs. She flopped to her back. For at least a full minute, his hot breath ran over her most sensitive area. She had to be as red as a third-degree sunburn as he clearly studied her. His large hands held her thighs open, and then his lips and tongue were on her.

Oh, God. The man not only knew how to kiss... he knew how to *kiss*.

Deep, heavy breathing indicated Declan had fallen asleep. His arm draped heavy over her waist, but she managed to slip free without jostling the bed too much.

She gently set her bag on the counter so as not to wake

the man sleeping not 30 feet away. He must have retrieved it as she didn't remember bringing it upstairs. The man was a thinker.

Wow. Bathroom mirrors were not as forgiving as stage makeup mirrors. Little wrinkles lined her eyes and tiny grooves etched across her forehead.

After splashing cold water on her face, she pressed her hand against the knot in her stomach. Her legs quivered a little—still. She'd had two orgasms that nearly plastered her to the ceiling. She hadn't been touched down there in years. Then to have a man's mouth work her over as he had? So much for Declan's gentlemanly manners. There was nothing civil about the man's oral skills. So why wasn't she overjoyed?

Declan didn't do anything wrong to cause the anxiety that had settled so resolutely in her belly—or her inability to reciprocate. It was her—all her. The man didn't ask for anything back. After she'd cried out a second time at the pure pleasure he'd provided, he'd crawled back up her body, encircled her with his arms, and told her to go sleep. *Sleep.*

He should have demanded something back, right?

What was wrong with her? Why couldn't she give this man what he deserved—pure love without reservation or hesitation? She did that with Starr and Luna. Why was it so hard with him?

She hadn't lied about not being afraid of Declan. But her body? It couldn't forget all the abuse it took in the past and how something that started out so wonderful could so easily turn to pain. She was damned sick of her twisted-up circuits inside.

Her fingertip found that little dent and scar above her hairline over her left eye. Then her hand drew up the back of her neck to the scar left from thirteen stitches. Her fingers found the little dent in her forearm next. More injury badges laced her skin, but she'd vowed long ago to stop counting them. She just touched the three most important—and most recent. The ones that reminded her of the day she got between Robert O'Malley and Luna, that *last* day before the great state of Alabama decided to step in and intervene. She'd never seen him again, at least until her eyes took in his shrunken body in that chair at Sunset House after Luna had stupidly tracked him down.

The bed creaked on the other side of the door. She opened the door a smidge. Declan had shifted but still lay asleep.

She should be there with him. Lying next to him. Maybe waking him up by curling her hand around…

Her body clapped back—hard. Her neck ached. Her thighs quivered. And that stupid muscle inside her chest that kept her alive thudded its fear as if to remind her she was no longer designed for such acts.

But maybe she could be… Declan might be right about her father and the supposed healing nature of letting it all out to the man who'd caused the most hurt. Luna and Starr certainly thought so.

What had Declan said that night at dinner about Tomas MacKenna? *I'm not going to be in reaction to him any longer. If I did, I'd lose my own power. I prefer offense to defense.*

She picked up her bag and sank to the floor. With any luck, Declan's bathroom wouldn't echo too much and he wouldn't hear the phone call she needed to make. With her eyes on Declan's form covered in sheets, visible through the crack around the bathroom door, she dialed the one person who would understand the most, who would go with her to her father's halfway house, and simply put the car into reverse and leave if Phee changed her mind on the street, which was a very real possibility.

Cherry answered on the first ring.

42

"Doll, you do not need to go in there by yourself." Cherry had twisted herself to lean against the driver's side door of her Buick. "How about I go in with you but go flirt with the others in there? Keep them occupied while you go all Terminator on Robert's ass."

"You want to eavesdrop."

"Oh, I'd be doing that, too." She waggled her head at her. "Momma Cherry does not like being left out of anything where her children are involved."

Phoenix's throat squeezed under her words, not because Cherry was being so gracious to her but rather because the queen believed every word. She had a way like that—made you believe you were chosen. Like Declan did.

He wasn't going to be happy she came here without him. She glanced up at the red door at the top of the concrete steps.

Some doors you had to walk through yourself.

"I'm not even sure he's in there." Her breath fogged the window.

"Where else would he go? He got lucky, that one." Cherry

stared hard at the townhouse where Phee's father lived, a halfway house for patients needing "memory care," as she'd learned from Luna a few weeks ago during one of her please-visit-him begging sessions. Guess they worked, because here Phee sat, waiting to go in and... *do what?*

She cracked open her door and stepped out before her maudlin internal talk took over. "He doesn't deserve this chance."

"Oh, honey." Cherry leaned over, her hand splayed on her seat, her red nails shiny in the sunlight. "This isn't his chance. This is yours."

"I have no idea what to say."

"Something tells me you do. You just don't want to say it." Cherry sniffed. "Want some advice on that front? I have had the practice."

She had. Her own family disowned her years ago. How anyone couldn't accept Cherry she would never understand. Phoenix didn't answer her, though, because Cherry would dole out her prescription for this scenario anyway.

Cherry's lips thinned. "No one cares if he gets in a single word. Just let it fly. It'll be cathartic."

Phoenix twisted her mouth into a half-smile. "I'm pretty good at that."

"Except maybe toward the one person who rightly deserved it and has yet to hear it."

Her belly rumbled in both recognition and fear. "I won't be long."

"I got time. Science Friday is on NPR and I love that man's voice." She clicked on her radio dial just as Phee slammed the car door shut.

Phoenix climbed the stone steps and rapped on the door. When no one answered, she tried the door, found it open, and stepped inside. Microwave popcorn—that was the first scent that wafted over her. The entranceway was tiny and sparse, with a rickety coat rack and a mirror hanging on the wall.

She could turn and walk back out, choose a better day, not one on the heels of Declan touching her, loving her despite her best efforts to thwart that from happening. And why was that? How about because she'd *not* been able to overcome her fears on her own and give herself over to Declan. Bravery was supposed to be her strong suit, but it wasn't, not by a long shot. There was a reason for her cowardice—and that reason lived in this house.

It pissed her off royally that she couldn't do what she wanted to do. Her father had taken away a choice from her by injecting her with a poisonous fear.

Further inside, she found an empty living room—more like a few couches and chairs, all appearing donated by their mismatched upholstery and some equally odd-looking end tables. A game board lay open on a coffee table, checkers stacked in neat rows of black and red to the side of it. Laughter sounded from down the hallway. Several male voices and a female. The floor creaked a little as she skulked down the hallway.

Three men sat around a yellowed Formica table under a window overlooking the backyard. A woman poured coffee into cups on the kitchen countertop. All eyes turned to Phoenix. She honed in on one man in particular—weathered, worn, familiar blue eyes widening at seeing her.

Every fiber in her body stiffened. "Robert." She said carefully.

The chair legs squeaked over the linoleum as he used it to help him rise and then as a crutch to help him stand.

The woman who'd been pouring coffee had set the pot back on the coffee maker and stepped forward. "Hello." Her warm smile beamed over at Phee. She held out her hand. "You must be one of Robert's daughters. I'm Maven, the day nurse." The woman had some grip. She was stocky and likely doubled as a bodyguard by her calm, take-charge way.

"Phoenix."

Her father hadn't moved or said a word. His eyelids fluttered in confusion.

"Well." Maven hadn't let go of her hand. "Why don't we settle in the living room? Chancey, help Robert over to his favorite chair."

No, "*Why are you here?*" No, "*What can I get you?*" This woman moved her down the hall and into the sitting room of incompatible furniture. Another one of the men—whose details she didn't bother to even notice—set her father into a ripped blue and red plaid wingback chair.

"I'll be right outside." Maven went out to the hall and sat down on a bench just outside two glass French doors that she'd closed behind her. So, they'd get an audience. It didn't matter. She'd likely never see the woman again, and she was responsible for these guys.

Robert had barely moved, sitting there like a shaky lump. A belt was cinched tight around his blue workman pants, one shirttail hanging out. At least he wasn't drooling.

She remained standing. "I have a few things to say." Though she still wasn't quite clear what they were yet. He'd once sent word through her sisters that he was remorseful. That he wanted her to feel better. Well, now was his chance to ensure that by listening.

He settled his hands in his lap. "Okay." So, the man could speak.

"I hate you." Cherry did say to let it fly. "I will never see you again after today."

He continued to blink at her, which only raised up more irritation. It fueled something inside because somehow, words then found purchase in her mouth. "Because of you, I can't be touched. I don't know how to be loved. I can't have children. Did you know that? The mere thought…"

His eyes widened. "Who did that to you?"

"Who do you think?"

His eyes clouded and he cocked his head. "Well, whoever did doesn't deserve you, pretty lady."

"I'm not pretty. Not anymore." She festered inside and it showed.

"You are. You remind me of someone long ago." His lips curled, revealing yellowed and rotting teeth. "Cara. A beautiful girl. Blue eyes. Same red hair. She had spirit, that one."

"Damn you to hell," she rasped. "You get to forget me and I'm left with…" She raised an arm and let it drop to her side. "This." Whatever this was.

She stepped forward, the sickening stench of old flesh wafting up. "I flinch anytime a man gets near me. Which is ironic as hell, given I'm a dancer and it's mostly men who like to see it. If you had just manned the ever-loving fuck up I could have done anything. Been *anything* other than…" Other than what? She loved dancing, but it was a risky business, not to mention one with a most definite shelf life. But it also wasn't like she'd ever wanted to do anything else.

His head cocked and he eyed her as if he didn't quite understand her words.

Her teeth ached. She'd been clenching them so hard in between words, surely she broke one.

He shifted in his seat a little. "Who are you again?"

The man had no clue as to who she was. That's when the real fury rose. "Fuck you, Robert O'Malley." Cherry was right about one thing. It felt good to say whatever words rose up. "How *dare* you get to forget what you did to me."

Fuck. Fuck. Fuck. Her throat seized and her last few words were nothing but a squeak.

"You beat us. All three of us. But that last time? Luna and I were the only ones home. Thirteen stitches were laid across my scalp. You did that."

He looked mystified—absolutely, positively perplexed.

"There's a man, a good man, who loves me, though why, I'll never know. And you know what? He doesn't care about why. He just does. He shouldn't have to put up with all the crap I channel from you. *You.*" A sob lodged itself so tightly in her chest, her throat burned from squeezing it back inside.

He raised his hands in surrender. "I—"

"You nothing." She yanked up her sleeve, a barely visible thin line across one wrist. She'd had a plastic surgeon remove the major part of the scarring, but it was still visible if one really looked. She'd done it with her own hand when things were really bad in that foster home. "See this? Never fucking again. I'm done. I'm sick of being the victim of your weakness."

Something thunked inside her. A heavy lump, ever-present in her chest, shifted. It wasn't gone, but it had most definitely moved.

Then came more thoughts. Declan wasn't getting what he wanted because of what this man did to her. This man had not only abused her and her sisters but everyone that they contacted was touched by what he did—or in Declan's case, not touched.

His eyes squinched but then cleared for a second as her epiphany had reached him. His mouth dropped open, and his face went slack. "You're..."

"Your nightmare. It's your turn to hold the pain. I don't need it anymore." She yanked her sleeve down. Truth was, she wasn't yet out of the woods. Rather, the *idea* of feeling good, of letting go, of being different was enough.

"It's over. Because I say so. Good-bye, Robert O'Malley. Tell the devil in Hell I said maybe next time." She turned away from him. It was the last time she'd ever lay eyes on the man—at least alive. She didn't need any more than the last 15 minutes with him to nail that proverbial coffin shut.

She cracked open the doors. "Thanks, Maven. He's all yours."

The woman merely nodded, a grimace across her face. "Oh, Miss O'Malley," she called. Phee stilled her hand on the front doorknob. "You take care."

Phee nodded once, yanked open the door, and headed down the steps. With each one, her lungs opened up a bit more. At the bottom, she took a moment to stand there. All the last few years she'd wondered how she'd handle seeing him again. Now she knew. Could someone get high off screaming at someone you've wanted to for so long? Why, yes, they could. She was living proof of it.

"So, how did it go?" Cherry asked as soon as the car door opened.

"It went." She dropped herself to the seat.

"Am I dropping you off at Declicious' house?"

"No. I need to go home." She wasn't running to him. There were two other people who needed to learn of her move more. "I need to talk to Starr and Luna. In person."

"Ah, of course. They need to learn of your triumph." She put the car into drive and peered over her shoulder at oncoming traffic.

"Is that what that was?"

She faced the windshield. "Girl, anytime someone speaks the truth it's triumphant. There's so little of it today."

"You should run for Congress."

Cherry's gaze flashed to her. "Oh, my God, have you seen what they wear on Capitol Hill? No way."

Phoenix threw her head back and let something else fly— a deep-throated laugh that she felt all the way down to her toes.

43

"Ruark made parole." Three words that curled Declan's insides into a tight fist. In two days, the man would be walking the streets again. To make matters worse, damnable Carragh MacKenna was at fault.

Nathan paced in the storeroom. "Carragh stood up for him. *Stood there* and said Ruark was going to work for him." He paused and stared hard at Declan. "That he would be the one to ensure he had a place to live."

His fiancée, Starr, hadn't said a word. But she didn't need to. Starr's eyes—so similar to Phoenix's—swirled with a hot blue fire. She raised her hand when Nathan reached out to her.

She stepped forward. "Declan, I haven't told Phee. I thought maybe you would want to. I don't think I could handle my anger and hers all at once."

"I can't begin to tell you how sorry I am, Starr."

"It's not your fault."

"But it's my responsibility." He swallowed everything else he thought because it didn't matter if anyone knew or understood his next move. But it was, indeed, time for him to move.

"Nathan. Starr. Doors open in an hour. I have some calls to place. Can you ask Phoenix to wait for me after the show?"

That at least got a smile from Starr. "I'll do my best." She moved as if leaving but stopped herself. "Oh, and I probably shouldn't tell you this, but I will. Phee went to see our father this afternoon."

"What do you mean, she saw your father?" He was overjoyed that she was ready to confront the man but not that she did so without him. That was not their deal.

"Yeah. And not with us but with Cherry. I think she'd finally seen the need to move on. You're the reason, aren't you? And I gotta say, if you could make that happen, then you can definitely handle the MacKennas."

"Thanks, Starr." He winked at her. Such faith in him meant something. But Nathan was right about one thing—one didn't handle that family. One bested them.

Once alone, Declan started that process.

He couldn't say why he'd been delaying the inevitable. Perhaps because he had more cards to play. Saving them as a last resort was prudent. Or perhaps he couldn't let go of the hope the MacKennas would just grow bored with him. But that was the problem with sociopaths. They never lost interest. They merely changed the game.

He'd introduce a new one himself.

His banker was the first call. After understanding his borrowing capacity, he called his real estate broker—the woman who had sold him the Shakedown property many years ago.

"Marta, I want every available property within a one-mile radius of Shakedown checked. I'm a motivated buyer. Anonymous as usual." No reason to alert the sharks to his appetite. He'd see what properties the MacKennas currently owned and buy as much left over as he could.

He also ran home, retrieved his mother's diaries from his home safe, and put them in his safety deposit box—after photocopying three key pages and dropping them in the mail. Tomas enjoyed courage from his adversaries, did he? The psycho hadn't seen anything yet. It was time to lay down his winning hand.

Then he'd deal with one burlesque dancer who still didn't understand going it alone was no longer necessary.

44

―――――

Phoenix was a sight. Her tumble of red curls hung loose and free and lifted and wrapped around her neck as she twirled. Her eyes sparkled at the audience and her smile was wide and relaxed. He thought she was fire before?

It took a minute to understand what was different tonight. She was in head-to-toe white. Not her usual color choice, but the pearly color was stunning on her. The long gown picked up fractured light as her hips swayed, not unlike a mermaid tail might in the sunlight.

The entire dance cast sauntered and pranced on stage—Phoenix, Cortelana, Aspen Snow, Nikki, Sally Mae, Starr, Luna, and of course, Cherry, who belted out a song he didn't recognize as the queen traversed the entire thirty feet, back and forth. Had the show morphed under his nose? He'd appointed Cherry creative director recently, and, so far, she'd never disappointed. Truth told, he enjoyed experiencing the show for the first time with the audience. Perhaps that was yet another reason to be drawn to Phoenix. She never failed to surprise him.

The dancers moved in a seamless braid, spinning around

one another, trading off an enormous peacock feather fan as if battling for the feathers like a prize. Red-lipped mouths fell into exaggerated "O"s as Nikki in a bright red tutu grasped the fan and tromped to stand behind Cherry, fanning her like a pool boy waving a giant palm frond. Aspen dipped under, her arm swiping the fan right out from Nikki. On and on they battled in a swirl of fringe and tulle and sequins.

The final notes of the song lifted and fell into silence—rather abruptly. The cast froze in various posts. Phoenix ended up in the center, flanked by the other dancers and holding the fan high to clamshell it behind her head like a trophy. All she needed was a giant Scallop shell to stand on—and be nude—and she'd be the perfect depiction of the *Birth of Venus*. He would drop to his knees at the sight.

Declan wasn't a man who often experienced the sensation of being overcome. He let the feeling wash over him anyway. He cleared his throat and expanded his ribs in a deep breath. And here he'd thought falling apart was for crises. No one told him the complete undoing that came from watching the woman you loved stand in joy. She was made to stand in the center—of everything good.

If only more people could learn what she did. She left her world behind when she performed. No one would ever guess this woman's past if they only knew her as Phoenix Rising, star of a burlesque revue.

The dancers disappeared one by one from the stage. Cherry gave off her final remarks, which, if tonight was like any other night, would take a while.

He turned to head to the back to catch Phoenix in the hallway. He didn't want to burst her joy bubble, but someone had to tell her about Ruark and it was going to be him. And that father visit? He'd play that one by ear.

In the hallway, Nathan leaned against the cinderblock

wall outside the bright pink door of the makeup room. Bright laughter echoed behind it.

"I see our dancers can still move in those heels." Their pace beat his.

Nathan lifted his gaze from his phone, and Declan set his back against the wall next to him.

"Yeah." Nathan chuckled softly. "They're inside. De-glittering or whatever it's called. It'll be a while. Trust me."

Declan's eyes cut once more to the door as the laughter continued. "Just waiting for Phoenix."

Nathan nodded once. "Glad to run into you. Max and I are taking Starr and Luna away after the show tonight. We'll be back on Tuesday for opening. To get away for a bit."

More like to get away from Ruark MacKenna, who would be roaming the streets in about 36 hours. "You said Starr and Luna."

"Phee doesn't want to go." The man didn't elaborate. He didn't need to.

"I'll watch her."

One side of Nathan's mouth quirked up, but he returned to studying his phone.

"If you need more than a few days…" he began.

"Thanks. But I'll see you Tuesday. Wouldn't have it any other way."

Damned emotion. Been creeping up on him at the oddest times, like when a man he still owed his life to declared he wouldn't run despite the fact his life could be in danger.

Declan clapped the man's shoulder and nodded.

The pink door cracked open. "Well, just the man I wanted to see." Phoenix was dressed in jeans and black flats. A black beret topped her head, her red hair still loose and curling over her shoulders and over a forest green velvet jacket.

He shook himself to the present. "Just what I wanted to hear."

She swished up to him and pecked him on the lips "I have something to tell you. I saw my father today." Like a flash, she was past him. "Are you coming?"

"Where are we going?"

She turned. "I thought I'd leave my car here. Let you take me home."

"My home?"

"Yeah." She pushed her backside against the exit door bar. "Two days off. I wonder what we could do."

Hushed words said with a smile? Today most definitely wasn't going in any direction he could have foreseen. "Well, good, because I have news, too."

"Oh, I know all about Ruark getting out on parole. I overheard Starr and Nathan so I made her tell me right before I went on stage. Starr has dibs on using her emery board on his balls first. But I get the second crack."

She was out the door and he barely caught the heavy thing before it slammed shut. "Nathan." The man hadn't moved from his spot, probably as stunned as Declan was about the alien that had taken over Phoenix's body.

"I'll help Jackie and Max close up." The man scrubbed his hair, seemingly as perplexed as Declan was.

He may have an exorcism he needed to perform because whoever had possessed Phoenix Rising was not someone that anyone at Shakedown had gotten acquainted with yet.

Or perhaps this is who Elizaveta was all along—and she was only recently let out.

Declan's front door clicked shut, and Phoenix turned. She took his cane, hooked it on the coat rack, and drew closer to him.

On the way over, she asked they not talk—not yet. He

obliged, held her hand, and rubbed his thumb over that spot between her thumb and forefinger, which turned out to be an erogenous zone.

They'd stopped by her apartment to feed and water Moonlight, but she didn't pick up any clothes, not wanting to be too presumptuous. She was unfamiliar with this man-woman who-stays-over-at-whose-house thing. She'd never once spent the full night with a man. It was time to cross off a few "firsts."

She placed both her hands along his cheeks, his five o'clock shadow rough under her hands. "Kisses?" She didn't wait for an answer.

She pressed her lips against his. His hand slid under her jacket and he yanked her closer. Her breasts mashed against his chest. Then the room spun. Her ass hit a piece of furniture. He'd moved her to where he could lift her up and place her on the console table. She only hoped it didn't collapse under her.

He peered down at her. "Who are you and where is Phoenix?"

"It's me."

"Or Elizaveta?"

She nodded once. After she and Cherry left that half-way home, an odd, jangly feeling wouldn't leave her. She wasn't anxious but rather vibrated with excitement, almost like a runner's high. Starr and Luna had been stunned by her report of her visit to their father but didn't press her for many details—thank God. She wasn't interested in revisiting any more pasts, not even ones that were mere hours old.

Now, she wanted to start directing her life to something new. Something big but not too big. And not exactly a baby-step either.

He cocked his head as if waiting for her to say more.

"I thought I'd... try. To be with you." Please, dear God, let him decipher what she meant, don't make her say it.

A slight rumble formed in his throat in answer. His hips jutted forward, his leg muscles hard and his cock even harder.

When Declan was merely her boss, like most men she encountered, it was easier to think of him as almost androgynous. She didn't think about male bodies at all.

Now? Declan was a man who could *do things* to her.

The drumbeat of her heart kicked up a notch. So what if she was nervous? Declan was a man who'd impossibly waited for six years for her to acknowledge him. Her body would get used to him. It was like learning a new dance. Nothing felt easy or comfortable at first.

He eased her down. "Are you sure?"

"No, but I want to anyway."

He sucked in a long breath, reached over to grasp his cane, and held out his other hand.

She took it and they walked like that, holding hands, up the stairs, around the bannister, a corner, and into his bedroom. Like they were an old married couple headed to bed after a long day. Nothing about them was "normal", but for a split second, she could see it. Night after night, following this path with Declan.

He led her to the bed, gestured for her to sit. Everything about the room was Declan. The scent of wool and cotton. The heavy dark wood furniture that would take four men to move. The muted dark blues and contrasting cream colors on the bedspread that her fists clutched.

"Anything you want to tell me about your visit to your father?" He dropped his cane into a brass umbrella stand by the door. The metallic thunk made her startle.

Oh, she supposed he would want to discuss *that*. She

shook her head. "Nothing to say. I said my piece. It was good. Freeing."

"And Ruark? I don't want you to worry."

"I'm not. Amazingly." Ruark was bound to get out one day. So what if it was early? The guy wasn't allowed near Shakedown, she or her sisters, or anyone associated with Declan. Maryland had many laws designed to protect victims. Plus, Declan's extra security had proven to be good. She hadn't been able to shake the sentinel's tail once over the last few days, not that she'd tried very hard. She also had noticed Declan was quite fond of security cameras, a few littered throughout his house. She'd caught that the first time she'd visited.

"What's changed?"

She shrugged. She wasn't sure herself, except perhaps feeling okay was a decision. That hold her past had on her had loosened. "Nathan will take care of Starr, and Max will of Luna. I see what prison does to someone so I don't expect Ruark to be able to do much except lick his wounds for a while."

"You know that because you saw me just after I got out?"

Her forehead tightened. Ruark and Declan weren't in the same league—hell, the same solar system. "You were twice the man just out of prison than he ever was in his whole life."

Little crinkles around his eyes deepened, and he drew closer. It made her wonder if he always needed that cane. He could walk, albeit with a slight limp, without it. The things she was desperate to learn about him now crowded in on her.

With a pop of his shirt button, he began to undress. "I want to show you something."

Oh. Getting nude was part of the deal, right? It wasn't like he hadn't seen a lot of her over the years. Hell, half of Baltimore had. But this wasn't about her body. Feeling Declan without those beautiful vintage suits between her and him would be more than physical intimacy. She was starting her new life—maybe *their* new life.

~

He hadn't been fully prepared for this sudden turn in Phoenix's willingness, but he was jumping on it. Whatever this woman gave, he'd take. She'd slithered under his covers, fully clothed. He, however, stripped himself down to his boxers and eased down to lie with her.

"This night is entirely up to you." He picked up her hand, kissed the back of it, and then brought it to his thigh. She wasn't the only one who had damage. A long, jagged scar ran down the side of his hip where his car door ripped across it. Not many plastic surgeons in prison to fix things.

She gasped when touching the raised flesh there. "Does this hurt?" Her blue eyes flitted over the scar from knee to hip bone. He barely noticed the old wound anymore, but to someone new, it had to appear severe.

"Not really. But this leg is weaker than the other. It's more annoying than anything. Do you mind it?"

"Not at all." She snuggled down to her side and nestled her hands under the side of her face. The loss of her hand's touch. "There's no part of you that matters that is weak. That's what's important."

He propped his head by his hand and stared down at her. He ran a finger down her nose, down her lips, neck, and to the swell of her breast. As he suspected. Every part of her was as velvety soft as a freshly picked peach.

"I won't push you."

She shivered a little, but it wasn't from fear. Her lips parted. She popped back up, the sheet tucked under her arms even though she still wore her top. "My turn."

She took his hand and lifted it to the back of her neck, pressing his fingertip to a place at her skull line. "This is my worst one. Thirteen stitches. Belt buckle." Her hand trembled in his, and her bottom lip quivered.

A raised, horizontal line lay hidden in all her hair, though if he lifted it he suspected there'd be a bald spot. Perhaps that's why she never wore her hair pulled up, her tendrils so often free and loose. They covered up a sin, one she should never have to bear.

"I hate that you have a worst anything."

She drew her knees up to her chest. "There are more. I'm afraid for you to see them."

"You'll show me when you're ready."

"Okay." She took his hand and placed it along her hipline. A small circular scar as if someone had placed a lit cigar to her flesh marred her skin. "This one is from Jones."

The man had always been on Declan's 'shit list,' and now Jones' placement shifted. He was on Declan's 'end-his-business list.'

"I didn't mean to make you angry," she said.

"I suppose I also wear things on my face." He willed his face to relax. "And this one?" he turned her wrist over, ran his finger over the barely visible line there. He'd seen that on her the first few weeks she'd worked for him. It was the kind of scar one didn't ask about.

She yanked her hand back. She drew her knees up to her chest and sent her gaze out over his room.

He joined her in sitting. "You're not ready, are you?" he asked.

"I thought I was." She quirked her mouth. "I'm sorry."

"I'm not. You're being honest with me. That means more."

"More than—"

"Yes." He kissed each fingertip. "More than." He tucked

hair behind her ear. A long strand hid one of her eyes. He always had to see her eyes. "It's okay to need more time."

"You see everything about me, don't you?"

"Not everything but a lot."

He thought she might turn away, but she didn't. "I think I don't mind anymore." She leaned against his headboard. "Can we not talk anymore about our pasts? I don't want them in this room with us."

He cupped her chin. "Yes. Let's have this time together. You and me. No one else is here. No ghosts. No pasts. Only us."

"Yes." She blinked over at him.

She then pushed off the covers and pulled her shirt off. She unhooked her bra with one hand in a move he'd seen a hundred times—but only on stage. He'd never had the pleasure of seeing her nipples, however. They were a perfect peach color to match the freckles that dotted her chest, the bridge of her nose.

His mouth ignited with a hunger he'd never felt. He needed to taste them.

She lifted her hand and brought his palm to cup her left breast. He thought all those years ago he'd felt soft skin during their brief lap dance at Maxim's. He knew nothing.

She stared at him. "I'm tired of living the same day over and over. I want something different. I want you."

She leaned back to the headboard and scooched down a bit but kept his hand on her breast.

He took a nipple in his mouth, tasting her sweet warmth. He worked both of the buds until they tightened and she was panting breath into the air above him. Her skin had pinked under his mouth's work, so he moved to the rest of her.

After ridding themselves of their clothes, he took long minutes to hold her nude body close to him, his hands roaming her thighs and her back. His scarred leg pressed between hers and his mouth worked hers over until he felt her body was ready. When her hips began to move, her breasts rubbed into his chest, and a soft mewl sounded into his throat, he pressed her to her back.

Six years of dreaming of her flesh yielding to him and they were finally here. Blue eyes gazed up at him, her lids at half-mast.

"Are you sure?" he asked.

She licked her lips and spread her legs wide. That's all it took for him to slip on a condom, and when his cock slipped into all her wet, he sent a thank you up to a God he still wasn't sure existed.

45

"Turns out they accepted your counteroffer. I still can't believe it, but apparently, there are some motivated buyers on your stretch of the waterfront." Marta's headshake came through the phone.

He himself could barely believe they'd take such a lowball offer. Perhaps word was out a certain family with nothing good on their mind related to the waterfront was enough. God, he hated being right about the MacKennas.

Then again, the city had shown no interest in developing this section and it didn't attract many visitors. Perhaps his notion of turning around the waterfront himself was foolish. He had to at least try. If he didn't, the MacKennas recent real estate buying spree would turn the neighborhood into a cesspool.

That's when it dawned on him. Perhaps they hadn't planned on running drugs or opening anything. They simply wanted the neighborhood to rot—and Shakedown along with it. Empty buildings quickly became crack dens and unsanctioned homeless shelters, especially areas rarely patrolled by the police force.

That only meant one thing. He had to put something useful in—enough for the neighborhood to become an asset and not the barely-holding-on-to-legitimacy that it was now despite Shakedown's upscale clientele.

"I'll send the paperwork over. Sign it fast, Declan. In case anyone tries to back out."

He killed the call.

Phoenix looked up from the book she was reading, *The Great Gatsby*. "Good news?"

One of her legs dangled over the arm of his leather club chair, her pink-painted toes such a contrast to his home. The masculine décor once suited it. Now, with her strong presence in it and a dose of good luck, things might change. Then she could read his entire library of classics if she so desired.

The last two days had blurred together. Phoenix hadn't been out of his sight for one second. They'd danced around his living room, even trying the paso doble, which he was horrible at. They made dinner together. They ate. And every night, she was in his bed.

Bit by bit, she opened up to him. Her most ticklish spot was under her chin. Kissing the backs of her knees made her squirm. And she handled his cock with her fingers in the shower until he came so hard he'd nearly doubled over and fallen to the tiles.

But then Tuesday morning came and ruined their bubble. Time to re-enter the world, especially now since he had a new business to launch.

While she spent the weekend reading his books, he had placed business calls. That was the thing about real estate—it didn't follow a Monday-Friday routine, which was good given an idea had formed during one of their living room dance sessions. Phoenix Rising wanted something more out of life? He could give it to her.

"Move in with me." His internal thought leaked out. He felt the need to have her around all the time that strongly.

Her eyes went planet-sized. "What?"

"Live here. With me."

"I-I…" She snapped her lips shut.

"Then think about it…" He set himself down on his coffee table, putting his elbows on his knees. "…while I propose something else."

She lowered her leg and sat upright. "There's more?"

"Shakedown is expanding. I'm buying the warehouse next door. That was Marta on the phone."

"Like another club?" Her eyes lit up and the book slid off her lap to land on the floor.

He picked it up and handed it to her. "A dance school. And I want you to run it."

She pressed her whole back against the chair. "Me? I don't know how to run anything. I have never done anything like that before."

He rose. "There's always a first time for everything. And something tells me you'd be great at it. Teaching girls." He snapped his fingers. "Like Naomi." Who had disappeared.

"But I never went to school for it or anything."

"Do you want to go to school?"

She swiveled her head around, her eyes searching the room like she chased a thought around the walls. "I never thought about it."

"The way I see it, girls like Naomi need someone they can look up to. Someone who hasn't had the gold star ballet school. The scholarship to Juilliard. They need someone to believe in them."

She chewed her lip. "That's a low blow. Bringing up Naomi."

"Her disappearance wasn't your fault."

Unhappiness colored her eyes and she picked at the pages

between the covers. "I know." She blinked up at him and pressed herself to standing. "Tell you what. You help me convince Naomi to be my first student and maybe first employee and—"

"Back to bargaining."

Her shoulders slumped, and she dropped the book to the chair. "You still have my napkin."

"I do. Paper burns easily, however." He pecked her on the forehead. "Okay. Deal. I'll go get Naomi—"

"I'll go with you."

"No, Elizaveta. *I'll* go."

"Bring Max."

He slapped his hand over his heart. "Don't believe I can do it?"

"Oh, you can. But I'd really like someone to get a punch in on Jones, and you're a gentleman."

He was hardly that after this weekend. When this woman lay in his arms—nude every night—he'd had to hold back the savage parts that wanted to slam into her over and over every other hour. He'd had to go slow, gentle, careful when he wanted nothing but to unleash his pent-up lust.

He grinned down at her. "No one's punching anyone. Oh, and about the moving in thing?"

"Pushing me?" She peeked up through her lashes.

"Seducing you. Now, hungry? You should eat before we go in tonight."

"I can't eat now." She stepped over to his bookshelf and slipped the book back into its place.

He gave her a side-eye when she faced him.

"Okay, a salad."

"Good. Then we'll talk about a move-in date."

She didn't object, just headed to the kitchen with an amused, "Tsk."

So, she wasn't the only one who could bring surprises.

And as for pushing her? He might have to start to—just a little.

46

Declan pulled into Shakedown's parking lot, yanking his car into 'Park.' Something wasn't right with Phee's car. It sat in the same place but appeared lopsided. She saw it right away, too.

She yanked open her car door and hoofed it over to Allegra. She placed her hand on the hood and bent over to get a look at the slashed tire. All four of them were slashed despite the fact they'd left it under a bright spotlight with cameras trained on every square inch of the lot. Not to mention the gate locked the lot behind tall fencing if the club was closed.

Max and Trick jumped out of the side exit so fast, Declan's heart nearly stopped in his chest.

"We got 'em on the security feed," Max shouted as he lumbered over. "Two guys, sweatshirts with hoods pulled down."

"Call the cops yet?" Not that calling law enforcement would do a damned thing.

Max crossed his arms. "No, thought you'd want to do it— or not. Because here's the thing. The guys knew where the cameras were. They kept their faces turned away the whole time."

Trick's eyes trained on his. "Could have been done by anyone."

"But it wasn't just anyone, was it?" Max growled.

"Ruark is out, but he got picked up by Carragh. It's only been about 24 hours. Can't be him." Trick shrugged when Declan swung his gaze to him. "I got word."

"This isn't their work. Too basic. They're more dramatic than this. It was random." Declan was sure of it. They could have been some disgruntled patrons once they learned a visit to Shakedown wasn't a strip club deal.

Couldn't they have just one weekend where nothing went wrong?

Phee had sidled up to him, tucking herself closer.

"I told you, you will always be safe." He circled her shoulders.

"I'm not worried about me. I'm pissed. Finding tires that fit Allegra? I shouldn't have left her here for so long."

He chuckled, and her beautiful blue eyes shone up at him.

Max and Trick eyed one another. Yeah, a lot had changed in the last few days so he supposed he'd need to clue them in somehow. Now that he knew his waterfront plans were possible, it was most definitely time to assemble his team. They had a lot of work ahead of them despite random acts of vandalism. It was time to clean up this neighborhood.

"Come on, everyone. Inside. I need to fill you in. We're expanding."

"Expanding. Now?" Trick followed him to the door.

"We're opening a dance school." Phoenix nearly danced herself to the doorway.

Trick stopped short. "Here?"

"I bought the warehouse next door. The first of many.

Gentlemen." He pushed open the door. "We are going to take over the waterfront ourselves."

He'd get Phoenix new tires first, of course.

47

―――

Since his declaration, a visible shift had occurred at Shake-down. Word about his plans caught like wildfire, and a renewed energy, an energy he didn't realize had been missing since the Ruark MacKenna debacle, caused the air to crackle with anticipation as if everyone had been waiting for him to expand.

Heard you might open a second club.

You thinking about a series of restaurants or something?

You going to put in a boardwalk?

Questions coupled with wide eyes and bright smiles made him question why he'd waited so long to consider any of that. In fact, he'd gotten so many questions, he had to put an NDA in place for his employees so they wouldn't let it slip to the wrong people.

So far, no one connected to one Irish crime family appeared in the audience, or had they and gone unrecognized? Or Ruark, Carragh, the lot of them may have mysteriously lost interest. Or they were biding their time. He could only hope it was adopted disinterest from what he'd shared with a bit of his mother's diaries. Then again, his delivery was just two days ago.

He and Max also took a little trip to Maxim's. They didn't recognize him, which was just as good. Their spiel hadn't changed. Naomi wasn't there but he left word he was looking for her, knowing full well she'd never get that message. They then were offered other girls—"better girls." He declined and left, though for a second he thought he'd have to drag Max out.

He and Phee never spoke of her Naomi request again. She didn't ask, and he didn't offer.

Tonight, he took his usual spot at the end of the stage and motioned to Jackie to give him his usual. Phoenix wasn't on stage. Wasn't she to dance next? He'd made a point of learning the schedule every night now. Instead of being tormented by her presence on stage, now he wouldn't miss it.

"Hey Jackie, you seen Phee?"

The woman set a tumbler of bourbon down in front of him. "I got my hands full with drinkers. Can't keep an eye on everyone." She winked.

With drink in hand, he scanned the place from the dressing rooms to the back storeroom. He found her in the unlikeliest place—out in the parking lot.

Max leaning against the cinderblock wall nearby with a lit cigarette. The scent of smoke—something he tried desperately to quit—lured him. The redhead staring at her car lured him even stronger.

"You got me new tires." A breath cloud formed in front of her face.

He shrugged off his jacket and placed it over her shoulders. "I did."

"This was the first thing I ever paid for myself." She turned to him. "With my first few Shakedown paychecks."

"Ah." No wonder she didn't want to replace it.

The brand new whitewalls gleamed under the streetlight.

"Thank you." She then inextricably moved closer and wrapped her arms around his waist. "Things really are going to be better, aren't they?"

He nodded.

"Hey!"

Declan and Phoenix turned to face Naomi. "Speak of the devil,"

"Heard you were looking for me." *Well, what did you know? She got the message.*

Phoenix extricated herself from him and crossed her arms. "You never showed up for your audition."

"Yeah, well, I got some extra nights at Maxim's."

"First rule of being a professional. Show up. On-time."

"You aren't the boss of me."

Oh, yeah, these two might not have been the best pair to team up. He had to intercept. "Naomi, what do you say to joining us here?"

"Are you shitting me? You'll let me dance?" The girl popped her gum—the first habit they'd rid her of.

Phee and Declan looked at one another. "Sort of," Phee said. "Come on in, I'll fill you in. But I meant it about showing up."

Naomi rolled her eyes at her, a familiar move—one he'd received from Phoenix a hundred times.

He chuckled. Never a dull moment.

48

——————

Phee's VW pulled in next to him. He'd lost her at a red light and had been waiting for her to arrive. They were early—too early, but he had payroll to run and she'd wanted to organize the dressing room.

The last few days had sped by, each afternoon, Phoenix and Declan arriving together to the club, and each evening after the show, heading home either to land in his bed or hers. She still balked at moving in with him, but she'd need to soon. Moonlight didn't like sharing Phoenix's bed with him and gave him the death stare out of her only good yellow eye. He woke up one night to the thing sleeping in between his ankles, however, which Phee declared a "good sign." *Good? Maybe.* Because clearly, they came as a package deal. He wasn't sure how his house would fare with a creature that made every surface, every seat, her own.

He cracked open his car door and stretched. The overcast day threatened yet another storm overhead with black clouds rolling in. The parking lot was nearly empty but would fill up soon enough given it was Saturday. He flicked his gaze to the choppy river that churned just fifty feet away. He understood how it felt.

The nights at Shakedown had been too quiet, too calm. With no response from the MacKennas to his mother's diary excerpts, his radar was up. Their silence warned him. Something was coming.

While Phee pulled her enormous bag from her front seat —he'd never understand women's need to haul around so much stuff—he jangled his keys to find the one that'd open the front door. From this distance, he could make out a package or something sitting at the front entrance. Strange, given the delivery guys knew to drop off anything at the loading dock area around back.

He drew closer. What the hell? He froze. He almost couldn't believe his eyes at what stood against the front door.

He spun on his heel, blocking Phoenix, who had skipped up to him.

"Phoenix, go home. I'm calling Max. He's going to meet you at your place."

"What's going on?"

"I'll fill you in. But I need you to go." He sidestepped as she tried to peer around him.

"What are you hiding?" She jogged around him but stopped short. A visible gasp sounded. She turned away. "That's…"

"Yes."

Her eyes flew up. "I need to stay here with you."

"No. Go. Now." She shuddered at the vehemence in his voice.

He stepped up to her, cupped her face. "Please." She nodded once and headed to her car. He watched her the whole way. Her blue eyes shone toward him through the windshield as she started up her car and put it into reverse.

Only when her taillights turned the corner did he turn back to the grotesque sight.

The headstone from his mother's grave leaned against his custom-etched glass door, a long crack splitting the dancer depiction in two. He'd just got that thing replaced. Fresh dirt still clung to the stone's base where someone had yanked it free from the ground that lay over her grave.

He forced himself to draw closer. Someone had taken a hammer or chisel to her last name. "MacKenna." It was barely readable. Some sick fuck had gone to St. Louis, found it, dug it up, and dropped it here. The possibility boggled his mind. Then the anger came. Defacing a dead woman's marker was deplorable.

He knew who'd have the mental sickness to do it, too.

Only one person was responsible for this act. That person had recently received three pages of a dead sister's diary that connected him to a well-known and crooked senator. Details so telling that the outstanding member of congress might take it upon himself to rid himself of such a connection, a connection pivotal to the MacKenna family's well-being.

He shut his eyes and tuned into every vibrating cell in his body. It seemed like his diary move would not get Tomas to stand down. It raised the stakes. Only now, he had a lot more to lose than a building and a business. And her taillights still burned in the back of his eyelids.

49

———————

The road vibrated under Phee's car. There she was, waiting at a red light in her VW on her brand new tires, and the man she loved was back at Shakedown without her. It wasn't right.

She'd spent six years avoiding Declan and now she wanted nothing more than to be with him—all the time. It was so strange, but a physical pull yanked at her insides to just turn around already.

Doing what he said by going home would be the smart thing to do. But she didn't want to. She made an illegal U-turn, prayed she didn't get seen by a cop, and headed back to Shakedown. She had a bad feeling. It was probably nothing, but she wasn't chancing it by not acting on it.

She pulled into the same parking spot, the lot still nearly empty. Despite recent tire-slashing events, a few of the employees often left their cars here as it was free parking behind a locked gate. Still, she could tell, no one had arrived for their evening shift yet. That meant Declan was in there *alone*.

She stepped out of Allegra and averted her eyes from the

headstone that still leaned against the front entrance. The side door opened with an echoing *clang*. She dropped her things in the dressing room and practiced a brief speech about why she turned back around.

You shouldn't have to deal with this alone.

I'm safe here with you.

Max has his hands full with... something. She didn't know much about Max's life except he was always around, watching like a sentinel.

The hallway was so quiet she could have heard a pin drop, or at least it was until she rounded the corner. Male rumblings came from Declan's office.

Max perhaps? It didn't sound like him. The voice, however, had a familiar edge.

"Beg for it." Who the hell was that?

She pushed open the carved door and nearly choked. If only her eyes betrayed her.

Ruark MacKenna held a gun to a kneeling Declan. Declan's eyes lifted to her, a furious fire blazing there like she'd never seen in them before. "Get out," he growled.

She couldn't move. Ruark was thinner, his skin grayer, but those unwavering, ice-blue eyes had locked on her, and her feet had grown roots. The man lifted the gun toward her. "Look who we have here." He used the gun to motion her inside. The guy swiped at his bloodied lip as if he'd just recovered from a fight.

The whole scene was like a movie, only somehow she'd gotten sucked into the screen. Everything about the scene was horrific and surreal, and her brain just couldn't lock on to this being *real*. The waving gun. Ruark's eyes. Declan's knees jutting out from his trousers on that carpet.

God, don't hurt him. Her brain kept returning to that prayer for Declan.

Ruark's lips curled. "Move. I'll have you later."

Her legs clenched. *Have you.* She'd claw his eyes out. He'd have to shoot her before he got an inch closer to her—or near Declan.

Cherry's words spun in her brain. *What if he was gone from this earth?* He couldn't be. The earth didn't rotate without him.

"Leave her alone." Declan fingered his cane that lay at his feet.

Ruark kicked at Declan, who fell to all fours but then quickly righted himself in a growl. He wasn't looking at her, rather his eyes sliced to where Ruark stood.

Maybe if she distracted Ruark, Declan could do something. He seemed to seek some opening. But she couldn't move her body.

"What do you want?" Men the world over felt some primal urge to be heard, seen, wanted. She could give him a moment of that. She'd been doing it her whole life.

"Want?" He sneered and spat blood onto the Oriental rug. "Where's Baldwin?" He glared down at Declan. "He's moved."

Shit. The man wanted to continue his plot against Nathan and Starr. Her mind cleared. A red-hot poker couldn't have jolted her aware more. "Yes, they've moved. They don't live here anymore."

Ruark pointed the gun at her. "Where are they?"

"St. Louis. Imagine that. You just came from there, right?" By the look of Ruark's eyes, she shouldn't have said that, but the pissed off side of her couldn't help it. Like hell, she'd let this guy continue to get away with his sick ideas.

Ruark's face fell into a laugh. "Shit, Declan. I don't know which one of those red-headed sluts this is… but she's funny. And probably too smart for her own good."

Declan had curled his hand around his cane. He was going to risk something, wasn't he?

Her feet inched forward. "Which one do you want me to be, Mr. MacKenna?"

The guy's head cocked. Jesus, he was easy. Call him Mister, give him an inch of power. He lapped it up like a kitten in front of a bowl of tuna.

If her dancing had taught her anything, it was this: The essence of how a story played out came from one thing—how much backstory existed. So, she'd find out his. "The headstone. It means something to you, doesn't it?" She might as well ask.

His hand shook, the gun scratching against his jeans. "It means I'm back in. And you..." He stared down at Declan. "Are dead."

"And then what?"

"You don't need to know shit."

"Maybe I'm interested." She inched a bit closer, her heartbeat threatening to revolt. Her body shook so hard he had to notice. Her hands gripped the back of her arms as if that would calm the tsunami of adrenaline in her body. *Fat chance.*

"Phoenix." Declan's warning tone couldn't stop her from at least trying to distract Ruark.

Ruark's eyes shifted. "Phoenix Rising. The hothead of the gang. I should've known. You like those fire crotches, huh, Declan? She must be real hot under the sheets." He stepped forward, and the urge to retch rose hard inside her.

The guy was five steps from her, and her legs danced with agitation.

"Yeah, I'd like to see you run." His gaze ran up and down her body. "I like it when a woman fights me. Makes it better when I fuck the bitch right out of them."

Declan lifted his cane and smacked it so hard into Ruark's legs, bones cracking shouted into the room. The man cursed and bent over slightly. He was turning and lifting the gun when someone or something shoved her—hard. She hadn't been expecting it, and the ground seemed to rise up to meet her. Her hands and legs burned as they hit the carpet.

A gunshot rang out and seemed to cut the air in half. It was so much louder than she could have imagined. Her ears rang, male shouts muffled behind the cotton in her ears. There was so much shouting. Her cheek rested against the carpet. Declan's carpet. Images crowded her mind.

Declan's dark gray eyes. His expensive trousers against the Oriental rug's pattern. The red and gold and... everything just ceased.

50

Declan hissed at Carragh. "Don't you go near her." Phoenix had fainted, which was probably a blessing. At least she landed on the carpet when Carragh pushed her. Then the man had shot his own brother.

Declan positioned his body between Phee and Carragh.

"She doesn't interest me." Carragh jerked his head toward his fallen brother and the two guys with him moved to an unmoving Ruark.

"You killed him."

"Maybe. We'll see."

The two guys hauled Ruark up by the arms, hooked them over their shoulders, and moved to drag him across his office.

"Where the fuck you taking him?"

"It doesn't matter. I'll see to it." Carragh wiped a handkerchief over his gun and pocketed the Glock into a holster inside his jacket. The thing had to burn. Carragh didn't flinch. "My brother is no longer your concern."

Where had he heard those words before? "He never was." He wasn't sorry for Ruark's fate but was still stunned as he wiped his lip with a Shakedown napkin. He'd at least got a punch on Ruark after he'd been jumped in his own office. He kneeled down to Phoenix and swiped hair from her face. She was out cold

Carragh hadn't moved. "I'm handling it from now on."

"If there is so much as one bruise on her…" He cut his gaze up to the man.

"Stand down, Declan. Your little dancer is fine. Now, let's talk." Carragh pocketed his handkerchief like he was a prince and not a stone-cold murderer.

Declan rose to standing. "Talk? Your brother just got shot. That your plan all along?"

"If my brother dies, then he dies." Carragh's flat tone was beyond compare. "If he lives, he's getting put away."

"Prison didn't work the first time."

"No. Mental institution. The man's a sociopath. Saw the gravestone out front. I'll see it's put back."

"Don't you touch it." Phee moaned a little near his feet. With one eye on Carragh, he reached down and helped her to sit up. She blinked.

Carragh sighed. "Declan, it's the least I can do given my brother went so rogue."

"You're the reason he got out in the first place."

"What can I say?" The man shrugged. "Like you, I believe in second chances. But sadly, Ruark is beyond saving. He snuck out in the middle of the night. Didn't know where he went until now."

To St. Louis, to his mother's gravesite.

"Lucky for you, I got word he was seen hovering by the waterfront. I figured he'd make a pitstop here."

"I don't care what you do with him. This is over. The shit I have on your family—"

"Yes, yes, I know all about the *diaries*."

"Remember that." He swiped hair from Phee's face. She scrambled to standing. He pushed her behind him.

"We could agree on many things, Declan. Like developing this waterfront. So, tell you what. I won't alert anyone there is DNA all over this office, evidence of a crime, and you keep your mother's things to yourself."

"Or I could torch the place." It'd be the only thing that would get rid of the blood all over his office for good.

Carragh gave him an amused smile. "But you won't." His eyes sliced to Phee, who wobbled a bit behind Declan.

"Why do you care about this place?"

"Turns out we're not so different, Declan. Your loyalty knows no bounds. Well, neither does mine. Like, I said. Family is everything."

"You're not my family."

"But I could be."

A female murmur sounded behind him. Phoenix grasped his arm.

"I want no part of your family," he said.

"You have no choice. And who knows? We might be more related than you know."

Fuck him. Another suspicion cemented into reality. "Stay away from Luna."

"You're in no position to tell me what to do." The man strode out, following the trail of blood his brother left as they dragged him out of the club.

51

Declan finally got Phoenix alone in her bedroom. Those sisters hovered like nobody's business when there was a fuss to be made.

He'd hauled Phoenix out of there as soon as possible. Taken her home—to Moonlight and her sisters. As much as he'd have loved to have locked her up in his home, she belonged at her apartment for the time being. That didn't mean he left. Phee was his now. Everyone around her needed to understand that fact despite that *Friends Forever, Sisters Always* thing they tried to pull on him as soon as he stepped inside the door. Luna in particular showed a fire when speaking that phrase to him tonight. It was her answer to his question, "Can you leave us alone for a bit?"

Of course, Declan had to shut the club down for the second time in a month. It took a supreme effort to rid his office, hallway, and parking lot of the MacKenna showdown. Max proved pivotal. Leave it to the ex-gangster to know of a cleaner who'd ask no questions. Within six hours, it was as if nothing had occurred. He'd lost the night's receipts, not to mention the payroll expense. It was worth it if it meant he'd live another day to love the woman who now lay cradled in his arms.

Sunlight streamed in from her window, making her hair light up like fire. She'd melted in his arms as he gently rocked her in her rocking chair for the last hour. Such a simple pleasure to feel the back and forth—except for the incessant whining from Moonlight, who sat on the edge of the bed and complained loudly.

"This her usual seat?" he asked.

"Every seat in this house is her usual."

That made him laugh for some reason. Maybe because he'd been worried such a display of violence had undone all the progress they'd made.

"I told you to go home and instead you came back to Shakedown. Why?" If only she had listened to him.

"You were alone there, and I just couldn't. I had to come back."

Always worried about others. Her compassion may have been buried for years, but it'd risen with a vengeance lately.

"Declan?" She pushed up to stare into his eyes. "What about your mother's headstone?"

"It's in the warehouse." Tucked away until he could return it to its rightful place.

"I'll help you put it back."

He brought her head back down to his shoulder. "I can handle it."

"If I hear the word 'handle' one more time, I'm going to make good on that napkin."

"Okay. You can come." He'd learned one thing over the last few weeks—his woman was stubborn but not always wrong about it. It would feel good to have her with him when he'd return his mother's gravestone—an act he couldn't have imagined having to do before tonight.

She settled her face against his neck once more. "I don't

know where my mom is. She wasn't buried. She was cremated."

"You don't have her ashes anywhere?" He adjusted her on his lap. His leg throbbed, but she didn't need to know.

"No. When we were taken from the house, they were left behind."

Pure sacrilege. "I'm sorry, Sunset."

"It's okay. They weren't her. Do you remember the night we danced all those waltzes? I said there was a reason I loved the 'Waltz of the Flowers'. It was the last song she and I had danced to in our living room together."

He murmured, unclear what to say to that.

"She was teaching me some ballet moves. I understand if you don't want to open that school now."

"Oh, we're opening. But only if you're leading it."

"Okay."

That was too easy. "What made you change your mind?"

"I don't want to dance for others anymore, and before anyone thinks it's because of what happened to me in the past, it's not. I want to make sure women like me have something else. Options, if that makes sense."

"It does."

"And something else Cherry said to me recently about not wasting time."

She pushed off him once more, easing herself up. Lifting Moonlight in her arms—because the thing hadn't gone far as if she understood the need to stay close—she turned to him. "So, yes."

He cocked his head in question.

"We'll move in with you." She brought Moonlight to her chest and their two faces stared at him. One yellow eye and two bright blue eyes that he could stare at for the rest of his life.

52

____

They say a picture paints a thousand words—or in this case, the image on his cell phone screen of the concrete retainer wall with Staunton Mental Institute etched into its side. So, Ruark MacKenna lived another day, albeit committed to a mental health facility.

Declan almost didn't click on Carragh's message, but he had little choice. Alive or dead, the mystery of whether Ruark was still a threat or gone from their purview forever also lived. Then there was that not-so-little mystery of the drugs that had been planted on him a few weeks ago.

Declan ran his hand down his chin. He'd been in such a good mood, too.

He stilled, thinking about his choices. He could give into the thought once again that life was fucking unfair. Or, he could tune into the greatest blessing of his life, who stood in the middle of an unfinished warehouse, peering up at the ceiling.

Time to choose, so he did. He chose Phoenix. He gazed up at her and pocketed his phone.

Ruark was like a cat with nine lives, though he had none

of Moonlight's charm. Yeah, he'd gotten used to the furball that had taken over his house the last few weeks like the prima donna she was. He'd almost lost a mid-century leather chair that she claimed as a scratching post. Phoenix got this spray that turned her away—for about half a day.

Phee's shoes made that wonderful brushing sound on the concrete as she spun in a wide circle. It reminded him of her time on the stage on those rare nights when the crowd was thin and he could hear every move she made. But she hadn't been onstage in a while. Instead, she'd been planning The Phoenix Rising Dance Studio.

"Well?" Declan rocked back on his heels and watched her face spread into a smile. "It's going to take a lot of work but we'll manage."

"Like that first time you brought us to Shakedown. It was little more than this."

True, the warehouse was nothing but concrete, steel girders, and late November gusts blowing through that could knock a grown man down. They could turn it into something. He had the funding, thanks to a little rumor about some "mob killing" at Shakedown—a rumor he didn't start and knew Max didn't, either. That meant only one person did—Carragh. Why, he'd never know because he was beyond done with that family.

At least business at Shakedown, just next door, was booming with nightly packed houses thanks to the holidays and Starr and Cherry's sudden interest in revamping the shows. He'd suspected they hadn't made many changes before to not upset one of their most popular acts—Phoenix, the woman who hated change. Yet now she was changing everything. Pushing, actually.

She stopped suddenly. "Everything okay?"

"Fine."

"Declan Phillips." She strode up to him. "No more 'fine.' No more 'handle,' remember?"

"Ruark was just committed."

The light in her eyes flattened a bit. "Oh, that means…"

"He lived."

"Well." She chewed her lip. "I can't say I'm glad. Does that make me awful?"

"It makes you human." He slipped his arm around her waist.

"To think he almost stole everything from us."

"And I'm still not over the fact you engaged him that day"

Just like that, the blue in her eyes churned like a stormy sea. "He was trying to take something from me."

His ego, not the most mature part of him, was pleased by that statement.

"But if I think about it, like really, really think about it…" she huffed, "he made me feel something that wasn't entirely bad. It was like he was trying to steal my future. And it dawned on me then. I can see the future now. Before, I couldn't. Not really."

If he was one tenth responsible for her giving up that past, he'd count himself the luckiest man in the world.

"Good. Because…" He slipped her hand into his and pulled her to the center of the space. "What kind of future do you see here?"

Phee let her head fall back and studied the ceiling. "We going to keep the height?" Her chin dropped down. "Because if you did, we could introduce some aerials acts. Silks, lyra hoops, trapeze. It's all the rage in dancing classes."

"Hell, yes." Naomi's booming voice filled the space. "We're doing it."

The girl who'd had her role as administrative assistant to Phoenix for only one week took her duties a tad too seriously. An unspoken threat to Phee's boss position always lay just behind her words, which were many. The girl talked incessantly. Phoenix could handle her, however. Declan had seen her put the girl in her place a dozen times—always met with familiar eye roll that Phee laughed off.

"And those bathrooms? Can we start with them?" Naomi hitched her thumb backwards. "They are na-a-a-sty."

"Well, they aren't finished. Probably just put in for the construction crew."

She snuffed her nose. "They remind me of Maxim's."

Declan's gaze shot to Phoenix, expecting a visible body shudder. Instead, a surprising smirk lifted one side of her cheek. "Declan will fix them."

Naomi glanced at the phone in her hand and frowned.

"Still no news?" Phee asked her.

"Nope. Rachel's still in labor. Man, is she going to be pissed. Twelve hours and still going? I'd be demanding diamonds after that." Naomi had appointed herself Shakedown's Grapevine Goddess, a title given to her by Cherry, who was more than thrilled to have another orphan in her midst to adopt.

"The baby's enough. Or so I'm told," Phoenix said in a pretty good mom voice impersonation. Something about Naomi made everyone "mom" her left and right.

"Naomi, go grab my bag from my car? I have some notebooks. I want to sketch out a few things for the architect."

And there went Phoenix, taking on *his* role. He chuckled internally. He didn't mind. Let her design the whole place. Which reminded him…

As soon as Naomi lumbered down the hall toward the parking area, he reached into his jacket pocket and drew out some papers. "I have something for you."

"Don't tell me. Liability papers to sign in case I make good on the aerial thing."

"Something like that. I mean, since liability is something you may want to consider going forward."

A pinched vee formed between her eyes. She took the tri-folded paper from his outstretched hand. She opened it up. A slow lowering of her bottom lip into an *"O"* warmed every inch of him. *Surprise, baby.* She stood there frozen. Oh, yeah, he'd downright shocked her.

"But…" She blinked.

"It's only fair. I'll have so little to do with this place that—"

She lurched for him and his face was suddenly full of red hair and cinnamon scent. He nearly lost his balance but righted her.

"We're co-owners of the place. Didn't want to burden you with the whole thing. So, Elizaveta O'Malley—" he tapped the paper in her hand "—your name is on the deed, and all decisions can be made by you. Provided I agree, of course." He held out his hand. "Partner."

A sheen of wet coated her eyes. She clutched the paper to her chest and took his hand. She pulled herself closer and kissed him. "Thank you. You didn't have to but… Thank you."

His blasted phone, which he'd stopped putting on silent, went off again. He hated splitting his attention between whoever was before him and the damned thing. "Why don't you take more time looking around? I'll go deal with this." He lifted the phone in his hand.

She lifted her chin and began to pace around the huge space.

He watched her slink around the room for a few minutes, unable to rip his gaze from her. It was a common problem.

"Yeah." He said into his phone.

"I expected to hear something." Carragh's rumbling voice made his gut curl.

"Nothing to say. You dodged a bullet on murder charges." Now that he couldn't be accused of murder, anyway. "Though your brother didn't get so lucky."

A long sigh emitted from the other end of the phone. "Happy Thanksgiving, Cousin." The line went dead.

He re-pocketed his phone. Fuck, that man wouldn't ruin today for him.

"The baby's here!" Naomi waved her phone as she galloped back into the space. "I just heard. Finally!" She stopped short and thunked Phee's considerable hobo bag at his feet. "Let's go to the hospital. We have to hear what they're naming him. Man, a birthday on Thanksgiving Day. I'd be pissed. Not getting any good presents or having little pilgrims all over the wrapping paper?"

Declan had to laugh at that description. It was good to see Phee join him in it. "We should go straight to Cherry's. Let Rachel and Trick have their moment. Besides, I had strict instructions from Cherry not to be late."

Naomi bounced on her heels. "It was nice of her to host all of us at her brownstone for Thanksgiving."

Phee gave her a knowing smile. "She just wanted to be in charge. Our group getting too large for our apartment was all the excuse she needed."

"Well, I've never been to a turkey dinner before."

His heart twinged a bit at hearing the girl's admission. Over the last few weeks, he'd noticed Naomi, at the oddest moments, showed a vulnerability that took people off guard —when she wasn't running her mouth.

Phee strode over. "There's going to be, what? Eighteen of us? I sure hope she let someone else bring food. We're only bringing pie." His girl was most definitely not a cook, but he didn't mind she wasn't a kitchen goddess. She was every-thing he needed everywhere else.

Naomi spun in a circle, mirroring Phoenix's early move.

"Maybe I could have one of those fancy townhouses some-day, like Cherry."

"You will."

"Maybe now I might." Naomi showed off her crooked teeth and then continued to spin with her arms outstretched like a little girl might.

Phoenix got a strange look on her face and turned to him. "Thank you, Declan."

He glanced down at the paper still clutched in her hand. "You deserve it."

"No, I mean…" She lifted her chin toward the back of Naomi's head. "For that. For the hope where there was none. For letting me be the one to bring it this time."

He grasped her hand and looped her arm through his. "I have a feeling it's just the beginning."

"Naomi," she called. "Meet us in the car? We'll be there in a sec."

The girl snapped her gum, a habit no one could seem to break her of, and nodded, never turning around before she strode to the parking lot.

Phee took both his hands in hers. "I have something else to tell you."

"Sounds ominous."

"No, it's just something I haven't said before." She glanced down at their joined hands then back up at him. "I love you."

He had to swallow, hard.

"And it has nothing to do with you making me co-owner of this warehouse," she said quickly. "I just… love you."

"You don't need a reason? Most people would."

She laughed a little at that. "No reason."

"Does this mean I can burn that napkin?

She cocked her head. "Mmm. Maybe frame it. In case of emergencies?"

"Expect any more of those?"

"On second thought, I'll burn it. My name is Phoenix Rising, after all."

He circled her shoulder and led her toward the exit. There was turkey and stuffing and sixteen of their chosen family waiting for them. "Yes, it is."

~

They pulled up to Cherry's brownstone with just five minutes to spare before being called on the carpet for arriving late. He opened the door for Phoenix and Naomi, who both stepped out, each holding a pie in each hand.

The girls only had eyes for the entrance as Luna stood on the steps waving at them.

Declan took in a long, deep breath of the chilly November air and slammed the doors shut. Hitting his key fob to lock the door, he paused to let a car drive by before crossing to the sidewalk where Phee, Naomi, and Luna stood.

The holidays hadn't been his favorite season before, but now he had an extended family who seemed to have finally caught a break, Phoenix catching the greatest one of them all —a new career and an opportunity to finally choose her life. Shockingly, that included him.

Luna hugged her sister, her eyes fixed on some spot in the distance. Declan felt pulled to turn. At the intersection just down the street, a limousine idled. The window slipped shut, hiding its inhabitants, but not before Declan caught ice-blue eyes staring over at the girls.

Jesus. It never ended.

Naomi and Phee were already climbing the steps, but Luna stood on the sidewalk, her face an unreadable mask. Her eyes found his, and she slipped on a practiced smile as if she was hiding something.

With any luck, what his imagination conjured next was wrong. Carragh and Luna were an impossible match.

He put his brain on silent mode and strode across the street. Today wasn't a day to worry about it. Tomorrow he and Phoenix left for St. Louis to install his mother's new headstone.

Max would have to go back on watchdog duty over Luna because Declan had learned his lesson.

He paused, stared up at the cold gray sky. "'All the world's a stage and all the men and women merely players. They have their exits and their entrances; And one man in his time plays many parts.'" He knew his part. The MacKennas didn't get near the girls again—at least not until his own body lay in a grave.

If you loved Tough Break, you'll love the next book in the Shakedown Series, Tough Love. Download or buy from your favorite retailer.

Carragh has waited years for the perfect moment to overthrow his father. Take the crown, the throne, and the fortune due him as the eldest son.
Then redheaded burlesque dancer Luna Belle sashayed into his view and refused to leave his dreams. Fine. He'll take her, too.

Never miss a new release!
Sign up for News From Elizabeth from her web site at www. ElizabethSaFleur.com

ALSO BY ELIZABETH SAFLEUR

The Elite Doms of Washington series

Elite

Holiday Ties

Untouchable

Perfect

Riptide

Lucky

Fearless

Invincible

The Justice Series

The White House Gets A Spanking

Spanking the Senator

The Shakedown Series

Tough Road

Tough Luck

Tough Break

Tough Love

ABOUT THE AUTHOR

Elizabeth SaFleur writes romance that dares to "go there" from 28 wildlife-filled acres, dances in her spare time and is a certifiable tea snob.

Find out more about Elizabeth on her web site at www. ElizabethSaFleur or join her private Facebook group, Elizabeth's Playroom.

Follow her on Instagram (@ElizabethLoveStory) and TikTok (@ElizabethSaFleurAuthor), too!